Forgotten

(Shattered Sisters #2

MAGGIE SHAYNE

THUNDERFOOT PUBLISHING, INC.

This is for Jessica,
my special heroine,
who has a heart as big as
the moon and a smile as
bright as the sun.
I love you.
Postscript: THANK YOU

The Shattered Sisters Series

CHAPTER 1

He was the key.

Joey Bradshaw shifted in the hard little chair and studied him. It was the first time she'd seen him...with her eyes. Everything was the same, though. The square, cruel jawline, the thick, dark lashes that tried to soften its effect, the tiny, crescent-shaped scar amid the curling black hairs at his wrist. His hair seemed blue black against the stiff, white linens. The only difference was that, at the moment, he was breathing. Even his scent was exactly as she'd imagined it. A blend of blatant male virility and some spicy shaving cream. Such a potent mix was a pleasant distraction from the disinfectant aroma of the hospital.

She'd left her half sister Toni in a hospital not far from this one only a few weeks ago. Toni was fine. All wrapped up in testifying against a drug kingpin, promoting her brand new true crime book, and house hunting with the man who'd won her heart and got her a puppy instead of an engagement ring.

Joey's other sister, Caroline, might not be so fine. And that was why Joey was here.

The handsome man's eyes opened, blinked into focus and narrowed as he studied her. Beyond his curious expression she saw nothing. They were empty, those deep brown eyes. Vacant, just as the doctors had warned her they would be. It was cruel, what she had to do to him. It might not even work. But what choice did she have, really? She'd foreseen her sister Caroline's murder. It was going to happen right after the murder of the man in the bed.

"Do I know you?" He sat up slightly as he spoke and the sheet slipped down to his waist. He wore no hospital gown. The sight of his tanned skin, stretched taut over a broad chest sent a little shiver of pure appreciation up her spine. In answer to his question, she nodded.

He shook his head, frustration showing in the way his gaze intensified. "Bad enough I couldn't remember my own name. I can't believe any blow to the head would make me forget *you,* lady, whoever you are."

Heat crept up her neck and yet another round of doubt came with it, She wasn't sure if his lighthearted flirting would make this easier or harder. Especially since the attraction was mutual. She'd prepared herself for the sexual magnetism that drew her to him. She'd sensed it before she'd ever come here—and decided she could handle it. But if it was a two-way street, traveling it might get damned complicated. For a moment she seriously considered getting out of her chair, walking out the door and never turning back. She'd spent too much time in hospitals lately. She'd almost lost one sister to the mob. Now another sister was in the sites of a serial killer.

No rest for the gifted, she supposed.

Then she glanced at his chest again, and in a flash that left her dizzy, she saw it bloody; pale skin between splashes of crimson. She felt the stillness of once-powerful lungs, and the deadening silence of a magnificent heart.

"Hey. Are you okay?"

Joey forced her white-knuckled grip on the chair arms to ease and dragged her gaze from his chest, back up to his milk-chocolate eyes. Numbly she nodded. She shifted in the chair, leather creaking against vinyl.

"You gonna tell me who you are, or am I supposed to guess?"

"You'd never guess in a million years," she said softly to the man she'd never met until today. "I'm your wife."

"My...*what?*"

"Your wife."

He shook his head slowly and she could feel how badly it ached. A white bandage at the back of his skull stood like a banner of surrender amid his soft, sooty hair. The car accident that had put him here had caused no other injury. Only that one blow to the head, and the resulting memory loss. For Joey's purposes, it was the perfect opportunity to intervene in a deadly situation.

"My wife." He closed his eyes briefly, then opened them again, studying her with poorly disguised skepticism.

"You don't believe me."

He shrugged, eyes narrow, almost mocking. What had happened to the emptiness? Her mind was wide open. The problem was, she had no control over what she "picked up," and what she didn't. The images, the feelings, were random. God knew there were some things she'd rather not feel at all. Sickening, horrible things.

"I don't believe much of anything until I see proof," he told her. "That's just the way I am."

She frowned. "And how do you know *what* way you are?"

The sardonic smile died and the clouds returned to his eyes. "I don't know. That just came out." He shook his head slowly.

Joey felt a rush of sympathy for him, followed quickly by a rush of guilt. Her presence here wouldn't make things any easier. "It must be pretty lousy, forgetting your entire life." Worse yet, with what she was doing to him.

He searched her face. "I've talked to the people I work with—"

"At the *Chronicle*," she inserted, just to show him she knew.

He nodded, his gaze intensifying, never wavering from hers. "They filled in a lot of the blanks for me. But no one mentioned a wife. How do you explain that?"

She wasn't unprepared. She'd known which bases would need covering, and she'd covered them. He had no family, or none she'd been able to trace. There would be no doubting in-laws to contend with. She called to mind the lines she'd rehearsed for this moment and cleared her throat. "Did they tell you about your weekend in Vegas?"

He nodded, his face wary. "I went there to follow up a lead on...a story."

"The Syracuse Slasher." His eyes widened, but he hid his surprise quickly. "Your lead was a dead end. But the trip wasn't entirely wasted." She reached down to the backpack on the floor beside her and pulled out the rolled, ribboned document. The scent of fresh ink worried her, but she doubted he'd notice that. She handed it to him, kept talking as he unrolled it. "When you asked me to go along, I had no idea what you were planning, Ash."

He frowned over the marriage certificate that

proclaimed Ashville Allan Coye and Josephine Belinda Bradshaw were husband and wife. For what she'd paid for the thing, he'd better not find a single flaw.

Finally he shook his head. "So I have a wife. It's so odd. It's like I've never seen you before in my life. I hope that doesn't hurt your feelings too badly."

"I knew what to expect." She swallowed, failing to remove the hard lump in her throat

"So we were just married on Saturday?" he asked. "And no one else knew about it?"

"That's right. We arrived back on Sunday night. I went to my house and you went back to your apartment...to pack a few things, you said. When you didn't come back, I didn't know what to think."

"And now that you know?"

She drew a bracing breath and steadied her jangling nerves. It was necessary, she reminded herself. If she let him out of her sight for a minute, it could mean disaster. And this was the only way. She couldn't very well go to the police. They'd laugh her right out of the building. They'd never believe her. Very few people ever had. It was sickeningly ironic that she could get people to accept lies more easily than the truth. The super at the building where Ash lived, for example. He'd bought this same story, hook, line and sinker, and unlocked the apartment for her. If she'd told him the truth, he'd have dialed 911 to report a woman having an obvious psychotic break.

Except with her dad. The one who'd raise her, not the one who'd sired her, He'd never doubted her gift. He'd never accused her of having an overactive imagination. But he was nothing to her now. Less than nothing.

"Well?" Ash prompted, reminding her he'd asked a question.

She straightened her spine, met his velvety brown gaze. "I'm hoping we can pick up where we left off." She let her eyes search his face, tried to put longing into her expression. It was easier than it ought to be. "That is...if you still want to."

Ash felt his eyebrows arch. So she wanted to play house with him. Well, that would require some serious consideration. He studied her again. Her hair was a mixture of honey gold and strawberry blond. It was wild and long. His gaze lingered on her exotically slanted, emerald green eyes and the black velvet forest surrounding them. She was small, no more than five feet tall, and she had incredible legs. No contour was hidden beneath the skintight leather pants she wore. The rest of her shape was concealed by her matching jacket. She smelled like fresh air and leather, and she looked at him like she was trying to see right through him.

"Can we do that, Ash? Pick up where we left off?"

He licked his lips. "I'm thinking." Who the hell *was* she, anyway? What was her game?

She rose, scooping her backpack from the floor and dropping it on the chair. Then, turning her back to him, she bent over it. He heard the rasp of the zipper, watched her rummage around in the bag. Watching the subtle movements of her black-leather-encased, perfectly round backside, he felt himself inclined to go along with her scheme, whatever it was.

When she turned, she held a pair of jeans—*his jeans*—and a pale gray button-down dress shirt. Holy shit, she'd been in his apartment.

"These are for when you're released." She opened

the narrow closet opposite the bed and busied herself hanging the clothes. She'd brought socks, too, underwear, his cross trainers. He noticed that her hands trembled just slightly as she stowed each item in the closet. "I wasn't sure what kind of shape your other clothes were in, after the accident."

He just watched her. She was obviously nervous, seemingly making things up as she went along. She couldn't seem to hold his gaze or sit still or stop filling the tense silence. "Is there anything else I can bring you? Magazines or books or—"

"No." He was baffled. "Look, um..." He glanced down at the marriage certificate in his hand. "Josephine—" She grimaced and her nose wrinkled. Damn. When she wasn't outrageously sexy, she was unbearably cute.

"It's Joey, and I'll only forgive that mistake once, amnesia or no amnesia.

He couldn't help but smile as he tapped the paper in his hand. "That's not what it says here. Josephine Belinda Bradshaw."

"Well, regardless of what it says there, my name is Joey." Her lashes lowered over those impossibly green eyes and she added, "Joey Coye."

He shook his head. He'd have to resist the cries of his body that were telling him to go along with her scam, whatever it was, just in case she planned to let him exercise a few husbandly prerogatives. He reminded himself that women like her were not his type. And that this was a serious game she was playing. She was up to something.

"Okay. Joey, then. Do you mind me asking how you got into my apartment?"

Her eyes focused on his, filled with enough innocence to fool the devil himself. "You gave me a key, Ash."

"Oh."

The investigative reporter inside jumped with questions. His libido was making noises of surrender. Loud noises. But the still-small voice of self-preservation squeaked its dissent.

Because, after all, the accident had been no accident. Someone was trying very hard to kill him.

Then again, forewarned was forearmed, right? And what better way to find out what she was up to than to play this out? She certainly looked harmless enough.

"Ash? Is anything wrong?"

He sighed. "No. As a matter of fact, you couldn't have come at a better time. They're springing me today."

Her eyes doubled in size at that instant. "T-today?"

"Yeah. Got the news ten minutes before you got here. So if you'll hand me those clothes, I'll be ready to leave by the time they bring in my discharge papers."

"Leave?"

"You *are* taking me home, aren't you?" He was enjoying her panic, but he was careful not to show it. He kept his expression blank, trusting.

"Home? I don't—"

"No." He stopped her before she could say anything else. Eyes downcast, he bit his lower lip to keep from grinning. "It's okay, I understand. I thought when you said you wanted to pick up where we left off..." He swallowed an imaginary lump. "It's all right. What kind of a husband would I be, like this?

He'd called her bluff. He'd watched her squirm, and now he was giving her a way out. Obviously whatever scam she was pulling wasn't meant to extend beyond this hospital room. He could wait until later to do a background check on her, figure out what this fiasco had been all about.

But wait a minute. Oh, hell no! She marched to that closet, gathered up his clothes, brought them to the bed, then perched on the mattress and gripped his shoulders. Her eyes stabbed into his with unmistakable sincerity and some kind of raw power.

No eyes had ever been that green. She had to be wearing tinted contacts. Didn't she?

"Don't ever let me hear you talk that way again," she told him. "I was just taken by surprise. I didn't realize they'd let you go so soon with a head injury this serious. I figured..." She shook her head fast and her crazy curls swung back and forth over her face. "Of course I'm taking you home. I wouldn't have it any other way."

He frowned, wondering how she managed to seem so genuine when she was lying though her teeth. Damn, she was good. "Are you sure?"

Her shoulders squared and her spine stiffened. Determination lit her eyes. "Get dressed, Ash. I'll go and see about getting your release forms and we'll get out of here."

He nodded and watched the sway of her hips, as mesmerizing as a hypnotist's pocket watch, as she turned and left. When the door closed, he shook himself, got out of the bed, went to the door and cracked it, just to be sure she wasn't standing outside. Then he grabbed his phone.

When he heard his editor's voice on the line, he didn't waste time with preamble. "There's a drop-dead gorgeous woman here claiming to be my wife, Rad. She wants to take me home. I'm going."

Radley Ketchum chortled. "You? Married? Ash, maybe they'd better x-ray your head one more time, huh?

What's going on?"

"I'm serious." Ash darted a glance toward the door and rushed on. "She has a certificate that says I married her in Vegas on Saturday."

"And she expects you to buy it? You? The most dedicated bachelor in the state of New York?"

"Well, she probably figures I don't know that, don't you think?"

Rad was silent for a long moment. "Look, you better not go with her. This whole deal was supposed to keep you alive, not get you killed."

He thought about the look in Joey Bradshaw's eyes when he'd pretended emotional agony. "I don't think it's her."

"Oh, no? What makes you so sure?"

Ash shook his head. "I don't know. Gut feeling, maybe."

"Does she smoke?"

"How the hell do I know if she smokes? Look, I'll let you know where I am when I get there, okay?"

"She lights up a cigarette, my friend, you get the hell out. You have any urge to stick around, you just think about those butts with the coral-frost lipstick stains on them that the cops found at the scenes of all three murders."

"Yeah. Don't worry, I'm not suicidal."

"One more thing. Get her address on record somewhere before you leave the hospital, just in case you can't call with it later. Phone number, too. Give me her name right now and I'll see what I can find out about her."

"Her name, she says, is Mrs. Ashville Coye."

"Very funny."

"The marriage certificate reads Josephine Belinda Bradshaw. Calls herself Joey."

"Got it. Take care of yourself. And, Ash?"

"Yeah?"

"Just in case she *is* our slasher, you be real careful not to let on that the amnesia is just a cover."

He disconnected and got dressed just in time. She was back at the speed of sound and, moments later, pushing him through the corridors in a wheelchair that was completely unnecessary, but required. Probably by the hospital's lawyers. She seemed nervous. Her eyes darted around, seemingly watching everyone. Ash steered himself toward the nurse's desk, taking her with him. He asked the nurse on duty for a pad and a pen and turned toward his "wife."

"What's your address?"

"Eight twenty-nine Gaskin, in Clay. Why?"

He jotted it down. "Just in case anyone tries to reach me here, I want to let them know where I am."

Her eyes widened. She reached past him to rip the top page from the notepad and then crumpled it in her fist. "I don't think that's such a good idea."

Ash got up out of the wheelchair and leaned negligently against the desk so he could see every expression that crossed her face, eye to eye. There was heightened color to her cheeks. Her full lips were parted slightly in agitation. She was one hell of an attractive woman. "Why not?" he asked.

"I just...I don't like my home address being...readily available to any nut case who happens to ask for it, that's all." She tugged the pen from his hand, leaned over the pad and wrote something down. She shoved it across the desk to the nurse. "If anyone tries to reach Mister—my husband—give them this number."

"So during my sentence, will I be allowed visitors?"

She whirled to face him, her hair flying. God, she was jumpy. He smiled so she'd know he was kidding. He wasn't, but it wouldn't pay to let too much show. His "wife's" expression eased slightly, and she picked up a large zippered bag from the desk, offered him a shaky smile, and started for the elevators.

Ash caught up within a second or two, waving off the nurse who started yelling about the mandatory wheelchair. "What've you got there, Joey?"

"What?" She thumped the down arrow repeatedly, gaze raking the halls.

"The bag."

Her brows lifted, but she handed him the bag. "Your personal effects. The stuff they took off you when you were admitted. You know, wallet, loose change." She averted her eyes. "Wedding ring."

Oh, man, she didn't miss a trick, this phony wife of his. If there was a ring in that bag, she'd put it there, just now. And he hadn't seen a thing.

"Wouldn't want to go too long not wearing that," he muttered. "Feel naked without it."

"Are you being sarcastic or making a joke?" She searched his face, her own worried, wary. He shrugged. The doors slid open and she shot a nervous glance at the people inside. It took her a few ticks, as if she had to study each face individually before she made up her mind. About what, he had no idea. Ash caught the doors before they slid closed again.

"We're holding people up, Joey. And here comes that wheelchair Nazi nurse," he said, nodding toward the nurse pushing the ridiculous chair their way. "Something wrong?"

Shaking her head, she stepped into the elevator. She stood very close to him as the doors slid closed, he noticed. Her attitude was damned strange. Not like someone who was pulling a scam just to get him in the sack—if that was what she was up to. God knew, it wasn't necessary. He'd have obliged her in a New York minute if she'd simply asked. One time and one time only, of course. She was not his type. She was his anti-type, in fact. Qualification number one for the future Mrs. Ashville Coye was that she not be promiscuous enough to have sex on the first date. He'd prefer she not be promiscuous at all.

But looking at her, all tight fitting leather and centerfold hair, he thought she was a walking advertisement for a good time. That's why he figured he'd have known Joey Bradshaw was no wife of his, even if the amnesia had been real. It was in those bedroom eyes that seemed to look right through him, to his hidden fantasies. And it was in those luscious lips, so full and plump that they made a man want to taste them.

He scoffed at his own train of thought. Probably collagen.

The doors slid open and she was the first to step out. She gave a quick glance around the lobby, following it with one over her shoulder to be sure he was right behind her. Then she started for the exit. No less than seven male heads turned as she passed, he noted.

She didn't seem to notice, just strode purposefully across the parking lot while Ash followed. The July sun rebounded from the pavement, making the asphalt feel like an oven. There was no hint of a breeze, and the air was heavy and stifling. She stopped beside a monster-size, glistening black motorcycle. Grabbing a black helmet with an angular, tinted face shield, she pulled it over her head. When he stopped right behind her, she held out one that matched.

"You're kidding, right?"

She thumbed her visor back, tilted her head to one side. "If I'd known you were being released today, I'd have brought the car."

"That's not what I—"

"Look, why don't you go back to that coffee shop off the lobby? I'll ride home and get the car." She frowned, and rushed on. "No, no, that won't work. Can't leave you alone." Then she she snapped her fingers. "I know, we'll call a cab and leave the bike—"

"You talk too much, you know that?" He grabbed the helmet and pulled it on, wincing as it slid past the bandaged wound on his head. The amnesia might be phony, but the damned concussion was real enough. "I'm fine. I was just wondering about you." He looked doubtfully at the bike as he fastened the strap under his chin. "Looks like a lot for a little thing like you to handle. Mind if I drive?"

"The last time you drove, you wound up in the back of an ambulance." She flipped her visor back down with a snap and swung one leg over the seat. Well, he'd managed to tweak her temper. He'd been wondering if her concern for his health and happiness would have any bounds.

The Harley was low slung despite its size. Still, her feet barely reached the pavement. She kicked the motor to life and revved it. Ash caught a whiff of gasoline and exhaust, sighed in resignation and climbed on behind her. He slid forward on the slanting seat until he was pressed to her backside. Putting his arms around her waist, he decided he might not mind the ride so much.

She caught his hands in hers and moved them until they just rested on her sides, above her hips. Again the visor was thumbed up. She twisted her head and shouted above the roar of the motor. "Move 'em and lose 'em... darling."

He thumbed his visor back, too, and tried for a pained expression. "I'm sorry."

Her anger vanished. Her huge eyes softened and she almost pouted. "It's just less distracting this way, Ash. That's all."

He nodded, a little surprised at how easily he could skirt her anger by acting hurt. A con artist centerfold with a heart of gold. He could hardly wait to find out what she was up to.

And whether it had anything to do with the Slasher murders.

He pushed his visor down. She did likewise. A second later they lurched forward and shot into traffic.

CHAPTER 2

Joey had done her research on investigative reporter Ashville Coye. In fact, she'd done little else for the three days since she'd heard of his highly publicized accident. She thought she knew him well enough to pull this off. She told herself that over and over again as she leaned into curves without easing her speed, and finally veered right, into the parking lot of the Three Rivers Inn. The bike dipped suddenly into the sunken lot, leaving her stomach somewhere in the region of her throat—God, she loved that sensation!—then zipped out the other side, onto Gaskin Road.

His hands tightened on her waist. She ignored the warmth that settled somewhere under her skin where he touched her, and smiled. He must be hating this. Aside from being a confirmed bachelor and a notorious playboy, he was a die-hard conservative. It must be killing him to ride on the back of a Harley driven by a woman.

But she couldn't take any pleasure in his discomfort. The man was in a terrible situation. He probably didn't even remember his political leanings. Even so, his remark about her letting him drive had ticked her off. Still did.

She swung right again, into the long dirt driveway, then onto the square paved parking area her mom had always called "The Strip," and pulled to a stop at the front patio. Killing the motor, she heeled the kickstand down and leaned the bike onto it. Then she tugged off her helmet and shook her hair. She glanced over her shoulder to see he'd already removed his. He was looking at the big, white split-level and shaking his head.

"This is yours?" He seemed skeptical. "What are you, independently wealthy?"

"It's no mansion." She swung her leg up in front of her and over the seat, landing with a little hop on the sizzling blacktop. The air smelled of the river out back, and there might've been a hint of rain mixed in.

He got off, as well, following her around the side of the house, over the well-worn path and to the back door. "Your backyard's as big as a football field...and it's riverfront." He shaded his eyes with one hand and looked over the smooth green lawn to the narrow brown river at its edge, some sixty yards away.

"Half a football field at best." She unlocked the back door and swung it wide, preceding him in.

"You don't want to tell me, is that it?"

She faced him and saw his suspicious eyes, and the stubbornness suggested by his set jaw. Uneasiness crept up her spine. But he was asking about the house, the property. Not her lies.

Necessary lies. Necessary to keep him alive. And Caroline.

"Ash, there's nothing I won't tell you. Just ask."

"Okay, I will. How does a woman your age afford a prime hunk of real estate like this?"

She wasn't ready to tell him about her business. If she told him a little, he was liable to go snooping around and find out more. He was just the type who'd write her off as a lunatic and count himself lucky to escape with his hide intact. So she answered a different part of his question.

"My age?" She added a smile, and said, "Thanks for that, Ash, but I'm thirty. Not exactly fresh from the cradle. But to answer your question, I grew up in this house. When Mom and Dad decided to move to a retirement village in Florida, I didn't want to see it go. Parents make very understanding mortgage holders." She slipped out of her jacket and hung it on a hook near the door. "They didn't even check my credit score." She tried to send him a grin, get him to relax a little with humor.

It didn't work. "What do you do for a living, Joey?" His tone said he wouldn't give it up.

"I'm an independent consultant."

"To whom?"

She wished he would drop it. "Businesses, mostly." To change the subject, she waved a hand to indicate the room they were in, a sparse area with cement floors, lots of padded mats, white walls, and several pieces of exercise equipment. "This is my torture chamber, as you can see. There's a bathroom through here, and that other door leads to the basement."

His gaze lingered on the weight bench and narrowed. "You pump iron?"

"You disapprove?"

"It's not very feminine."

"The results are."

He looked her over thoroughly, his gaze traveling a deliberately slow path over her. For the first time in her life, Joey felt uncomfortable in skintight pants and a skimpy bustier. "I'll let you know," he quipped.

He was being obnoxious, and it was deliberate. She knew it was. The pig. So why did a small, hot shiver zip up her spine like an electric charge?

"Why'd we come in this way, instead of through the sliding doors at the front?" He was glancing around with something more intense than curiosity.

"Mom was vigilant about her carpeting. It wouldn't have mattered if the president had come to the door, she'd have told him to go around back."

He finally laughed, just a little, and the sound was so comfortable she relaxed her tensed up muscles. "Come on, I'll show you the rest." He followed her up a set of shallow stairs, into her cozy kitchen. A doorway at each end led into the L-shaped living-dining room. He moved around, eyes seeming to take in everything at once.

It occurred to her that maybe he was looking for something familiar, something that would jog his elusive memory, and she felt a twinge of conscience. "Ash, you really didn't spend much time here. Your own apartment will probably seem more familiar to you, though. We'll spend some time there later on, if you want. See if it stirs up the past for you."

He frowned at her. "Why would you want to do that?"

She frowned right back. "Why wouldn't I?"

"Now there's an interesting question." Before she could form a reply, he was walking away from her. She swallowed. He must suspect that she wasn't being honest about their...relationship. She'd have to watch herself. He'd stepped into the living room and was looking up another set of stairs.

"Three bedrooms and a bath up there. Go ahead, look

around. I want you to feel at home here." She meant it, she realized. She wanted this to be as easy on him as possible. The man was going through what was probably one of the worst things any human could experience. Loss of his own identity. And to make things worse, she was giving him a false one to latch onto.

He started up the stairs, but the sound of a horn blasting out front stopped him. He joined her in looking through the sliding-glass door with the broom handle in its tracks to prevent it being opened. He gave that a closer look, and shot her a puzzled glance.

"Same broom handle has been there since I was a kid. I told you, nobody comes in the front door."

His smile was real, and for a moment it distracted her. Then she returned her gaze to the car outside. In the driveway, Caroline and her girls spilled from their minivan and trooped over the path, waving gaily.

Joey felt the bottom fall out of her stomach as she realized the implications of her sister's untimely visit. She hadn't been prepared to begin this thing so soon. She'd expected to have time to figure out a way to talk to Caroline.

"What's the matter?" He said it as if he already knew and was poking fun at her. "You're so pale all of a sudden. Who is that?"

"My...sister, Caroline." She closed her eyes. Think! "Ash, I...I haven't told her about you...about us." She felt sick.

"You didn't tell your own sister you ran off and got married?" His dark brows made surprised arches over his brown eyes and he shook his head, tsking repeatedly. "Shame on you, Joey."

There was no time to beg him to keep his mouth

shut. There was no knocking among family...not in this house. Never had been. In a fraction of a second, two blond, giggling girls were racing up the stairs and hurling themselves into Joey's arms.

"Aunt Joey, we came for a picnic!"

"Can we go fishing?"

"We'll throw them back, we promise."

"Please? Please?"

"Slow down, you two. Easy." Joey hugged her nieces, feeling the surge of affection they always inspired in her. She adored them, and she knew part of the reason was probably the unlikelihood of her ever having children of her own. She was not mommy material. "Go on to the kitchen. There's candy in the lazy Susan. Go on now."

They peeled themselves from her and raced back into the kitchen. Their mother, dressed as always in baggy sweats and an oversize T-shirt, which she thought hid the fact that her figure had suffered a bit from carrying the two girls, stood behind them. Her hair, so like Joey's in length, texture and coloring, was pulled into a bouncy ponytail, and her smile was bright, but curious.

"Hi, Joey." She glanced uneasily between her and Ash, questions all over her face. "Sorry we didn't call first. I never guessed you'd have company. We can go if—"

"Oh, I'm not company." Ash stepped forward, extending a hand. "My name's Ashville Coye. You must be Caroline. You're more beautiful than your sister told me you were."

Oh, his amnesia hadn't made him forget how to ooze charm. Stunned, Caroline shook his hand weakly. Her gaze still jumping from Joey to Ash and back again, she blinked, and said, "Ashville Coye—the reporter who's doing the series on the Slasher murders?"

He shot Joey a quick glance. "I guess that would be me."

"Well, what a coincidence! It's nice to meet you." She seemed a bit confused. "I heard about your accident. I hope you're...better now."

"Your sister is helping me through."

Caroline smiled brightly, then glanced apologetically at Joey again. "Look, the girls and I will go to the park instead. I'm really sorry I—"

"I think you'd better stay," Ash said in a deep, steady voice. "Joey and I have some news."

Joey swallowed hard, feeling as if a fist had just punched her in the solar plexus.

"News? Joey, what does he mean?" Caroline's voice went a shade higher. "Is anything wrong, honey? You're not sick are you?" A hand immediately went to her sister's forehead, then her cheek. Why was that always the pattern with mothers? Any mother, anywhere in the world, would do it in exactly the same manner. Palm to forehead, then to cheek. And not just to her own brood, but to anyone, friend or foe, who showed signs of having a fever.

Joey shook her head. "Nothing's wrong. I'm not sick, Caro."

"Is it Toni? She's not in trouble again, is she?"

At Ash's curious look, she said, "Toni's another sister," Joey said.

"Half sister," Caroline corrected. "Joey and I have the same mom. Joey and Toni have the same dad."

"Toni's fine," Joey told her sister. "She and Nick have set a date, and they've narrowed their dream house search down to three Victorians. One of which is down this side of Ithaca, so that's the one I'm obviously pulling for."

"So what's wrong then?" Caroline asked. And then she frowned. "It's this Slasher thing, isn't it? You've gotten yourself into some kind of trouble and—"

"No, Caroline." Joey glanced up—because Ash was at least a foot taller than her—and knew there was no way out of this. Next she looked into her sister's blue eyes and felt her own sting. Caroline might never forgive her for this when she learned the truth, but it would be worth it to save her life. There was no one in this world closer to her than Caroline.

"I...that is, Ash and I..."

She couldn't go on. Her mouth felt as though she'd rinsed it with ashes. Caroline would never believe this. She knew her too well.

Ash's hand closed around hers and lifted it. "I think this says it all."

Frowning, Joey glanced down to see the simple gold band she'd bought and placed on her left hand. It was a prop. Nothing but a prop.

Caroline's eyes widened. Then she made a face. "This is a joke, right? It has to be a joke. Look, Mr. Coye, no one knows how much my sister detests the institution of marriage better than I. You can't seriously be standing here trying to tell me that she...that you... Oh, my God, you're not kidding. Are you?"

When he saw the tears pooling in Joey's eyes, Ash thought maybe he'd taken his challenge a bit too far. He didn't have a clue why she wanted him to believe she was his wife. He'd thought she would cut the act if forced. He'd been wrong. Whatever was going on in her head, she must be damned serious about it. Otherwise, she never would have continued the charade in front of her sister. It was pretty obvious how close they were.

It was also increasingly and uncomfortably obvious that Joey had some kind of involvement in the murders. He'd wondered about that from the beginning, and her sister's cryptic comment about the killings added credence to his suspicion. But, damn, it was tough to look at her and suspect her of being a serial killer.

A moment later he found himself enveloped in a hesitant but genuine hug. Then Caroline hugged Joey even harder. Fiercely, really. And she was crying, too. She sniffed and straightened. "I never thought it would happen." She sniffled some more. "Joey, honey, didn't you even have a wedding?"

"It was a...sort of a...spur-of-the-moment decision."

Caroline frowned, this time at both of them, finally settling her gaze on Ash. "Did you get my sister pregnant? Is that what this is—?"

"Caroline, please!" Joey diverted the woman's attention. "Look, you've been after me to settle down for years. You ought to be happy for me."

Her lips thinned as her gaze moved downward to Joey's admirably flat belly. "I'm sorry. It's just that it's so sudden. I'm in shock, that's all." She took Joey's hands in hers and stared into her sister's eyes. "Are you happy, honey? Because if you are, then that's all that matters."

Joey kept a remarkably straight face. The tears were a nice touch. "Yes, I'm very, very happy, Caro."

Caroline swallowed. Without releasing Joey's hands or even turning her head she called, "Girls, come in here. I want you to meet your new uncle."

The incessant stream of high-pitched chatter died abruptly. Two angelic blond faces peered into the room, quieter than they'd been since they'd arrived.

"Ashville, these are my daughters. Bethany is seven, and Brittany is six. Girls, this is your Uncle Ashville... Aunt Joey's new husband."

Two pairs of blue eyes rounded. "Husband?"

"Uncle?"

The older one came forward, and Ash, feeling more guilty by the minute, dropped down to one knee. He felt a new anger at his make-believe wife. Playing head games with him was bad enough, but to start in with a couple of helpless kids, and, in effect, to force him to play along, that was too much. Then again, he was the one who'd forced the issue. He just hadn't expected her to take it this far.

One pair of eyes probed his. "Are you going to turn Aunt Joey into a boring-baby-machine?"

That question, coming from such a pint-size spokesperson, almost made him laugh out loud. "A what?"

The second one, Brittany, joined her sister. "That's what happens when you get married," she explained seriously. "You never get to have any fun anymore. You have to stay home and do laundry and have babies."

"And husbands boss you around and tell you what to do."

"We're never getting married."

"Never."

Both girls stood before him, pudgy arms crossed, jewel blue eyes hostile, pale golden brows furrowed. They could have passed for twins.

"Just who told you all that?" he asked, amused.

"Aunt Joey," they chorused.

All eyes turned to her, and she shrugged helplessly.

"Well, you see, when your Aunt Joey met me she decided it wouldn't be so bad to do laundry and have babies, after all."

"The hell I did." She clapped a hand over her mouth, but her eyes shot daggers at him.

The little girls studied him, tilting their golden heads to one side.

"Look, we'd better go." Caroline took the girls' hands. "I want to have you over for dinner. Soon. I'll call you, Joey. *We'll talk.*" She paused at the stairway, glanced at her sister and frowned hard. "Is everything all right?"

"Yeah. Stop worrying."

Caroline nodded, hugged her sister once more and opened the back door.

"He's very handsome, Mommy." He thought that was Brittany. It was hard to be sure. They were dressed alike in denim bib overalls with little pink bows down the seams. The only difference in them that he could detect was that Brittany was about an inch shorter. And they wore different colored hair ribbons.

"Will he make Aunt Joey stop riding the motorcycle?" That was the yellow ribbon. Bethany, he thought.

"Will she still get to take us sp'lunkin' when we're big enough?" And that was the red—wait a minute. *Sp'lunkin'*?

That was all he heard, because the door was closed and the girls hustled outside. He cocked a brow at Joey. *"Sp'lunkin'?"*

"Caving." If looks could kill, Ash figured he'd better start on his last will and testament.

"Caving?"

Her glare was ferocious. "How could you do that? Just stand there and blurt out that we were married? I could kill you!"

Interesting choice of words, considering that someone had so recently tried. "Well, what was I supposed to do? You *are* my wife. Aren't you?"

She shook her head fast. "I wanted to tell her in my own way. She's going to think I've lost my mind!"

"No doubt, seeing your views on marriage. Boring baby machine?"

Her eyes narrowed. "It's accurate. Look at Caroline. She used to be crazy, fun, confident. Lately Ted's turning her into a—" She bit her lip, stopping herself.

"Go on, into a what?"

She shook her head. "Doesn't matter. It's a whole different situation. You're nothing like Ted."

"Are you sure?" He really wanted to hear more about her views of male domination. Caroline looked perfectly content to him. Obviously loved her girls. Then again, who wouldn't? They were heart grabbers, those two.

She glanced up at him from beneath her lashes. "That you're nothing like Ted? The day you prove otherwise, you're out the door, pal."

He shrugged. "So what's for dinner?"

She held her anger for a moment longer. Then it dissolved and she laughed. It was a small laugh, but a laugh all the same. For a second he was insanely glad he'd managed to douse her blazing anger and make her smile. Just because she wasn't the type of woman he'd spent most of his life looking for didn't mean she had to be his enemy.

But if she was plotting something, like his murder, for example, she definitely was.

"I'm not much of a cook. And I don't aspire to be. There are more exciting ways to kill time, you know."

Figured. Not only did she dress almost as provocatively

as his mother had, she didn't cook, either. A sudden suspicion hit him. Maybe that was why she wouldn't tell him what she did for a living. If she was a business consultant, then he was a brain surgeon. Maybe she was a prostitute.

He searched her face and glanced again at the surroundings. It certainly didn't look like the kind of place where men trooped in and out at all hours. The kind of place where a young boy would huddle in the darkness, afraid of the sounds coming from his mother's room, afraid of the harsh, deep voices of strangers.

"Is anything wrong?"

He shook the idiotic idea from his head and doused the surge of memory with a supreme and practiced act of will. "If you don't cook, then what do you eat?"

"You have anything against pizza?"

"Nope."

She frowned, tilting her head to one side. "What is it, Ash?" She took a step nearer, searching his face with those sparkling green eyes that seemed to exude laser beams. "You remembered something, didn't you?"

He shook his head. "No. I was trying to remember, but no luck." Actually, his childhood with his sex-for-hire mother was something he wished he could forget. "So are you going to call for that pizza, or am I? I'm starving."

Something was bothering him, she was sure of that much. But if he wouldn't say, she sure wasn't going to press him. It wasn't as if she had any right to. She wasn't *really* his wife.

Still, the preoccupied look in his dark eyes remained throughout dinner and right up to the late news, when he finally seemed ready for conversation.

"I take it ours wasn't a long courtship," he said.

She swallowed hard and faced him across the room. He was in the forest green recliner, but not tipped back. She sat curled with her legs under her on the matching sofa. "What makes you say that?"

"Your sister had never met me until today."

He was watching her face as she answered, and she couldn't help but avoid his probing eyes. She hated lying. If there was any other way, she'd have taken it. "It was kind of a whirlwind thing."

"Swept you off your feet, did I?"

"Something like that."

"Wined you and dined you until you couldn't resist me?"

"God, no. Wining and dining would bore me." Her answer was spontaneous, and honest.

He leaned forward in his chair. "Then what? What kinds of things did we do together?"

She pressed her lips tightly. She'd rather say nothing than spin blatant lies. Best to stick as near the truth as possible. She could tell him the kinds of things she liked doing, even though she'd never done any of them with him.

"I have an aversion to all things mundane, but even for me, an occasional night vegging in front of the TV is just what the doctor ordered."

"And what do we do when we aren't vegging?" He was just a little pale, and there were lines of tension in his face, like he was just barely restraining himself from grimacing. She felt a dull throbbing in her head, and knew it was his, not her own.

"Sometimes we'd jump on the bike and ride south

till we'd see more cows then people. Then we'd find a likely patch of wilderness and do a little poking around. Sometimes we'd just stay home and laze in the backyard. Especially on a warm, clear night, with the river sloshing along and the crickets raising a ruckus. I'm a die-hard stargazer, you know."

"No. I didn't know."

She felt a little uncomfortable under his intense gaze. "No, how could you?"

He shifted in the chair, elbows on his knees. "No nightclubs? No dance parties?"

"Do I look like a party animal to you?"

He nodded.

She couldn't hide her surprise. "Really? Well, I'm not. I like excitement, but that doesn't do it for me."

"What does? Spelunking?"

She nodded hard. "Ever tried it?"

"I don't know. Have I?"

She could have slapped herself for making a slip like that. "Like I said, we haven't known each other that long. You've never tried it with me. But that doesn't mean... I keep forgetting you can't remember."

He shrugged. "I can't imagine it's anything I'd find to be much of a thrill. Find a cave and snoop around inside. Stir up a few bats and step in stagnant water. Doesn't sound all that interesting to me."

She laughed a little, but she was getting the strangest feelings from him. Like unease. He didn't like talking about caves, much less, she imagined, exploring them. The idea of the small, dark spaces gave him an unreasonable amount of trepidation, or something. Something he was trying not to feel.

"There's a lot more to it than that, Ash. I've been

miles into a cave, miles underground, in places where no one's ever set foot before. I've crawled through passages on my belly, only to emerge at a hundred-foot drop, then rappelled down it with nothing but my rope and carabiners." She shook her head, remembering that particular trip, and a little thrill raced up her spine. Then she sensed the small tremor that raced up his, only his wasn't caused by excitement. It was something darker. And then it was gone.

"Sounds dangerous."

"Risky is a better word. Of course, the more experienced you are, and the more care you take, the less the risk."

"And you're experienced?"

"Um-hm."

"And you take the utmost care?"

She averted her eyes. "Pretty much."

"Interesting."

She glanced at him, saw his studious frown and wondered what he was thinking. Then his gaze dropped to the neckline of her blouse and narrowed.

"Ready for bed?"

She drew a sudden breath, then caught it, releasing it in a controlled manner. "I've been meaning to talk to you about that."

"I figured you had."

She licked her lips and swallowed. His eyes followed the motion. "For all practical purposes, Ash, we're strangers. I mean, for all you know about me, we could have just met today."

"Can't argue with you there."

She squared her shoulders. "So I think it would be best if we used separate bedrooms."

He bit his inner cheek. "Because you don't believe in sleeping with strangers?"

She frowned hard. "What kind of a question is that?"

"A fair one, I think. Does that apply to all strangers or only the ones you're married to?"

For a second she gaped. Then she snapped her jaw shut with an effort and tried to control a surge of anger. "You're really a jerk, you know that?"

"I've been called worse." He was silent a moment. "Don't you think a night of unbridled passion with my wife would jog my memory?"

"I don't give a damn what it would jog! Newsflash, asshole, amnesia isn't a free pass for bad manners." She got to her feet, her anger simmering. "At the top of the stairs, turn left. That's your room."

He stood as well. "You know, for a newly married woman, you're not acting very wifely."

"I don't feel very 'wifely,'" she said.

He took a step forward, bringing him very close to her. He caught her shoulders in his hands. "I could fix that." With a tug, she was flattened to his body. She felt the hard planes of it through his shirt and a tiny tongue of heat curled in some unexplored cave within her.

She drew back her hand and slapped him.

He released her, blinking in shock. "What the hell was that for?"

"You figure it out."

"But you're my wife."

"And you assume that means I provide sex on demand, right? And if I refuse, you just go find it elsewhere. That's the way it works, isn't it?" She was angry, blurting things out as they entered her mind without thought to what he'd make of them.

"You have one hell of a warped outlook, lady."

"I've seen enough to confirm it as fact. Good night, Mr. Coye." She turned on her heel and marched up the stairs.

"Night...Mrs. Coye."

She stopped on the fifth step, her back stiffening. Then she forced herself to continue.

CHAPTER 3

His head throbbed, reminding him painfully of the very real injury behind his feigned memory loss. He had a hell of a concussion. He was lucky that was all he had, considering his brake line had been cut, and his car totaled from the impact with a city dump truck. He was still more tired than a man his age had any business being.

Still, he'd found Joey Bradshaw's limits. She wasn't willing to take him to bed to perpetuate her little lie. Was that a real sense of morality, or just another cover? Did she know, somehow, what kind of woman he'd been looking for and intend to convince him that she was it? He didn't want a woman like his mother. He wanted a sweet, shy, sensible woman. One who would raise his kids the way kids ought to be raised...not the way he'd grown up. One who would make pot roast for Sunday dinners. One who wouldn't hop into bed with a man on the first date.

He didn't want a biker babe or a thrill seeker. Joey didn't even come close to the model wife he was looking for. So it was a bitter irony that she was the first woman in a long time to say no to him.

But he was pretty sure she was just trying to convince him that she was on the up-and-up. All that talk about stargazing and hiking in the woods. Right, next she'd want him to believe she was fond of daisy picking and orphaned puppies.

It was time to do a little serious investigating. He'd take out his frustration that way.

He knew perfectly well that he hadn't got married in Vegas. He'd been checking the details of a string of murders committed five years ago. Murders remarkably similar to the ones taking place in the Syracuse area now.

In the past, the victims had consisted of four men and one woman. All killed by a single, swift slash to the jugular. They had all been attacked between midnight and 3:00 a.m. No one had reported hearing anything, not a scream, not a scuffle, though the bodies had been found in busy areas. And none of the victims seemed to have had a thing in common, besides the manner in which they'd died.

So far, in Syracuse, three bodies had been found. All men. The MO was the same. Only this time, there was one more clue—cigarette butts found at all of the crime scenes, coral-frost lipstick stains ringing the filters. And for the first time, the police were entertaining the notion that the killer was female.

She'd have to be strong, but not unnaturally so. Just enough to grab a man from behind and draw a razor-sharp blade across his throat. It would only take an instant.

Ash thought again of the trim, firm shape of Joey Bradshaw's arms, and then of the weight bench downstairs. He shook his head, still finding it difficult to believe it could be her.

Then why's she lying, pretending to be my wife? And why did her sister make that remark about the murders getting Joey into trouble?

Again he shook his head. It just wasn't credible. But he found himself recalling her nasty remarks about men a few minutes ago, and wondering what made her so disdainful of his gender. Just how much of a man hater was she?

He began in the living room, and he went through everything. Every cabinet, every closet, every drawer. He found little of interest. Some deep-treaded boots in the closet, along with a pair of helmets with lamps on top, and several neatly looped ropes with some sort of hardware attached. Looked as if she hadn't been kidding about the caving.

Then, on the top shelf of the living room closet, his hand closed around a cool metallic object. A chill raced through him as he pulled it down. A nine-millimeter Ruger. A full clip.

"Damn."

He glanced up the stairs. If there was anything to find, he'd more than likely find it in her bedroom. But how could he look with her sleeping right there?

Maybe the opportunity would arise later. He slipped into the kitchen and picked up the phone, quickly punching in Radley's number. A sleepy, female voice answered, and Ash kicked himself.

"I'm very sorry if I woke you, Amelia," he said to his boss's wife. He should not be calling at this hour. Amelia wasn't well. Cancer that had metastasized to her brain. Poor woman needed her sleep.

"Don't be silly," she said. "Radley's right here. I'll put him on."

A second later Radley's voice came on the line. "Ash? Do you have any idea what time it is?"

"I know, I know, I'm sorry. I just...it was the first chance I've had. Have you dug up anything on my make-believe bride?"

"Nothing yet. I'll have something for you tomorrow. I've got people on it." Ash could hear Rad's footsteps, then a door closed. He was moving into another room to let his ailing wife rest. "How's it going?"

"Damned if I know. She's not...she's not a run-of-the-mill-type woman, Radley."

"In what way?"

Ash sighed hard. "She packs a cannon and rides a Harley, for starters."

"She rides a—listen, Ash, this might be something. I got a look at the police reports today. They put a woman on a motorcycle at the scene of two of the three murders. She showed up when the bodies were found. A gaper, you know."

"Description?" Ash wondered why he felt so disappointed.

"Small woman, large bike, dark helmet with a tinted visor over her face."

Ash swore fluently.

"Maybe you ought to pull out of there, Ash."

"I think I'll stick with her a while."

"If you're sure."

"I am. Let me know when you get the rest of the info, Rad. And I'm really sorry I woke Amelia. How's she doing, anyway?"

"Still in a cast." Ash remembers Rad saying his wife

had taken a fall and broken her hand several weeks ago. "Still, we have more good days than bad," he said. "That's the most we can ask for at this point. I'll talk to you tomorrow."

Ash disconnected. Before he mounted the stairs, he took the clip out of Joey's cannon and replaced the gun in the closet where he'd found it.

Joey knew she was asleep. It wasn't a normal dream; it was lucid. And she knew she didn't want to see it, but she also knew she had to. She might learn something, see something she hadn't seen before. So she didn't struggle against it. Struggling wouldn't make it go away. It would only distract her from paying attention.

There was Ash. He was falling in slow motion, his back hitting the carpeted floor hard, then his head. His eyes were closed. He wasn't getting up. A hand came up in front of her face, then, blocking her view of Ash. The hand seemed to linger before the lens of her vision. It was gloved...a black glove. Buttery-soft kid leather. She could smell it. And there were two small buttons at the wrist. The hand clutched a jeweled dagger, dripping thick red blood.

The vision clouded, faded and began to solidify again in her mind's eye. This time there was only a still form, facedown on the floor. The baggy T-shirt's back was covered in crimson stains. The long, multicolored hair reached into the blood, its ends soaked in it. Near her head, the bloody jeweled dagger rested.

"Caroline!"

Then she felt it, the insidious creeping sensations that were not her own, but echoes of someone else's feelings. Rage, so intense she felt her body shake with it. The shadow of a black soul eclipsed her own for just a moment, and terror held her in an unshakable grip.

Joey sat up in bed, eyes wide in the darkness. She couldn't go on like this! She wouldn't! Tears flooded her eyes, and her throat spasmed. She wished to God she could escape this thing people called a "gift." It was a curse and she didn't want it anymore. Why should she be the only one to know what was going to happen? Why should she be the only person in the world who could prevent her sister's murder? God, she was so afraid she'd fail. What if she failed?

Her bedroom door swung open and Ash filled the doorway, wearing nothing but a pair of boxer briefs. "Joey? You okay?"

She reached out, flicked on the lamp. "I'm okay. Bad dream."

He came in, approached the bed and finally sat on its edge. He did it all slowly, as if waiting for her to object. She kept quiet

"You don't look okay." He lifted one hand, brushed the tears from her face, then looked at his hand as if it had acted without his consent. "You're shaking all over."

She realized slowly that she couldn't keep him from being killed while she slept. She had to be close enough to prevent it at all times. It meant her sister's life. She had to break the killer's chain—and she had to break it with Ash.

"You screamed...your sister's name, I think. Was the dream about her?"

She bit her lip. It was hard, lying all the time, hiding the things that troubled her the most. "I don't remember." Her throat closed off. "It scared the hell out of me, whatever it was."

She tried to catch the sob before it escaped, but she failed. She heard him swear softly just before he slipped his arms around her and pulled her to his chest. "It's okay, Joey. It was just a dream. It's over now."

Her tears dampened his skin. Her cheek was pressed tightly there, and his scent completely invaded her senses, drowning out the memory of that alien presence in her mind. His arms around her were strong and hard and felt as if they could be barriers against the dark invader. She snuggled nearer without quite meaning to. That damned chemical attraction she'd felt before she'd even met him came to life inside her.

"You want me to stay?"

She sniffled, glad he'd offered, so she wouldn't have to ask. She did have to be near him at all times, attraction or no. It had been foolish of her to let her temper make her forget that earlier. What if the killer had struck tonight? Ash could be dead already, and the Slasher on his way to his next victim.

Caroline.

She lifted her head and met his gaze. "I'm not going to have sex with you, Ash."

"I didn't ask, did I? What do you think, that's all I ever think about?"

She felt something then, and it made her frown. Nightmares. God, he had them too, all the time. They'd started a long time ago. That's why he was reacting this way to hers.

That was all. Just that tiny kernel of revelation. Then nothing.

She sighed, shook her head and settled back under the covers. Ash lifted them and slipped in beside her. They both lay on their backs, looking at the ceiling, saying nothing. She wondered if his body was as stiff with tension as hers was.

She had her answer a second later. He swore and rolled onto his side, facing her. "This is ridiculous. Neither one of us bites. Roll over."

She did, facing away from him. A second later she went rigid as his arms came around her from behind and his body snuggled closer to hers. "Relax, Joey. I'm not up to anything. I promise."

She did relax after a moment. Actually, it was cozy lying this way. Incredibly warm and sort of...safe feeling. It was a real shame she had to lie awake and wait for him to fall asleep. It would have been so easy to just curl into his strong embrace and drift off.

But an hour later, when his deep, rhythmic breathing told her he slept, she eased his arms from around her waist and slid carefully to the edge of the bed. Then she paused, listening. His breathing pattern didn't alter. She slipped to the floor and tiptoed out of the room, going down the stairs.

She went to the closet in the living room and took down the gun. She knew by its lack of weight that it was empty. A little chill snaked up her spine.

She could have sworn she'd left the gun loaded. She'd deliberately put it out of reach of her two nieces, but in a spot where she could get to it quickly. So who had taken the clip out?

A tremor worked its way up her spine as she dragged a footstool nearer, climbed onto it and reached farther into the closet, to the shoe box in the back. She removed the shoes and pulled out a box of cartridges and the extra clip. She didn't get down first. She filled the clip right there, while standing on the stool, then slipped it up into the hollow handle of the gun. On unsteady legs, she stepped down and went through the house, rechecking every lock. But they were all still secure. No one had been there.

So who had taken the clip out of her gun? There was only one answer. Ash. And if he'd found the Ruger, then he must have been snooping. And if he was snooping, then he must not trust her. He must suspect something.

She had to be more convincing. She couldn't mess this up. Not when her sister's life—when Ash's life—depended on it.

Her nerves jangled. Her muscles twitched. She paced the floor for a while, until her pacing took her to the kitchen cabinet where she kept the cigarettes. She'd quit smoking a decade ago, but since these murders and her visions about them, the urge to light up once in a while had become overwhelming. She opened a window to let the smoke out, and tried to clear her mind.

Something was wrong. Something more than just the suspicious mind of the man upstairs, sleeping in her bed. Some darkness loomed too close, reaching out its gnarled, ugly claw. She shivered, took a final drag from the stump of the cigarette and ground it out in an empty tuna can she snatched out of the recycle bin.

Only then did she slip silently up the stairs, the gun at her side. She paused by her side of the bed, glanced once at Ash and frowned. He wasn't in precisely the same position as before. She watched him a moment. His dark lashes rested on his face. A shadow of beard darkened his jaw, giving him a fierce look and making her want to rub her hands over his bristles. His arm was on the outside of the covers, and she could tell easily that his disapproval of weight training applied only to women. She wanted to touch his arm, to feel the iron in those bands of muscle when he tensed beneath her fingers.

This was stupid, this moon-eyed staring at him as he slept. She was a grown woman, not a love-struck teen. But even with the dread embedded in her soul, she felt the attraction. It was impossible to forget it, even for a minute. It had been a little easier when he'd come on like a cave man earlier. But she knew that wasn't the real Ash, she sensed it. Him coming in here in his shorts because she'd had a bad dream—that was the real Ash. Knowing that made it harder to stay immune to him.

She thought about slipping the gun under her pillow, but was afraid he'd touch it in his sleep. If it hadn't been Ash who had taken her bullets, then he still didn't know about the gun. What on earth would he think if he knew? She decided on the drawer in the nightstand beside the bed. She could reach it quickly and with a minimum of effort. She'd just have to remember to keep the bedroom door locked when the girls were around.

As she closed the drawer, Ash moved. She swung her head around quickly, but his eyes remained closed, his breathing steady. He'd only rolled onto his back, exposing the chest that so disturbed her. It also revealed the ripples of his abdomen. She could see the six-pack beneath his skin even as he lay there, completely relaxed. She had the absurd image of running her hands over him, feeling the hard shape of his muscles, the warmth of his skin against her palms. She almost groaned aloud.

Shaking her head, she gently eased herself into the bed. A second later she was imprisoned by his arm snapping her waist, and one hair-roughened leg covering hers. Rather than struggling free, she opted to relax and go to sleep. She told herself it was so she wouldn't wake him. In truth, his weight was more a comfort than a burden, even if such closeness was more likely to keep her awake than lull her to sleep.

He couldn't rest easy after she'd sneaked away to get the cannon and had returned, tucking it within easy reach. He told himself it was okay, that he'd removed the bullets already. But he couldn't be sure she hadn't reloaded it, because he hadn't searched the place for bullets yet, and he couldn't be sure she wasn't a lunatic who was planning to shoot him. He figured at least with his arms around her, he'd know if she went for the gun.

Unfortunately this close he could smell the lingering aroma of cigarette smoke that clung to her hair. Radley's words floated into his mind like filmy ghosts. *She lights up a cigarette, my friend, you get the hell out...think about those butts with the coral-frost lipstick stains on them....*

He tried *not* to think about those butts, even as he wondered what shade of lipstick she used. Then he asked himself if he was the one who was stark, raving mad. Despite the fact that he had every reason to believe she might roll over at any minute and try to blow his head off, his body was beginning to respond in some very primitive ways to the feel of her.

Beyond the clean, crisp feel of the sheets, he felt the silky texture of the nightgown she wore. Beyond the musky smoke in her hair, he could smell the shampoo she used. Under the weight of his thigh, hers was like silk, and firm, and so shapely he wanted to trace the length of it with his lips.

The image jarred him, and he had to back off a little

so she wouldn't feel his response to her tight, rounded backside pressing into his groin.

How could he lust this way after a woman who might be out to kill him? Maybe that head injury had done more damage than he knew.

Eventually, after hours of restlessness and several changes in position that did nothing to ease his discomfort, he must have slept. When he woke she was not in the bed. He couldn't believe it. The rising sun slanted through the window, spilling over the empty pillow where she'd been. He sat up quickly, glanced around the room and found it empty. He yanked the drawer open. The gun sat there like a stern reminder. A quick check and revealed that the damned thing had been reloaded...to the hilt. He slammed the drawer, swearing, threw back the covers and got up just as she stepped in from a door that linked the bedroom directly to a bathroom.

She wore a pair of low slung jeans and a tank top that fit like a second skin. Her hair was a mass of long wet straggles. Water beaded on her neck. His gaze moved lower, to the round breasts beneath the clingy material, to the luscious rise of them visible at the scooping neckline and the droplets that clung there. A rush of blatant, animal lust seared him from the inside out, and he cursed himself for idiocy. Even then, he let his glance sweep down to her denim encased thighs, curving calves and sexy bare feet

He swore yet again, and didn't realize he'd spoken aloud until she said, "Sorry. I tried to be quiet."

"You were." He lifted his gaze, by sheer force, to her eyes, slanting and green and full of mystery. "Leave me any hot water?"

She smiled, and he felt an inexplicable hope that

whatever she was doing, she had a good reason. "I left you plenty. And while you're showering, I'll make us some breakfast."

"I thought you couldn't cook."

"I didn't say I couldn't. I said I didn't...much. I can scramble eggs and nuke sausage."

"Well, I can butter toast and mix up frozen orange juice, so we ought to survive." He glanced down at his body, clad only in skivvies. "I don't suppose I have a change of clothes here?"

"No. Sorry. Right after breakfast we'll go over to your place, if you want. Maybe being in your own apartment will sweep some of those cobwebs out of your rafters."

And that was when he noticed the running shoes dangling from one of her hands. "You going out?"

"Coming in, actually." She walked to the closet and tossed the shoes carelessly inside.

He frowned. Dammit, how could he have slept right through her leaving the house? He was lucky he didn't wake up dead. Why hadn't he heard the car, or the bike? "Where did you—?"

"I run every morning. I hope I didn't bother you when I snuck out."

Snuck out.

"I never even knew you'd left. What time—?"

"A little after five." She smiled softly and her eyes traveled over his face. "You were sleeping like the dead, Ash. I think your body has a little recovering to do yet."

Right. He must have been out cold. And the last time he remembered glancing at the clock's luminous digits, it had been twelve twenty-something. She could have been gone half the night, for all he knew. He had nothing but her word for it.

The entire time he spent in the shower, he kept thinking about the famous scene in *Psycho*. But nothing happened. He emerged, groped for a towel and smelled the scent of scrambled eggs and sausage wafting up the stairs.

He pulled on his jeans, but didn't snap them closed. The sight of the clothes she'd left discarded on the bathroom floor distracted him. He bent to pick them up. Shiny black spandex leggings with hot pink racing stripes. Little white ankle socks. Her damp towel was still there, too. He stuffed the clothes into the hamper, then opened the medicine cabinet, rubbing one hand over his scruffy face and hoping to find a new razor.

There was a tap on the door. He went to it and swung it open.

Joey didn't say a word. Her lips were parted, as if she'd started to speak, but nothing came out. Not even, he thought, a breath. Her wide green gaze moved down his bare chest, pausing for a moment at the slightly gaping fly of his jeans, then jerked upward to his face again.

His ego spiraled upward and he leaned one shoulder against the doorjamb. "Did you want something?"

She shook her head. "No. I just—the razors. They're in the closet, top shelf. Shaving cream, too. I thought you'd be looking for them."

She wanted something, all right. Her eyes said it all. And why the hell did it give him such a thrill to know a murder suspect was lusting after him?

"Thanks. I was just looking for them." He turned and opened the closet, pulling down the cream. She still stood in the doorway. He glanced at the pink can. "Powder-fresh scent?"

A mischievous smile played with her lips. "It's the best

I can do for now."

"It won't be so bad. I like the way *you* smell."

She cleared her throat and lowered her gaze.

"So how's that breakfast coming? *It* doesn't smell half bad, either."

Her head flew up again. "My eggs!" She turned and raced down the stairs. He chuckled and turned back to the sink to begin applying the lather to his face.

A few minutes later he heard a phone ring, and then her voice, cussing long and fluently. He stuck his head out the bathroom door. "I think it's mine," he said.

"Thank God," she yelled back.

He wiped the last of the lather from his face and ducked into the bedroom to snatch his phone from where he'd left it on the nightstand.

"Ash?" Radley's voice was strained. "We've got another one."

"When?" Ash tried to keep the turmoil from his voice.

"He was found half an hour ago. Coroner's putting the time of death between two and three this morning with what he has so far. We'll know more later."

Ash swallowed hard. He couldn't be sure of Joey's whereabouts between two and three this morning. He only had her word that she'd left the house around five. He didn't want to ask the next question, but he knew he had to.

"Where?"

"Phoenix, Ash. A couple of miles from where you're sitting."   .

Ash shook his head as it began to throb again.

"Ash, did she leave the house? Was she away from you at all between two and three?"

"It's circumstantial."

"Dammit, Coye—"

"I don't know, okay? I fell asleep."

"You fell—"

"I know. I'm an idiot. Shoot me. Save her the trouble."

"You really think—?"

"It was a sick joke." He didn't think Joey was out to kill him. Or anyone else. Hell, the idea was ludicrous. "Look, we don't know anything yet. Keep this to yourself until we do." Why in God's name was he trying to protect her? He ought to call the cops himself.

"Too late for that, Ash. They have the plate number of that bike from the last time. Now, with this murder practically in her backyard, don't think they won't be over there to grill her."

Ash closed his eyes. His mind was spinning. He just couldn't make himself accept that the woman he'd held in his arms last night, the woman whose tears he'd wiped away after a nightmare had scared her half to death— could also be a cold-blooded murderer. "Thanks for the warning, Rad."

"You want me to be there when they show up?" Radley asked.

Ash chewed his lip. He looked up at the sound of Joey's footsteps, light and quick. She stopped in the doorway, her eyes huge and round and green. "I burned our eggs."

She looked so damned remorseful he couldn't help but smile at her. He covered the mouthpiece. "That's okay. I hate eggs."

Her face brightened immediately. "Raisin bran?"

"My favorite," he lied.

She grinned and trotted back down the stairs. Ash stared at the empty doorway until Rad's voice brought him out of his trance.

"You want me to come over or not?"

Ash stiffened. "Only if you're going to back me up. And I mean one hundred percent"

There was a long pause. Then, "What are you going to do?"

"Trust my instincts. They haven't been wrong yet, have they?"

CHAPTER 4

Ash's facial muscles were too tight. There were a pair of brackets etched between his dark brows. He kept looking at her across the table. Not saying anything, just *looking* at her between bites. It gave her a squirmy kind of feeling. As if he was searching for something, as if he was trying to read her mind. He finished his raisin bran and rose, rinsing the bowl, then stacking it in the dishwasher.

"Are you going to tell me what's wrong, or just keep frowning all morning?" But she already knew, didn't she? She'd felt the eerie restlessness in the middle of the night. She'd paced and shivered and given in to her craving for a cigarette. She'd sensed the ugly blackness closing in. She'd tried to run it off with a morning jog, but she'd been too afraid to leave his side, to go far. She'd jogged up and down the driveway a dozen times, keeping the house always in sight.

He turned to face her, smiling a little. "I didn't realize I was frowning."

"It was that phone call. You've been messed up ever since." She rose, too, leaving her cereal bowl, spoon still inside, on the table. "Who was it?" She felt sick to her stomach. The dread she'd felt so strongly last night returned, and she braced herself for his answer.

"Rad Ketchum." He didn't elaborate.

"Your editor." The darkness gathered around the edges of her mind. Something bad had happened last night. Something she'd sensed...maybe even as it was happening. Something she should have been able to prevent. What good was the damned "gift" if she was too afraid to use it? God, when the coldness, the darkness, came to her, she did her utmost to push it away, to ignore it, when she should look closer, examine it and try to see what it meant. And it was coming again now, the cold, clammy hand clutching her heart and squeezing. It was getting harder to breathe. And then there was white heat searing her throat.

She gasped in pain and sat down hard when her knees buckled without warning. Tears choked her. Ash shot forward, startled, grabbed her shoulders and asked if she was all right. She lifted her head and stared up at him, the most horrible, gut-wrenching fear she'd ever known throbbing all through her. "It isn't her," she whispered. "It isn't Caroline. Tell me it isn't Caro."

His puzzled frown—or was it a worried one?—deepened just before Joey closed her eyes against a flood of tears. "Why would you think...? Joey, Caroline is fine. This has nothing to do with your sister." He shook her a little, hands tightening on her shoulders. "You hear me?"

She drew a deep, shuddering breath. Then another. She forced her eyes open as the tide of panic receded. "Then who?"

His dark eyes narrowed, and through the haze of dread she realized she was giving too much away. He'd wonder how she knew. If she told him, he'd think she was insane, or worse. She bit her lip and tried to think logically, coherently, even with that shimmering gloom hovering in her peripheral vision. It was getting closer. Getting harder to ignore.

"Something's happened to someone. I can see it in your eyes. Your editor called and told you something and..." She bit her lower lip and watched as some of the suspicion faded from his eyes. "Just tell me."

"Okay. There was another murder last night. Early this morning to be exact."

He watched her face, observing her every reaction, she thought. "The Slasher?"

He nodded. "The victim was found a little over an hour ago...in Phoenix."

She knew her eyes widened. She felt them expand until her head ached. Phoenix, New York was only a few miles from Clay, where she lived. She'd sensed the darkness was getting closer, but this was too close.

She shot to her feet, catching the front of his shirt in both fists. "Caro lives in Phoenix—"

"She's fine, I told you—"

"And the girls? Brit? Beth?"

"The victim was a *man*, Joey. His name hasn't been released yet."

She sighed as every muscle in her body went limp. The hands bunching the material of his shirt relaxed, and she sagged forward without even thinking about it. His arms came around her, maybe as automatically as hers encircled his waist, as instinctively as her buzzing head rested against his warm, hard chest

It felt good. Like some kind of armor against that darkness, that chill. Like she was being infused with calmness and strength, and she'd be able to stand on her own again if he'd just hold her a little longer. She hadn't known being in a man's arms could feel like that.

When his tight hold on her eased, she stepped away and looked up, seeing the same surprised expression on his face that must have been on hers. And there was something else. As if he'd come to some kind of conclusion, or made a decision.

"Joey, the police might come here this morning. They might want to ask you some questions."

"*Me?*"

He opened his mouth to say more but the doorbell chimed. The *front* doorbell. Ash licked his lips. "If anyone asks, Joey, you don't smoke. Never have. Okay?"

She shook her head, bewildered, searching his face for an explanation.

"Just trust me."

She nodded, sensing that she *could* trust him. Too bad he was the one person she had to lie to in order to save her sister's life...and his own.

He gave her shoulders a final squeeze and let go. Joey walked through the living room, looked through the glass door to the police officers standing there. There were two men in uniform, and a very tall blond woman in plainclothes. She exuded the kind of raw, rugged sex appeal men find hard to resist, and her cold blue eyes on Joey seemed to be trying to intimidate her from the first glance.

Joey stared right back, not blinking, and pointed one finger at the decal that read, Please Use Other Door.

"Go around back." She said it loudly, and her voice

didn't shake at all.

The cops show up to question her about a murder, and she tells them to use the back door. Ash's admiration for Joey went up another notch. She had backbone, he had to give her that much. Not that she'd seemed all that solid a few minutes ago. But he'd known her fear for her sister was genuine, even if it didn't make much sense. And if it *was* genuine, then she couldn't have been the killer, right? She'd have to know who the victim was if she'd committed the crime herself.

He stood beside her at the door as Homicide Detective Beverly Issacs and two male officers filed in. Bev dwarfed them both by a good four inches. Her head was level with Ash's when she stopped in front of him. Joey, at his side, looked like a pixie in comparison.

"Hello, Bev."

"Well, Ash. Seems like every time I turn up a clue in this case, I find you there before me. You wanna tell me why that is?" Her voice was frosty, but her eyes glinted so he knew she wasn't really angry or suspicious of him. Just running out of patience.

"Oh, I'm not here for any clue. I got married. Hadn't you heard?"

Her smile was wide and instant. "Right. And I'm running for mayor."

He felt Joey's gaze on him and looked down to see her frowning. "You *remember* her?"

Whoops. "Bev and I go way back, Joey. But I only remember her because she questioned me at length right after my accident." He'd almost slipped. Even the police weren't aware his amnesia was anything but genuine. He had to be more careful; Bev was sharp. He glanced at her again. "Bev, meet my wife, Joey Bradshaw...Coye," he added quickly, hoping Bev hadn't noticed the slight hesitation.

Bev's ice blue gaze darted from him to Joey and back again. "You're serious."

Ash nodded.

Bev shrugged. "Well, newlyweds or not, Ash, I have some questions for your wife here." She glanced down at Joey. "You don't mind, do you, Mrs. Coye?"

Ash smiled inwardly as Joey stiffened her spine and rose to her full height, which was still a head shorter than Bev's. Her chin came up, and her gaze never wavered from Bev's for a second.

"I don't mind at all."

Bev nodded and nudged one of the officers. The officer yanked a pad and pencil from his pocket and stood ready.

Bev said, "Mrs. Coye, you own a motorcycle. Is that right?"

Joey didn't blink. "Yes."

"A black Harley-Davidson, New York plates, 352H4?"

"It's a black Harley. I don't have my plate number memorized, but you're more than welcome to take a look."

"Not necessary. It's registered to you."

"If you already know, then why are you asking?"

Ash slipped his hand around Joey's and gave a warning squeeze. It wasn't a great idea to be hostile toward the police. They would wonder why.

"That bike's been seen at a couple of crime scenes recently, Mrs. Coye. You want to tell me why?"

"I was curious. Is there a law against that?"

Beverly's gaze showed a hint of her temper. Ash had felt it coming. Damn, Bev was not a good person to tick off. "What kind of cigarettes do you smoke, Mrs. Coye?"

"I don't smoke, Ms. Issacs."

"*Detective* Issacs," Bev said, jaw kind of stiff.

"Whatever."

Bev looked at Ash. "You *married* this?"

"Easy, Bev. She's upset. You would be, too, if someone implied you were a serial killer, wouldn't you?"

Bev sighed and swung her head toward Joey again. "Where were you last night and early this morning?"

She opened her mouth, but Ash spoke first. "She was in bed, with me."

"All night?" Bev looked skeptical.

"All night," Ash replied.

"But she could have slipped out, while you were sleeping."

"We're newlyweds, Bev. We barely had two days together before the accident, and I've been in the hospital ever since. You really think I *slept* my first night back?" As he said it, he slipped an arm around Joey's shoulders and squeezed her to his side.

Bev's wary gaze kept shifting to Joey and Ash hoped she wore a convincing expression on her face. He kept his own gaze level with Bev's, not looking away once.

Bev shook her head. "You lost your memory—"

"But not my mind."

"If I find out you're lying—"

"I'm not."

She nodded, casting a skeptical glance down at Joey, then turned on her heel and left the house. The two officers followed, and Ash closed the door.

For a long moment he didn't turn to face Joey, knowing

the questions he'd see in her eyes.

"You lied to her."

"Yeah." He turned around slowly and looked at her. There was some sort of ache in her eyes that he hadn't expected. As if he'd hurt her somehow. Impossible.

"Why?"

"A husband wants to protect his wife. Human nature."

"Or maybe you thought I needed an alibi."

"If I thought you were a killer, Joey, I wouldn't be here."

She blinked three times, each downward swipe brushing more moisture from her eyes, only to have it quickly replaced. "You know this Beverly pretty well."

He nodded. Then added, "I used to, anyway. Or so I'm told."

She stared at him harder. "You've slept with her."

He had, but how the hell could she know that? Was his face that transparent? He squirmed for a second, then remembered he didn't have to give her a direct answer. "Maybe. I don't remember." For just a second she looked furious. Then she covered it. For crying out loud, was she actually jealous?

"*She* does." Joey looked at the floor. "And she'd like to do it again."

He gave his head a small shake. "Did I miss something? Did you and Bev have a heart-to-heart while my brain went out to lunch, or what? Where are you getting this? What the hell did she say or do to make you think—?"

"Nothing. She didn't have to. It was obvious."

She turned to walk away, but he caught her arm before she reached the stairs and turned her to face him. "Obvious, how?"

"I know what I know, okay?"

She knew, all right. And she didn't like it a bit. And for some reason, he *liked* the idea that she didn't like it.

He followed her up the stairs to the kitchen, trying not to grin in satisfaction. She was more worried about his one-nighter with Bev Issacs than she was about the police department's suspicions of her. Further indication she was not the Slasher, to his way of thinking.

She stalked into the living room and paced the floor. He sat down in the recliner and watched. He watched the sway of her hips as she walked away from him, the way her thighs moved as she walked back. She was no killer, He didn't know why he felt so certain of that now, but he did. He didn't know what she was, but he knew he wanted to find out And he knew something else, too. She was in trouble. It was fear he saw in her eyes at times, not cunning or cold-bloodedness. She was lying to him out of ice-cold fear.

He rose and took her shoulders, stopping her nervous pattern. "Hey." She looked at him, those eyes so wide and vulnerable he thought he'd probably believe anything she told him. "Whatever it is, Joey, I'm on your side. Okay?"

He saw the guilt that flashed over her face along with the surprise. "You don't even know me. How can you—?"

"I want to know you."

Her eyes widened. Her lips parted and she stared at him.

"I might be able to help, if you'd just talk to me."

She shook her head, but her gaze remained riveted to his. "I...can't"

He shrugged. "You will. I can wait." His eyes focused on her full lips, and he felt himself tightening up inside. He wanted to kiss her. He wanted it badly. He moved his head lower.

She stepped away, turning around quickly, averting her face. "If we're going to your apartment to pick up your things we ought to get at it, don't you think?" Her voice was strained and too soft.

He steeled himself against the desire stirring inside him. "Sure. Okay."

There was just too damned much to deal with!

Joey paced Ash's living room while he rummaged around in the bedroom, tossing clothes into a suitcase. She couldn't shake her attraction to him. It was absolutely monstrous in proportion and growing all the time. And he felt it, too, which complicated things still further.

To top it off, he was protecting her. Probably only because he thought it was his duty as her husband. But he'd lied to the police, jeopardized his career, for a woman who was no more than a stranger to him. How would he feel about her when he learned the truth, that she was nothing to him, that he'd put himself on the line for a woman he didn't even know? She hated the guilt she felt because of that.

And what about his relationship with Detective Amazon? Maybe they'd actually had some kind of affair, and he just didn't remember. Maybe Joey's lie was now going to ruin whatever they'd had together. That Beverly Issacs still wanted Ash practically appeared in boldface type across her forehead whenever she glanced at him, at least it did to someone as sensitive as Joey. But how did he feel? Was he attracted to the woman? He must have been once. It was hard to imagine any man who wouldn't be. And why did the thought make Joey feel like throwing up?

She paced faster. Another man had died last night. She'd felt it coming and done nothing to prevent it. She'd have to do better if she was going to keep her sister and Ash alive.

He emerged, suitcase in one hand, laptop in the other. She frowned at it.

"I'm still on leave from the *Chronicle*," he said, "but I'd like to work from the house."

She nodded. His face was pinched, and she realized his head was throbbing. She picked up a lot of his feelings, more than she usually did with anyone—except perhaps, for the Slasher. She shook that thought away. "You need to lie down, Ash. Didn't the doctor prescribe anything for the pain?"

His eyes narrowed. "How'd you know my head was splitting?"

She forced a smile as she sought an explanation. If she kept slipping like this, he was going to catch on. She gave him what she hoped was a sly glance. "I'm your wife. I can read you like a book."

He nodded, but was still looking at her oddly when he followed her out the door.

She fed him Ibuprofen when they got home, and left him lying in her bed. *Her* bed, he noted with interest, not the one in the room she'd assigned him originally. She'd hustled him up there the second they had returned from his place and insisted he lie down. It was almost as if she could feel the way his head was pulsing every time she looked at him.

But pain or no, he had work to do. While he believed

Joey was innocent of the Slasher killings, he was still all too aware of her dishonesty. He thought she might have a good reason for the lies, or at least what she must believe was a good reason. But he couldn't help her unless he found out what it was. And he had a feeling, a bad, creepy kind of feeling in the pit of his stomach, that it all revolved around the Slasher killings. She'd known something had gone down last night. She'd known it before he'd told her. There was no doubt about that.

He slipped out of bed after she'd been gone for a while. His gaze fell on his suitcase. She'd left it here, in this room. It was pretty obvious she intended for him to stay there, in her room. His ego would have liked to believe it was out of pure, overwhelming desire for him. His brain, however, knew there must be more to it.

He sat on the edge of the bed, took out his cell and tapped Rad's number. When he heard Radley's voice on the other end, he kept his own low. "What have you dug up on my wife?"

Rad snorted. "Wife, huh? You getting attached to that phrase, Ash?"

"Knock off the comedy and give me an answer."

Rad was quiet for a moment, then he said, "Are you falling for her, Ash?"

"Don't be ridiculous."

"It's not ridiculous. I know what it's like, don't forget. You can talk to me. Any time."

It was true. Few people were as deeply devoted as Rad was to his Amelia. Broke Ash's heart that she was sick. Rad didn't like discussing the details. He just knew it was bad, and got the impression it was terminal.

Papers riffled and Rad said, "As for your girl, all I can say is, it's damned weird."

"Weird, how?"

Rad cleared his throat. "She does free-lance work for some major corporations."

Ash frowned. "That's what she told me, but I didn't believe it."

"Yeah, well, I find it kind of hard to believe myself."

"Why?" A ripple of alarm went through him.

"She's a self proclaimed psychic, Ash, though she seems to try to keep that part of it quiet. Calls herself a consultant. Her business comes by word of mouth. One corporate big shot tells another about her skills, and so on."

Ash didn't say anything for a long time.

"You still there?"

"Yeah. I'm just not sure I get it."

"Okay, here's the skinny. Say a company is considering a merger, or a major move, or maybe they have an employee embezzling funds but aren't sure who. They take it to J. B. Bradshaw. She comes into the firm as a secretary or some such, snoops around a little, talks to people, gets a feel for the place and then she gives them their answer."

"Right. You want to get serious now, Rad?"

"It's gospel. I've had it triple-checked."

Ash shook his head. He didn't believe in mind readers. "And she gets results?"

"Sometimes she does. Word is, she doesn't charge unless she can help. She hasn't always been able to. But she's never been wrong. She either comes up with the right answer, or no answer at all."

"Uh-huh." Ash wasn't buying a word of this. "And she lives off this?"

"Her fees are pretty hefty, Ash. And she's getting

quite a reputation in corporate boardrooms. I've heard she works pro bono for small, struggling firms who can't afford—"

"Have you got anything legitimate for me, Rad, or just fairy tales?"

Radley made an aggravated noise into the phone. "Skeptic. Okay, she doesn't have a police record. Not so much as a traffic ticket. She holds a valid handgun permit, and the records list a nine-millimeter Ruger as her only weapon."

"Anything else?"

"What do you want, a biography? Nothing you don't already know. She was raised with her mother, deceased, stepfather who is retired in Florida, and a half sister, Caroline. Her birth father was Tito de Rio, and she has another half sister, Toni Rio, the writer. There are other sisters—apparently the guy got around, but I stopped digging at that point. Toni is engaged to a cop, Nick Manelli out of Brooklyn. Caroline is married to Theodore 'Ted' Dryer, formerly of Clark County, Nevada. The have two girls, aged six and sev—"

"Clark County, Nevada?" Ash jumped to his feet. Vegas was in Clark County.

"I already checked, Ash. Dryer's lived in New York State for eleven years."

"That doesn't mean he hasn't gone back to visit... maybe five years ago, the summer the Slasher did his hunting in Vegas."

"Maybe."

Ash swallowed. He hadn't wanted to believe Joey was involved in this ugliness. But maybe she was. Maybe she was protecting her brother-in-law. Or even her sister. Picturing Caroline as a murderess was harder than envisioning Joey in the role. He shook his head. Anything was possible.

"Thanks for the help, Rad."

"You lied to the police, didn't you?"

Ash frowned at the phone. "I thought you didn't want to know."

"You could get your ass tossed in jail. Especially if you're withholding evidence."

"I know that."

He could almost see his friend's frown over the phone. Rad said nothing more, just broke the connection. Ash sighed and hung up. He went to the door, opened it and listened for a minute. Not a sound, so he slipped down the stairs and glanced around. Joey was sitting on the couch, legs curled under her. Her face registered extreme agitation as her eyes scanned the pages of a fat book. A thick, wavy lock of silky hair fell down over one eye, and she shoved it back with a sweep of her small hand. Her brows bunched tighter, her green gaze intense. He glanced at the title and almost swore out loud. *Inside the Mind of a Serial Killer.*

Dammit straight to hell. He shook his head in frustration and backed up the stairs. Psychic. Hell, she was no more a psychic than she was a killer. But it was becoming increasingly evident that she was obsessed with the Slasher. Why? Did she know anything, or was it just morbid curiosity? He wondered if he'd ever figure her out.

Well, at least she was occupied for a time. He went to her dresser, pulled open the bottom drawer and pawed through it, then opened another.

The landline phone rang, and he stiffened. Then he relaxed when it didn't sound again and she didn't call to him. Must have been for her. Good, she was still distracted.

His headache eased slightly, probably due to the Ibuprofen she'd insisted he take, and the hot, herbal tea she'd made him drink afterward.

His hand dipped into the top drawer, and his gaze was drawn downward. He was wrist deep in sheer, silky underthings. He couldn't move for a minute. When he could, he found himself pulling a nearly transparent, lace-edged, ruby red teddy from the drawer. He held it up, eyeing the high cut of the leg openings, the sheer lace that bisected the bodice. He couldn't help but picture her in it.

Then he blinked fast and shoved the garment back into the drawer. What was he, some kind of a pervert? Had this ridiculous attraction got so bad that he had to resort to pawing her underwear? He looked again at the mounds of lace and silk and satin in the drawer, and an ugly, unfamiliar feeling crept into his mind as he wondered when she wore them, and for whom. From the wide selection under his hand, she must find need for these kinds of garments often. Too often.

Disappointment and irrational anger flooded him, along with burning, red-hazed memories.

His mother had called herself Lila, and her brassy red hair came from a bottle. She always looked so beautiful on those nights, just before she'd lock him in. But it was fake beauty, like a Halloween costume. He would sit in the corner, in the tiny, pitch-black closet. He would hear the sounds she made. Sounds that made him think someone was hurting her. And he would wonder if they might kill her and then she'd never come to let him out. Sometimes she didn't, not until very late the next day. Those were the times when she'd been too drunk to think of him sooner. Those were the times when he'd see the ugliness behind her pretty mask.

Her name wasn't Lila, it was Liz. And she wasn't pretty. Not with her watercolor hair in matted straggles and black mascara smeared under her eyes and the stench of puke and liquor on her breath.

When the closet door opened on those mornings, he didn't want to look at her. And he couldn't anyway, because he'd be in a hurry to run to the bathroom. And always, on the way, he would pass the empty bottles and unwashed glasses, the overflowing ashtrays, the rumpled bed, and always, always, there would be sheer, silky lingerie lying on the floor.

He felt something out of place against his fingers, and looked down at the price tag dangling from one thin strap.

Unable to resist, he picked it up again, frowning. Then his gaze moved over the other items in the drawer, spotting more tags, and still more.

"Ashville Coye, what the hell do you think you're doing!"

He spun fast, still clutching the teddy. Joey stood in the doorway, her face as red as the satin that caressed his fingertips. "I, uh, I was just...looking for a place to put my clothes." He stuffed the teddy back into the drawer and slammed it shut. "Sorry."

Her expression didn't ease. Her cheeks were pink with embarrassment. Her eyes glittered with anger at his invasion of her privacy. "Did you ever think to ask?"

He just looked at her and shook his head. How could she look so innocent? Was he a complete idiot?

"I'll make some room for you. In the meantime, you

really ought to be lying down." She still didn't meet his gaze. She lifted a hand that held a pair of tightly rolled dampened cloths. "I brought a hot pack for your head. Thought it might help."

He complied and went back to the bed. She perched on its edge, leaned forward and gently laid one of the moist, hot cloths on his forehead.

The swell of her full breasts was so close to his face he could feel the heat rising from her skin to his. He could smell the scent of her. A rush of desire seared him from within, and he knew he still wanted her. Good or bad, chaste or promiscuous, he wanted her, and it was infuriating to admit that, even to himself. He puckered his lips and blew gently, warm breath bathing her breasts.

She straightened at once, eyes widening.

"When are you going to be willing to sleep with me, Joey?" He'd asked the question before he could tell himself not to.

She blinked fast, avoiding his eyes. "When you get your memory back."

"What if I told you I was getting it back already? What if I said I remembered every minute of our...wedding night?"

She swallowed hard. "I'd say you were lying."

He nodded. "Can't blame a guy for trying." He looked toward the dresser. The strap of the teddy still hung out of the drawer. A confused jumble of anger, disappointment and desire pummeled him. He tried to ignore it and licked his lips. "What if I never remember?"

She shook her head. "You will. I'm going to help you."

"I think seeing you in that red number would help me a whole lot, Joey."

"I really wish you wouldn't talk to me like that."

He smiled slowly. "Makes you hot?"

"Makes me angry. You're obnoxious as hell, you know that?" She glanced down at the second hot cloth in her hand and slapped it onto his chest. "Here. This one's for the back of your neck. You can do it yourself."

She stood and turned to go. Driven by his own demons, Ash lunged from the bed. "You've never worn them, have you? Not any of them."

Her back stiffened. She said nothing.

He grabbed her arm, turned her slowly to face him. He forced himself not to hold her too tightly, or to jerk her around. It made no sense to feel this angry. This was about him, not her. And yet he was driven to know. "Answer me, Joey. You've never worn them, have you?"

"No. I've never worn them. Why is it so damned important, anyway? What do you think, that I put them on and parade through the streets? Jump out of cakes? What?"

Why this feeling of relief? She could be lying through her teeth for all he knew. God knew it wouldn't be the first time. And why the hell did he care what she wore, or for whom?

He released his breath and sat down on the bed. He lowered his head, and for the first time he really wondered why she would buy the things and not wear them.

"So you're stocking up on silk and satin," he said. "You must have big plans. Expecting a prince on a white horse to come along?"

She stood perfectly still, her eyes searching his, hurt, but more than that. It felt as if she was trying to see what drove him. "Princes turn into frogs, Ash. Happens every time. I almost forgot that for a little while today. Thanks for reminding me."

He heard the real confusion, the pain in her voice and wished he could take back his words. Dammit, the idea of her wearing those things for someone else had filled him with rage. The thought that she could be anything like his mother. He'd just wanted her to deny it.

"No danger of that with you, though, is there, Ash? You were a frog to begin with." She turned away, reached for the door handle. "By the way, we're having dinner with my sister and Ted tonight. I hope you'll try and fake a few princely qualities while we're there."

CHAPTER 5

Dinner.
Pot roast with baby potatoes and tiny carrots and whole onions cooked right with the meat. Thick, creamy gravy, mashed potatoes, sweet peas, homemade rolls, still so warm the real butter melted when you spread it on.

Damn, it was too bad Caroline was already taken. She was the type of woman Ash had been looking for. The kind who'd have babies and not go all to pieces because she'd put on a few pounds. The kind who would adore her life, not go looking for excitement elsewhere.

But there was something wrong with the picture. Because no matter how hard he tried to make Caroline's image fit the one in his mind, just to remind himself of what he wanted—what he'd *always* wanted—he found himself looking toward Joey, instead.

All right, he might as well cut to the heart of the matter. He wanted Joey...in a purely physical way. But lust wasn't everything. Just because it had hit him between the eyes like it had never hit him before didn't mean he had to rethink his priorities. And to be perfectly frank about it, he probably wouldn't want her so badly if she wasn't holding out on him so well.

"I had no idea you two even knew each other, and then you stand there and tell me you're married," Caroline was saying.

Ted's laugh was low and contained. "I wish I could have seen the look on your face."

Ash frowned. He couldn't remember the look on Caroline's face. Only the devastation and panic on Joey's. "I'd have married her sooner if I'd known your dinners were a fringe benefit, Caroline." He made an effort to keep up the conversation, to appear the polite, friendly new brother-in-law trying to get to know his wife's family.

"What blows me away," Ted went on, "is that you two were able to put it together at all, after the accident and everything." His brown hair was sprinkled with gray, and his face was too lean—like a weasel's face.

"Ted, maybe Ash would rather not talk about that," Caroline put in.

"No, it's okay." Ash reached out and grabbed the glass of milk Bethany had just set on the table's edge just before it tipped into her lap, sent her a wink and kept on talking. "Truth is, I don't remember a thing about Joey and me. It's like that day she showed up at the hospital was the first time I'd ever met her."

Ted's gaze narrowed, and he sent Joey a probing glance. She ignored it.

"Where *did* you meet, Joey?" Caroline asked her sister.

Ash speared a succulent piece of meat and relaxed in his seat to listen to her answer. Ought to be entertaining.

"I'll bet it was something to do with that Slasher case, wasn't it?"

Ash frowned, his brain instantly going on alert. He swallowed his food and sat straighter. "Why would you think that, Ted?"

Ted shrugged. "Well, you were investigating it. She's been obsessed with it since the first—"

"I haven't been obsessed. You're exaggerating."

"Interested is probably a better term," Caroline put in quickly, as if she was jumping to her sister's defense. "But no more than most of the people who live around here."

Ted frowned hard at his wife, and she sent him a silent message, a powerful one. A puzzled expression settled over his face, but he shrugged and leaned back in his chair.

"I certainly understand her interest in the murders better now. She was seeing you, Ash, and you were investigating them. It's only natural she'd want to know all she could."

Ash nodded, but kept glancing at Joey's face. She looked as if she were sitting on a pile of thumbtacks.

"There was another one last night, you know," Ted put in, and when Ash glanced at him it was to see him watching Joey's face, as well.

"Another what, Daddy?"

"Another of the great ice-cream robberies," Ash said quickly, not missing a beat. "Three gallons of Heavenly Hash. Someone's going to have a whale of a belly ache this morning."

Brittany giggled, and Caroline shot Ash a grateful glance. Ash felt something warm press against his calf and looked down. A black-and-white cat the size of a small cow looked back, purring loudly. "Well, now. Who's this?" Ash stroked the cat's head and fed it a bit of his meat

"Felix," the girls chimed in unison.

"He likes you, Uncle Ash."

"I think he likes everybody who feeds him."

The cat moved on to the next seat, panhandling for scraps, and Ted picked up the conversation. "Where *did* you two meet?"

Joey shifted in her seat. "At the theater...the one at Destiny, USA. We were both there to see the same movie and we ended up sitting together."

It wasn't bad, as far as lies went. Wasn't good, either, but it wasn't bad. "And the next thing she knew, I'd spirited her off to Vegas and married her," he said. "Right, Joey?"

She bit her lip, nodded and applied herself to her dinner.

"You ever been there?" His question was directed to Ted. He couldn't quite get a read on the man. There was sheer adoration in his eyes when he looked at his girls. He fed the cat a scrap every few seconds. Those things seemed to lend credence to him being a decent guy and a family man. But when he met his wife's eyes, there was something decidedly uncomfortable there, and he was watching Joey with a depth of scrutiny probably similar to Ash's own. As if he knew or suspected she was hiding something.

"I used to live there," Ted said, glancing away from his sister-in-law for once.

"You miss it much?" Ash asked.

"Not really."

"Oh, yes, you do, Ted." Caroline smiled in Ash's direction. "You ought to hear him in the winter."

"Well, who wouldn't miss the sun when there's three feet of snow outside the door?" Ted chuckled, but it seemed strained.

Ash nodded, smiling. "You get back there often?"

Ted paused with his fork halfway to his mouth.

It was Caroline who piped in with the answer to Ash's question. "We used to take vacations there, but it's really not much fun for little girls. They were toddlers last time, remember, Joey? It took all three of us just to keep up with them."

Ash's stomach clenched. "Joey went with you on vacation?"

Caroline nodded. "To help with the girls. These days, we opt for places with theme parks nearby."

Ash was itching to ask if that trip happened to occur during the summer of the Slasher's Vegas killing spree. But he couldn't just come right out with it. These people were not stupid. They'd know he suspected something, even if they might not know what.

"Time for dessert?" Bethany asked.

"It's Aunt Joey's favorite," Brittany sang.

"Caro, you didn't—"

"Of course I did." Caroline rose and began clearing away dishes. Joey got up to help, and Ash automatically stood as well.

They accomplished the cleanup within a few minutes, then sat around the living room with luscious cheesecake and wonderful coffee, groaning almost in unison that they couldn't hold another bite.

"You play pool, Ash?"

Ash almost answered yes, then caught himself. "Damned if I know." He tapped his head with a forefinger by way of explanation.

Ted laughed. "I have a new table downstairs. What do you say we find out?"

"I'm game…if you'll show me around your shop first."

Ted frowned. "It's pretty boring."

"It's your business. I'm fascinated by sole proprietors." And curious to see if the shop held any clues to whatever Ted was hiding.

Ted Dryer was an electrician. TD Electric had its "headquarters" in a shoe box of a building he'd put up beside the house. He had a professionally crafted sign over the door, and a company pickup with magnetized signs stuck to its doors in the driveway. Ted walked Ash outside to show him around. The pickup was less than two years old, the building freshly painted. From all appearances, business was good. Ted unlocked the door to the shop and ushered Ash into the office portion. It consisted mostly of a desk and chair, a phone, a file cabinet and a little rack to hang keys on tacked to the wall just inside the door. The pickup keys dangled there on a key ring that read, My Other Car's a Mercedes. There was a computer on the desk. It was turned on. Ash was dying for a moment alone with it.

"What's through there?" he asked, pointing at a door in the back.

"Workshop area." Ted unlocked and opened the door, led Ash into a room about the same size as the office, with a workbench and tools and lots of small electronic items with their guts exposed. "Hell, I shouldn't have left that out," Ted said, and began picking up a set of tools and replacing them in a box.

Ash grabbed his phone from his pocket, looked at the screen and then at Ted. "My boss texts me at the damnedest times. I'll just be a sec." Then he walked back into the office while tapping on his phone's screen. The second he was out of Ted's sight, he leaned behind the desk, grabbed the mouse and clicked on HISTORY. A list of recently visited websites came up and he flipped up his cell phone, snapped a photo of the screen, then paced back into the workshop barely missing a beat, tapping the phone as if he'd never stopped. He paced out and back in again once more for good measure.

Ted finished putting his tools away and then they returned to the house and knocked balls around on a green felt pool table in the finished basement. Joey's brother-in-law seemed friendly, but maybe just a little too curious.

"So tell me about you and Joey," he said at one point during the game. "I can't quite picture her settling down to be someone's little wife."

"Me neither." Ash met Ted's glance and they both laughed. "Hell, Ted, you can probably tell me more about her than I could tell you." He shrugged. "I must have known her so well once, but now..." He let his voice trail off, hoping Ted would take the bait.

"She's pretty up-front," Ted said. "I mean, she's not the kind with hidden agendas and plots. She's just about what she seems. Calls 'em like she sees 'em, says what she means...most of the time."

"Most of the time?"

Ted shrugged and bent over the table, drawing the cue stick back slowly, aiming its tip at the white ball. "We all have our hang-ups." He struck the cue ball. It struck two others, one of which rolled neatly into a corner pocket. Ted straightened and walked around the table, reaching for the chalk.

"And what's Joey's?"

Ted's brows raised. "Damned if i know. I thought I

had her figured out. Thought she hated anything male and always would." He laughed and shook his head.

But Ash didn't feel like smiling. "Why'd you think that?"

Ted chalked the cue. "Always assumed it was because of her father. Fathers, I should say. The one who raised her cheated on the girls' mother through most of their marriage. Not that she didn't cheat right back with Joey's birth father. But the daughters don't seem to consider that anything but payback. From what I hear, Joey's birth father was even worse. Has kids by several different women. Course, Joey didn't know that until recently. She's only met one of them, a semi-famous crime writer, Toni Rio." He looked up to see if Ash recognized the name, but he didn't. "They really seem to have bonded. I think Caroline's a little bit jealous. Up until a year or so ago, she was Joey's only sibling." Then he frowned. "Hasn't she talked to you about any of this?"

Ash shook his head, sensing Ted was volunteering a lot in hopes Ash would reciprocate. "No, she hasn't. At least, not that I can recall."

"Well, she ought to. The girls' relationship with their father has left scars. And in Joey's case, finding out the man who raised her wasn't her father at all, probably left a few more more.

"Ted, telephone," Caroline called from upstairs.

Ted sighed, set the stick down and went up the stairs. Ash followed. They joined Joey and Caroline, who were standing in the living room, close to each other. He found his gaze drawn to Joey's face. She seemed worried, and watched Ted as he spoke quietly and hung up.

"Well, I'm afraid I have to go out."

"But, Ted—"

"It's an emergency, hon," he told his wife. "Mrs. Peterson's power is out, and she says the box smells hot. I really have to go check it out." He gripped Caroline's shoulders, drew her forward and kissed her quickly. Ash didn't miss the way she turned her head so his lips fell on her cheek instead of her mouth. Then Ted turned to pump Ash's hand. "Good meeting you, Ash,"

"Same here," he replied.

Ted faced Joey. His jaw tightened as he looked at her. "Take care, Joey." The words were heavy with meaning. And then he was hurrying out the door.

Caro sank onto the sofa, her face obviously straining to hide her misery. Ash wasn't sure what to do, but he caught Joey's glance. She nodded her head toward the two girls stretched on the floor watching television. She looked worried about her sister and Ash knew she wanted some time alone with her.

"Hey, you two," he said to the kids. "Isn't it getting close to bedtime?"

Two blond heads turned in his direction. "Not yet!"

"Can't we stay up? Mommy?"

Ash shook his head in mock disappointment. "Oh. All right then. I was gonna read you a story, but…"

They were on their feet in a flash, and Ash felt himself being tugged, one girl holding each of his hands, across the living room and through the open bedroom door at its far end. He'd be out of earshot, but still within sight of Joey and her sister. He glanced over his shoulder at Joey, caught her grateful smile and sent her an encouraging wink.

She was worried. Right now, it was about her sister,

but it went deeper, Ash thought. She hadn't relaxed all night. And while it was obvious she was still lying to him, and to her sister as well, it was equally obvious that she hated every minute of it. And it did nothing to dampen the desire he felt for her every time he looked at her.

Joey went to the bedroom door and peered inside. Ash sat in a rocker, a girl on each knee, a book open on his lap.

"And as the princess gently kissed the frog, something magical happened. The spell was broken, and he turned into the handsome prince he truly was. Falling down on his knees, he took the princess's hand in his and told her how much he loved her. They were married in a great celebration, and of course they lived happily ever after."

He closed the book. "Well, how was that?"

Joey smiled, an unfamiliar warmth curling in the pit of her stomach. She'd been furious with him earlier, but she'd reasoned with herself until she thought she understood him. He believed she was his wife. He probably felt frustrated and hurt that she'd rejected his physical advances. His rotten attitude was no more than another result of all he was going through right now. She had to forgive him. "They're asleep," she whispered.

Ash glanced at the blond heads lolling upon either of his shoulders. Joey stepped forward and scooped Bethany from his lap. She carried her to the white four-poster and tucked her in. When she turned, Ash was installing Brittany in the bed's twin, on the other side of the room. Felix had already settled himself on the foot of her bed and looked dead to the world.

"You know, these two are just about the most precious

things in my life."

"I'm not surprised," he said, his voice low. "They've charmed my socks off already."

She met his gaze across the room. "You're terrific with them."

"I love kids."

She went to the rocker and picked up the book. The process of forgiving him was suddenly complete. "*The Frog Prince*?"

Ash met her in the room's center. "Seemed appropriate," he said softly. "It's a fascinating theory, don't you think?" He took the book from her hands, set it aside. "I know I acted like a frog earlier. I didn't mean it."

"I know."

He slipped his arms around her waist, drawing her close. She stiffened, but he shook his head quickly. "One kiss, Joey. Not so much for a husband to ask from his wife, is it? Besides, how else will you know if there's a prince hidden under this frog skin?"

She moistened her lips. What she saw in his eyes made her blood warm, and she was assaulted once again by the attraction that wouldn't go away. She wanted to kiss him, not to convince him that they were truly man and wife, but to feel the touch of his mouth on hers, the pressure of his arms around her, the strength of his chest against hers. She nodded. "All right," she said, glancing at the girls to be sure they were still sound asleep. "One kiss."

Ash smiled. Then his mouth covered hers. His arms around her waist tightened, drawing her body to his. She parted her lips, curious, eager, excited, all at once. It seemed as if he was tasting her, and liking what he found.

The flash flood of desire that rushed through her

shocked Joey. Her arms curled tighter around his neck. Her body pressed harder against his, and her fingers threaded into his hair. This was good. Whatever this was, it was incredibly good. It was more than a kiss. It was a firestorm of feeling. And she thought he was losing himself in her as much as she was in him. She felt his heart hammering, heard his rapid breathing. All because of her. The feel of his hands at the base of her spine, their pressure holding her tight, was bliss. And then the sound of Caroline clearing her throat sent her to the opposite extreme. She stepped away guiltily, suppressing a shiver. The fire in Ash's eyes , though, still burned bright.

"Caro...I—I'm sorry. I...we just—"

"It's okay. I remember when it was like that. Go on home, you two."

Ash blinked, then turned, slipping a possessive arm around Joey's shoulders. "You sure you don't want us to stick around until Ted gets back?"

The pain that lanced her sister was obvious to Joey, and probably to Ash as well, but Caro only nodded sharply. "No, he's liable to be...late. As long as the girls are asleep, I guess I'll turn in myself. It's been a long day. Good night."

Joey sighed as her sister turned and walked away. Ash kept his arm around her while they walked together to the front door. He looked down at her and she held his gaze for a long moment before she had to look away. He wanted her. His eyes were telling her so in no uncertain terms. And dammit, she wanted him, too. But she couldn't let this thing with him develop into anything more than it was. She couldn't let herself begin to feel anything for him. God, she didn't ever want to suffer the way Caro was...the way their mother had.

He walked her to the car, opened the driver's door and stood aside. Joey shook her head and handed him the keys. "You mind driving, Ash? I'm too worried. I'd probably put us in a ditch."

He got in and she went around to the other side. "You want to talk about it?"

She frowned hard as he started the car. Strangely enough, she did. Why, for God's sake? What good would telling *him* do? "Caro thinks Ted's cheating on her." Joey shook her head and thumped her fist on the dash as the car backed out into the street. "Damn him. How can he do this to her?"

Ash shook his head. "Don't you think he deserves a trial before you string him up, Joey?"

"My sister wouldn't think it unless the evidence was pretty strong. She doesn't *want* to think it now, but it's getting harder not to."

"Why?"

She looked up at him, looked at the way the lights of other vehicles played over his face. His beard was coming in again, a darker shadow on his jaw. Her fingers itched to run over it. "There's money missing from their accounts, and he won't explain it. He has these murmured conversations on the phone and hangs up when she comes into the room. He's secretive. She knows he's keeping something from her. And that was the second emergency this week for Mrs. Peterson."

"So?"

"Mrs. Peterson's first name is a thirty-five year-old widow who'll take on anything wearing pants."

"And you know this because…?"

She scowled at him.

"Well, have you ever met the woman?"

She lifted her chin. "No. But Caro has—"

"And you don't think she might be a little biased?"

"My sister isn't like that." She felt his gaze on her, but didn't look back. "Why do men do it, Ash?"

"What? Cheat?"

She nodded, still not facing him.

"Not all men do it."

She released a clipped burst of air. "Right."

"Your stepfather did, though. And your birth father, too. And to you, that means all men must be the same."

She looked up quickly, startled.

"Ted mentioned you had a problem with your dad. Dads. You've talked about your mother several times. You and your mother must be very close."

"We were." She swallowed the lump in her throat

"Damn," he muttered. "I'm sorry, Joey. I didn't know. Was it...recent?"

"Last year. Stroke." She drew a breath and willed herself to go on. "Dad, my stepdad, the one I thought of as my father my entire life, was with his mistress the night my mother died. He moved her into my mother's house two months later."

"And you can't forgive him?"

"I hate him."

He nodded. "Hating people takes a lot of energy, Joey."

"I'm used to hating him. I've had a lot of practice."

"Been doing it a while, hm?"

"Since the first time I saw him with someone else. I was twelve. The thing I never understood was why my mother put up with it. She had to know. God, if I could see it, I know she could. Why did she stay with him?"

"That's probably something only she could answer."

She nodded, but remained quiet.

"You know, growing up like that might make a lot of women wary. Maybe even a little quick to jump to conclusions."

She faced him as he turned her car into the long, graveled driveway and drove slowly over it. "You think that's what Caro is doing?"

He shrugged. "Could be. I got the feeling Ted was hiding something, but it didn't seem like it was an affair."

She frowned "What else could it be?"

"I don't know. Whatever it is, he'd be better off being honest with Caroline about it. The truth probably isn't as bad as what she's thinking."

Joey blinked, for the first time wondering if there could be another explanation for Ted's behavior.

"It's important, I think. Being honest," he went on. He steered the car onto the blacktop portion of the driveway and killed the headlights, then the motor.

She had to turn her head away. Even though he couldn't see her in the darkness of the car, she could feel his eyes on her. Obviously, he knew she'd been less than honest with him. She couldn't even deny it.

"You're right." Her voice was almost a croak. "But sometimes there are things that are more important." She thought of her beautiful nieces, growing up without their mother, of the beautiful man beside her lying still and cold in a grave.

"Okay, I'll concede that point." He was silent a moment. "Will you answer me one question?"

"If I can." She lifted her head.

She heard him move, and then the interior light came on. He looked at himself in the rearview mirror, rubbed his stubble-coated chin. "You see any signs of a prince emerging here?"

"Not a one." He looked crestfallen, and she laughed softly. "But you know, I'm beginning to think the frog isn't as bad as he pretends to be."

Ash slept in her bed again that night. It was an unspoken conclusion that he would. He still wasn't sure why she wanted him there, if she didn't want *him*. Of course, she *did* want him, she just wouldn't let it happen. So why share a bed?

It made it a lot harder to check on her brother in law's recent internet browsing, but he managed it. After she was asleep, he looked at the image on his phone, and one by one, keyed in the URLs Ted had visited.

Dissociation and Dissociative Amnesia as a Criminal Defense.

Violent Crime and Mental Illness.

Dissociative Identity Disorders and Violence.

In-patient care for Violent Dissociative Disorder Patients.

He did a quick Google search and learned that Dissociative Disorder was the current term for what used to be called Multiple Personality Disorder.

Very interesting. He cleared his browsing history before he slept.

Sometime that night he had the dream again. He tried to wake up, but as always, he couldn't. He could only lie there, his heart racing, his skin beading with sweat, and live the damned thing over again. He should have been used to it by now.

But then it left him, all at once. Suddenly there was warmth in the cold, dark closet of his childhood. There was light. Someone was there with him, and it was all right.

In the morning, he almost choked. Joey was curled into his arms, her head nestled in the crook of his neck where her breaths bathed his skin. Her hair tickled his chin. Her legs twined with his, one lying over his thighs.

She'd worn an oversize football jersey to sleep in. It was hiked up to her waist. Her panties were brief, and they were too small a barrier. He was in hell. He'd died during the night and this was to be his eternal torment. He couldn't move without waking her. And if he woke her, and she felt the undeniable proof of where his mind had wandered, she'd probably be furious with him for the rest of the day. As if he had a choice in the matter. *He* wasn't the one twined around *her* like a jungle vine!

She moved slightly, and the friction made him bite his lip. Then he bit it harder. Maybe pain would dampen his responses. He tried to back away a little, but her leg tightened around his.

He groaned out loud.

Her eyes fluttered open, unfocused. He closed his fast. Maybe he could pretend he was still asleep.

Joey couldn't believe the way she'd wrapped herself around Ash as she'd slept. Then she remembered the dream, and she knew why.

It had been vivid, the nightmare. And it hadn't been her own. It had been his. She'd experienced every part of it right along with him. There was no imagery in the dream. Only darkness, and the sensation of smothering in it. There had been a deep fear that made his heart race. Fear of being abandoned, alone in the dark, crushingly small place for a long, long time, had smothered her. And then there had been the sudden awareness that he wasn't alone.

She wasn't really there, in the small, black prison. *He* was. It was Ash's nightmare. But in the midst of sleep, she'd gone to him. She'd wrapped herself around him, wanting to shelter him from the darkness, the cruelty, the fear.

He'd clung to her, and the dream had lost its power.

She shook her head and gently loosened her grip on him. Easing her head from his chest, she moved her leg away from his. Then she looked at him, lying there in the golden light of early morning. So big. His long, powerful legs stretched to the very edge of the mattress. And so strong. His bare chest bulged, rippled.

Yet he hadn't always been this way. He'd been young and small and helpless once. He'd been afraid, and so very alone. He'd had nightmares.

And somewhere, right now, today, beneath all the sinewed strength of the man, that little boy lived still, as vulnerable as he'd ever been. Ash kept that child in tight control. But he couldn't control the boy in his dreams.

Why, God, why did that one small glimpse inside him make her want him even more?

She lifted her trembling hand to touch his face. She ran her fingertips very lightly over his cheek and felt tears well up in her eyes for the boy he'd been. She slipped her arm around his waist and lay close to him again, wanting him to feel that closeness, wanting to keep his nightmarish memories at bay.

Tears spilled over, dampening his chest. Then his hand came to her face and very gently brushed them away.

"You're crying." He moved away from her, looking

down with a deep frown. "Joey, what's the matter?"

She shook her head, staring into his eyes and seeing more than she ever had before. There was so much more to him than she'd known. So much she still had to learn.

"Bad dreams," she whispered.

And Ash's frown deepened.

CHAPTER 6

She was a puzzle.

No matter how he tried, he couldn't figure her out. And he was beginning to feel more desperate to understand the workings of Joey Bradshaw's mind than he was to identify the Syracuse Slasher. Because he wanted her...more than he'd wanted any of the women he'd dated in search of the elusive Miss Right

Across the table, he watched her delve into the omelet he'd made this morning. She closed her emerald eyes—those rare precious gems that seemed to hold the secrets of the universe when she was serious, and seemed brighter than the sun when she smiled. She licked her full lips, and Ash felt his gut twist into a hard little knot

"God, this is good. Where did you learn to cook like this?"

"Trial and error, mostly," he admitted. It wasn't his best effort. It definitely needed more salt.

"No, it's perfect," she said. But as she said it, she reached for the saltshaker and handed it to him.

He took it, shook a little onto his eggs, then stopped. He looked at her and blinked. "I didn't ask for the salt."

"Didn't you?" She pretended his remark meant nothing, but she seemed to have trouble swallowing the next bite. "I must have seen you looking for it and guessed."

"I wasn't looking for it." He shook his head and studied her face. His conversation with Rad came back to him. *He* thought she was some kind of psychic. "You do that a lot, you know."

"Do what?"

"Answer a question before it's asked. Hand me something I want, but haven't mentioned." He recalled that she'd appeared in the bathroom just when he'd been searching for a razor, to tell him where they were.

"Maybe it's just that I know you so well, Ash."

But she barely knew him at all, so again she was lying. She just had a keen instinct, he supposed. It was no more than that. There *was* no more than that.

"You know what I was thinking?"

He swallowed his coffee. "Nope. I'm not the mind reader." He said it just to gauge her reaction. She tensed and shot him an alarmed look. So maybe she'd rather he didn't know about her hocus-pocus leanings. He grinned to ease her mind and was rewarded with a smile that nearly knocked him off his chair.

"I was thinking we ought to stay a night at your place."

"Why's that?"

"Well, your memory doesn't seem to be improving at all. It worries me. Maybe if you were around familiar things."

Even the aromas of the ham and cheese and onion he'd added to the eggs hadn't drowned out the freshly showered scent of her skin, or the whiffs of strawberry her hair was emitting. He thought there just might be another reason behind her suggestion, but he didn't say so. He would only find out by going along with it and keeping an eye on her. "If you want to. We can go over tonight. I ought to be working, anyway, and most of my projects are on the desktop at my place."

"How much time off are they giving you?"

He detected a hint of worry in her voice, and he wondered about that. "Only what I'll take sitting down. I'm itching to get back to that story, especially since there's been another—" He stopped when he saw her go a shade paler and replace her forkful of food on the plate. "What is it, Joey? You don't want me to go back to work?"

She lifted her head and met his gaze. "What did the police tell you about your car accident?"

He frowned, trying to keep up with the way she hopped from subject to subject. "Not much. Wasn't much to tell. Brakes failed—"

"I thought it was a new car?"

He sipped his coffee, giving himself time to collect his thoughts. Nothing had been mentioned about his car having been tampered with. The cops were playing this one close to the vest. "New cars break down, Joey. Accidents happen."

"What if it wasn't an accident?"

He set his cup down and stared at her. Did she know something? And if she did, was it because of her alleged ESP, or because she had an inside track with the Slasher? "What do you mean?"

She lowered her gaze, shook her head. "You were trying to expose a serial killer. What if... what if you were making the Slasher nervous?"

He drew a deep breath and released it with utter control. That was exactly what had happened. So how did Joey know about it? He pasted a false smile on his face and chucked her under the chin. "Hey, I'll go along with any theory that makes you worry about me. I kinda like it."

"This isn't a joke, Ash. I really don't want you going back to the office. Not until..." Her voice trailed off.

"Not until the Slasher's caught?" He reached across the table, closed his hand over hers. "You really are worried about me, aren't you?"

She nodded, and Ash found himself believing her. It felt kind of warm and fuzzy having someone worry about him. It was a feeling he thought he could get used to. "Let's not stress about it at the moment, okay? I have a full week to go before I get the doctor's okay to go back to work."

She sighed long and low, but nodded.

"You haven't been working yourself, lately."

"I'm self-employed. There's nothing pressing right now."

"Have you been turning down jobs, Joey?"

She met his gaze and he thought she was going to lie to him again. He was relieved when she didn't. "A few. But I can afford it."

"Why?"

"Why?" she repeated.

"Why haven't you been working?"

She shrugged and picked up her fork, pushing her omelet around her plate. Finally she met his gaze. "What I do takes a certain amount of...concentration. And instinct." She shook her head slowly. "Lately I just haven't had it."

So her supposed *powers* were failing her. "What's distracting you? Me?"

She looked up fast. "No. I don't know what it is. It doesn't matter, anyway. It'll pass."

Now she was lying. He had no doubt. The way her eyes couldn't quite hold his, the quick tightening of her jaw. It was surprising how quickly he'd learned the signs.

She shoved her plate away, obviously ready to change the subject. And again it was clear to him how much she disliked lying to him. "You know, I'm getting a little bored with this sitting around the house all the time. Are you up for a little recreation?"

"What did you have in mind?"

"Something that requires physical exertion."

He cocked one brow. "You're not thinking of dragging me into a cave somewhere are you?"

She laughed aloud. "Not until your head's a little better. And we won't bother with the exercise room because I don't want to hang around the house." Her gaze traveled down to his chest and a speculative gleam lit her eyes. "You're in great shape. What do you do to keep from going to pot?"

"You mean you'd be willing to try a little one-on-one?"

She leaned forward, hands propping her chin, elbows on the table. "Only if you're talking basketball."

"You wouldn't stand a chance. Too short."

"Sounds like a challenge to me."

An hour later she was standing on a concrete outdoor court, wearing a loose-fitting tank over a pale gray sports bra, a pair of black spandex shorts, and high top Chucks.

Red. The court was behind a school, but school was out, so they had it to themselves. The grass had been mowed that morning, and it smelled so potently fresh that the air was almost tinted green. The ball wasn't old. It still had that new-ball smell.

She dribbled close to the ground, which was an advantage of being short. The rough texture of the ball felt good on her palm. The sun on her back felt even better. Ash towered over her, arms spread, trying to keep her from making any progress. She faked right, then drove left, ducking under his arm and charging to the basket for a layup worthy of the WNBA, she thought.

The ball hit the hot blacktop, bounced twice and rolled to a stop at Ash's feet. He didn't look at it. He was looking at her with something that might best be labeled amused wonder.

"I never would've guessed."

"Don't just stand there, big guy. We're here to sweat, remember?"

He picked up the ball and began a lazy dribble away from the net as she came nearer to guard him. Then in a burst of speed he spun backward, pivoted to face the basket and executed a perfect jump shot from a foot beyond the line.

In no time at all, they were both damp with sweat beneath the July sun. Joey's once-neat ponytail dripped straggles that stuck to her face no matter how often she swept them away. Ash swiped a hand across his forehead. His dark hair curled wildly and his face was alive with color. The sleeveless, collarless sweatshirt he wore had dark spots in the center of his chest and back.

"What do you say we take a break?" Joey tossed the ball into Ash's chest. He caught it with a quick, reflexive move.

"Admitting defeat, are you?" He smiled as he said it.

"Not on your life. I just don't want to have to carry you back to the car."

"Fat chance. You're just afraid *I'll* end up carrying *you* to the car."

"Ha!" She put her hands on her hips in a taunting gesture. "You're so wiped out you couldn't if you had to!"

"Lady, you just made a tactical error." He dropped the ball and lunged forward, scooping her up so fast she didn't have time to dodge him. She struggled, but she was laughing so hard it weakened her. He held her tight to his chest, one strong arm under her knees, the other just beneath her shoulders.

"What about the ball?"

"Oh." He bent over it, letting her pick it up, then straightened and strode off toward the car. He picked up speed, nearly running over the sidewalk.

"We'll see who's wiped out."

"Watch out for that cat!"

He skidded to a halt, frowning at the sidewalk just ahead. "What cat?" No sooner had he spoken, however, than a calico cat scrambled across the sidewalk just ahead of him. He looked down at Joey and shook his head. "How the hell do you *do* that?"

"Don't be silly. I saw it coming."

"Then you must have eyes in the back of your head."

She waggled her brows up and down. "Well hidden by my hair, aren't they?"

His gaze changed just a little. He looked down into her face, into her eyes, and something stirred in his. Her arms around his neck held on tighter as he lowered his head.

His lips found hers, nuzzled, then parted and possessed. She let her head fall backward and clung to him for dear life as her pulse rate skyrocketed.

This wasn't fair. She wasn't supposed to feel this way toward him. It was an act...an act that was necessary to save his life, and Caroline's. And yet she had no defenses. As his wife, how could she refuse even to kiss him? She was lucky he hadn't charmed her into a lot more. She didn't need ESP to know he wanted her. And if she kept refusing, he was going to guess the truth, or at least wonder about it. Kissing him was another part of her cover.

Right. Get honest, she told herself. She was kissing him because she *wanted* to kiss him. The feel of his mouth covering hers, the warm dampness at the back of his neck where she clung, the taste of him, all combined in an ardent assault on her senses. He was storming the gates she'd erected, and she had the insane urge to help him tear them down. Deep down inside, she knew she wanted more than his kiss. Much, much more.

They stopped at a convenience store for deli meat and sub rolls on the way back. When they arrived at Joey's place, clothes still damp and hair in tangles, Caroline's car was in the driveway. Ash was craving a shower, and he figured he'd probably get first crack at one. Joey would want to speak in private with her sister.

He sent her a reassuring glance as she shut off the motor and then they both got out and walked around the house. Brittany and Bethany were chasing each other around the back lawn, near the house. It looked like a spirited game of tag. Caroline sat in a lawn chair, watching them. Her hair, as always, was up in a ponytail. She wore sweats again. Ash took a moment to note how alike the two women were. If Caro would get some spunk and hold her head up a little higher, she'd be a knockout. He didn't think he'd realized until that very moment what a difference confidence made in a woman's appeal, at least to him.

What was that? Was he just thinking Caroline ought to be a little more like Joey? That the dedicated soccer mom should be more like her hellion sister?

Then he recalled the way Joey had let him kiss her on the sidewalk, the way she'd kissed him back, and he knew he hadn't yet succeeded in convincing himself she was all wrong for him. His mind knew it. But, God, he was having trouble proving that to the rest of him.

Caroline rose and met Joey halfway. Her eyes were red and her cheeks showed tear tracks. She hugged her sister and a sob ripped through her. I'm...l-leaving him."

Joey met Ash's eyes over Caroline's shaking shoulders. "It's all right. It's going to be all right, I promise. You're tough. You can get through this." She sent him an apologetic glance. "You and the girls can stay right here with Ash and me."

He made a grimace, then remembered that they were planning to spend some time at his apartment anyway to help restore his memory. For someone who would be found out as a result, Joey certainly seemed eager for him to get his memory back.

Joey released her sister and turned to unlock the back door as Bethany and Brittany came running toward her. Caroline averted her tearstained face while her daughters crowded inside.

"You should have gone on in, Caro. You didn't need

to wait for me."

"I didn't want to intrude."

"If I minded, I wouldn't have given you a key, silly."

Ash stopped in the doorway, sensing the turmoil in Caroline and the pain it caused Joey. "I'll get the groceries," he said. "Leave you two alone."

"No need." Caroline sniffed and seemed to stiffen her spine. "You're family now, Ash. And please don't worry that we're going to move in on you. I'm taking the girls to Miami to visit Dad and Rhonda for a couple of weeks."

Joey frowned as she and her sister stepped back outside. "I'd rather have you here."

"You're newlyweds—"

"So are they." Joey's voice was tinged with bitterness. She shook herself, though, and put an arm around her sister as they followed Ash along the path around the house. "We'll talk. Look, at least stay for lunch. Ash is making subs."

"I don't want to impose..."

Ash turned, letting them catch up. "Hey, you haven't lived until you've had an Ash Coye special. Make you into a new woman." He sent Caroline a smile and felt Joey's gratitude bathing him as he walked with them around the house to get the groceries from the car.

Ash clicked the key bob to open the trunk, then reached in for a bag, vaguely aware of the slamming of the screen door coming from the out back. Joey bent to grab the second bag, her worried eyes scanning her sister's face. Caroline bit her lip as tears filled her eyes once more.

"I don't think I can stand this. God, Joey, what am I going to do?"

Joey shifted the bag she held to her hip, freeing one

arm. Her big green eyes moistened as she reached for her sister and hugged her for a long moment. And then all of the sudden, Joey went rigid, jerking away from Caroline. Her eyes rounded and her face went white. "Brittany," she choked. The grocery bag slid from her grasp, spilling its contents onto the blacktop. "Brittany!" It was a scream the second time, delivered as Joey took off running full tilt around the house.

Ash didn't take time to wonder what the hell her problem was. He followed her, dropping his bag back into the trunk. Caroline ran alongside, keeping pace with him when she should not have been physically able to.

Joey flew over the back lawn, heading for the river. Ash's stomach knotted when he caught sight of one little girl, only one, standing dangerously close to the riverbank. Bethany. She was near the red wooden dock, her small body convulsing with sobs. Ash ran faster. His feet hit the dock just as Joey sprang into the air over the side, knifing into the murky, fast-running water.

In the space of a heartbeat, he was following Joey's path into the cold, muddy water. If she thought Brittany was in the river, then he wouldn't waste time questioning it.

He submerged, but was unable to see in the greenish water. When he broke the surface again, he caught sight of Joey. She was out farther, in the force of the current, moving away from him rapidly. As he watched, she dived under. He stroked toward her, his heart hammering forcefully enough to break his ribs, his eyes straining, his arms putting forth superhuman effort.

He almost jumped when Joey broke surface a few feet ahead of him. Her face was pale, haggard, her eyes a dull green, a color that seemed to scream with pain.

Something was wrong with her!

Then she tugged Brittany's limp body from beneath the water, and struggled to hold the child's face above the waves as he stroked toward her.

"Ash..."

Then he had her. But there was no way in hell he could fight the current and hold onto both of them.

She pushed Brittany into his arms. Joey looked horrible, and he had a sickening feeling there was a lot more wrong with her than the cold, dirty water or exhaustion. He held the little girl firmly with one arm as she began to whine and struggle and choke. He reached for Joey with the other.

"You'll sink," she said. "I'm okay, just get Brit out of the water."

He shook his head. "You're hurt Joey, what is it?"

"She needs to get out of the water. Go now. I'll be right behind you."

Her pupils told another story. Ash pulled her arms around the child, speaking softly to calm Brittany as he did. Then he hooked his own arms around them both. "Hold her tight, Joey. Don't let her go." He sidestroked toward shore. They would end up yards from the dock, since the current was pulling them downstream. His head was under more than it was above, but he managed to keep both Brittany's and Joey's faces out of the water.

Then he was in the shallows and Caroline was wading in up to her waist, reaching for her daughter, sobbing hysterically. Bethany came running along the shore, eyes wide.

As soon as Caroline had Brittany in her arms and was carrying her onto the bank, Ash wrapped his arms around Joey and picked her up. Her head fell backward.

Her eyes were glazed. He swore and trudged onto the shore.

A jagged tear through Joey's black spandex shorts as well as her tanned thigh gushed blood at a rate that made him dizzy. He lowered her to the grassy ground, tugged the baggy tank top over her head and wrapped it around the wound, tying a knot and tugging it fiercely tight. Her eyes fell closed.

"Joey?" He caught her face in his hands.

"Dizzy," she whispered. "Brit?"

He looked up to see Brittany sobbing and choking, white-faced, in her mother's arms. "Caroline, you have to call an ambulance."

"I did." Bethany's trembling voice came from beside her sister, and it shook with fear. "I r-ran to the house and called 911. The lady said they would be here soon." Her lower lip trembled. "Is my sister gonna die?"

Caroline opened her arm to encircle Bethany's shoulders. "No, honey. She'll be fine." Caroline looked toward Ash for the first time. "Joey... Oh, God, Joey..."

"It's okay, Caroline. She cut her leg on something, lost some blood, I think, but the bleeding's stopped now. She'll be okay." Ash's hold on Joey tightened and he searched her pale face. "You'll be okay." It was almost a prayer. Something inside him moved, twisted, ached. How had she come to matter so much to him in such a short time? What the hell would he do if she *wasn't* okay?

CHAPTER 7

"**M**ommy, I'm scared!"

Joey tried to whisper reassurances as Brittany was settled onto the stretcher next to hers, which sat beside the river on the green mat of lawn. Her mom would've had a fit about them driving over her grass. The thought flitted in and out of Joey's mind like an errant breeze.

She was dizzy and having trouble keeping her eyes open. Her voice, when she spoke, was slurred and the words came slowly. She felt drunk and weak and very, very cold. All she could smell was river water. She was soaked with it.

Caroline looked helplessly from frightened, still-pale Brittany to sobbing, terrified Bethany, clinging to her waist. "I thought they were inside. I should have been watching." She'd whispered the same two phrases over and over until Joey worried she was more shaken than Brittany was.

"I don't want to go in the amb'lance," Brit whined.

108 | MAGGIE SHAYNE

I'm *scared.*"

"How about if I ride with you?" The deep voice was Ash's. He was right there, beside her, close to Brittany, one hand smoothing Bethany's hair. He was calm and strong and solid, and Joey couldn't imagine anyone she'd rather have by her side right then. "Your mom and Bethany can follow right behind us in the car. If you want, I'll hold you up so you can see them out the window."

"Mister, there isn't going to be much room," said the prematurely balding EMT. "You'd be better off changing into dry clothes and following us yourself."

Joey focused on Ash, saw the stern look he sent in the paramedic's direction. "I'm riding in the ambulance."

"I want Uncle Ash," Brittany said softly. Her voice trembled as she was installed in the ambulance. Then Joey's gurney was lifted and snapped into place. Ash climbed in, settling himself between the two, and Joey was ridiculously glad he was here.

Caroline stuck her head in the back. "I'll grab you some dry clothes from the house and be right behind you." She leaned in farther, snagged Ash by the neck and hugged him hard. "Thank you," she said on a broken sob.

A moment later they were bounding over the lawn and then the driveway. Brittany twisted until her head was off the litter, resting it on Ash's knee. Joey saw his crooked half smile. She watched his big hand stroking Brittany's wet hair away from her face, Then he stopped long enough to tug a blanket over her shoulders.

When the driver gave a siren blast to clear traffic, Brittany jerked and began to cry.

"C'mon now, kid, you're not afraid of a little noise, are you?" Ash asked.

She nodded, choking on a sob.

"Would a story help?"

A short sniffle, wide blue eyes gazing upward, another nod.

Joey felt his warm gaze on her and she forced a weak smile for him. "Do you have a favorite, Brittany?"

"Red Riding Hood."

"Its been a while. But maybe I can remember it." He pretended great concentration, a furrow forming between his brows. "Okay. There was this little girl, and they called her Red Riding Hood because..." He looked at Brittany with mock seriousness. "Because she was a redhead and she liked to go riding dressed up like a hood."

Brittany released a peal of laughter. "Noo, Uncle Ash."

"Hmm. Wait, wait, I remember now. Because she had a red car and she was always riding on the hood."

"No." Brit giggled, relaxing back onto the pillow. "Because she *wore* a red hood."

"Right. That would have been my next guess. Anyway, she was walking through the woods one day...I think she missed the bus. And along comes this big, bad raccoon." Brit squealed. "Squirrel?" Ash attempted. "No, wait, it was a 'possum. I'm sure it was a 'possum. A big, bad 'possum."

Joey closed her eyes, soothed by her niece's musical laughter. And then....

"I love you, Uncle Ash."

"I love you, too, kiddo. No more swimming in the river, okay?"

"I didn't mean to. I fell."

"I figured that."

"I caught a frog, but he got away, and when I tried to

get him, I slipped."

"Well, no more frog catching near the river, then. At least, not without me. I'm a world-class frog catcher, you know."

A miserable feeling settled over Joey like a shroud. What had she done? How devastated would Brittany and Bethany be when they found out the uncle they were fast growing to adore was no uncle at all? And Ash? How much pain would the truth cause him?

Ash left the treatment room when Caroline arrived. Brittany was fine, and glad to see her mother and sister. Ash hurried through the corridor and started toward the room where they'd taken Joey, only to be stopped outside the door by a nurse.

"You can't go in there."

Ash shook his head, frustration pulling at his nerves. "The hell I can't—"

"Sir, the patient is—"

He started to go around her. "The *patient* is my *wife.*" Then he stopped and stood still, blinking. For a second there, he'd believed it was true. For the briefest moment, he had stopped playing a role. He wasn't pretending. He actually felt like a man desperately worried about his wife. He drew a calming breath.

"At least tell me what's going on."

The nurse smiled gently. "She's fine. The doctor's suturing her leg. Why don't you sit down? I'll let you know as soon as you can go in."

He clenched his jaw and stuffed his hands in his pockets to keep himself from bodily moving the slight woman out of the way and charging into the room. He couldn't sit, so he paced, keeping that closed door always in his sight. The nurse went in and it took all his will to keep from following. What seemed like hours, but in truth was only minutes later, a doctor emerged. The nurse came out behind her and sent Ash a nod.

He rushed into the room, then stood inside the door as relief sapped his nervous energy. Joey sat on the edge of a bed wearing a thin white hospital gown that covered her thighs. Her bare legs dangled over the side.

She met his eyes and smiled. "You look like a drowned rat."

He glanced down at his wet shorts and the sweatshirt that still stuck to his skin. Then he glanced back up at her, and quick crossed the space between them, pushed the gown up, away from her injured leg. Thick, white bandages padded the length of her outer thigh. The memory of the way it had looked before, torn, bleeding, made him close his eyes for just a second.

He felt her palm on his cheek. "Hey, it's all right. I'm fine."

Reaction must be setting in. And it was a powerful reaction. He felt sick. He stared hard at her face, the green eyes that were already regaining their sparkle, the slightly puzzled smile. He studied it, just to prove to himself that she was really okay, and wondered just when she had dug her way under his skin.

"Brittany is fine, too," he told her. Mainly just for something to say to cover his jumbled emotions.

"I know. Dr. Fritz told me."

"Dr. Fritz?"

She bent her head and tugged the rubber band from her wet, tangled hair. "Her last name is unpronounceable. Ouch." She scowled at the hairy rubber band before tossing it toward a wastebasket.

She was okay. It was finally sinking in, and as it did, the questions that had been overshadowed by his worry came to the surface. Questions that made him uneasy.

"So what happened?"

She ran her fingers through her hair, trying to comb out the snarls. "I think it was a rusted-out barrel. I felt it slice into me when I dove in. Didn't see it, so I can't be sure."

He bit his lip and watched her intently. "That's not what I meant." He caught her hands, stopping their movements. She faced him again, frowning. "How did you know, Joey?"

"How'd I know what?" She knew what he was asking. It was clear in her eyes.

"That Brittany fell in. We were all there together. You just went white all of a sudden, yelled her name and took off for the river. So the question I'm asking is, *how did you know?*"

Her tongue darted out to moisten her lips, and she hesitated before answering. "I...heard a splash."

"From that distance?" He shook his head. "No one else heard a thing, Joey."

"Well, I did."

"So how'd you know it was Brit, and not Bethany?"

She bit her lip, her gaze lowering. "Bethany is afraid of water. Brittany is a little fish. Or, at least, she used to be. Maybe that will change now."

Ash stood close to her, his thighs touching her legs where they dangled from the edge of the bed. He studied her face, wanting to be angry with her for holding things back. But he couldn't. He was just so damn glad she was alive. He replaced her hands in her hair with his own and shook the still-damp tangles out. For the first time he questioned his own skepticism. Maybe there was actually something to this psychic thing.

"You saved my life, Ash. Brit's, too. You could have drowned trying to pull us both to shore."

She was grateful. She meant it. Her eyes were like billboards announcing her true feelings. He knew when she was lying, when she was hurting, when she was scared. He knew when she was wanting him and fighting it. "No chance of that, princess. Frogs are great swimmers."

He stiffened then, because she slid her arms around him, beneath his, and lowered her head to his chest. "I'll never be able to repay you for this. There aren't any words. If I'd lost that little angel..." She shook her head. "How am I ever going to thank you?"

"You could try trusting me, Joey."

She lifted her head, meeting his eyes.

"All frogs aren't the same, you know. Some of them are pretty decent characters, given half a chance."

She blinked as moisture gathered in her eyes. "I'm afraid..."

"Of what?"

She shook her head quickly. "That you'll go away...that you'll stay. That I'll become a gullible fool like my mother, and my sister Toni's mother, and so many others." A tear spilled onto her cheek.

"You're a lot of things, Joey. But gullible isn't one of them. Maybe you ought to try trusting your instincts."

She shook her head. "That's what my mother did, and then my sister. Look where it got them."

"It doesn't have to be that way."

She looked at him then, her eyes so intense he felt them penetrating his mind. He leaned forward intending to kiss her senseless. He'd show her, make her believe... He was brought up short when the door opened and the same petite nurse stuck her head in.

"Your sister asked me to bring you these." She set a plastic grocery bag on the floor. "Dry clothes." She left them alone again, and the door swung closed.

He cursed the woman's timing. The mood was broken. Joey lowered her arms and averted her eyes. Sighing, Ash picked up the bag and pulled a pair of shorts and a T-shirt out of it. Joey slid from the bed to the floor and winced when she put weight on the leg.

"Easy now." Ash set the clothes on the bed and gripped her around the waist, lifting her right back up to the bed again. He grabbed the shorts and crouched in front of her to slip them on, over her feet, pulling them to her knees.

She grabbed the waistband. "I can take it from here." She slid down, landing only on her good leg this time, and tugged the shorts up under the gown. She tried balancing on one leg while reaching behind her to undo the ties in the back, but wobbled and would have fallen if he hadn't caught her.

"Enough with the modesty, Joey. Turn around."

She sighed and presented her back to him.

Ash untied the gown. He couldn't keep his eyes from traveling over the gentle curve of her spine. And he knew it wasn't really necessary to slide his palms slowly over her skin as he pushed the gown down from her shoulders, but he did it anyway.

The hospital gown landed on the floor. He stood still for a moment fighting the demon that drove him to turn her around, to look at her, to touch her. It was a hard battle, harder because it was one he didn't want to win.

But he stiffened his resolve and reached past her for the T-shirt her sister had brought for her. As she gripped the bed for support, he pulled it over her head, holding it in place while she inserted one arm, then the other. And it really was accidental that the backs of his fingers brushed over her breasts as he pulled the shirt down over her body.

He felt her shudder, though. He lifted her hair out of the shirt's collar, and then he held it aside and lowered his lips to the back of her neck. He didn't think about doing it, wasn't even aware he was going to until his lips brushed over her nape. He heard the breath escape from her in a rush, and something like pain squeezed his chest.

Then he straightened and stepped away from her. He had to, or God only knew what the little nurse would see the next time she popped through the door.

There was too much tension, too much confusion inside his head. He cleared his throat as she turned to face him. "You, uh, want to hobble, or ride on my back and let me hop you out of here?"

She smiled, but it was shaky, uncertain. "I can walk." As if to prove it she took a step, but then gasped audibly.

He got in front of her, bent his knees and crouched down. "Climb on."

"Ash—"

"Don't argue with your husband, lady." He looked over his shoulder at her with mock severity. "Climb on. I'm about half dry already so you won't get too wet."

She gripped his neck and slid her legs around his waist. Ash held her soft-skinned legs to his sides. She started to droop, so he reached behind him, palms to backside, and shoved her up higher. "Rrribbit."

She laughed aloud. "You're crazy, you know that?"

He walked with her on his back into the corridor and down it. "No wonder you were so great with Brit in the ambulance. You're just a kid yourself."

He frowned, remembering the fear in the little girl's huge blue eyes. "I can't stand to see a kid scared, and she was ready to climb the walls in there."

"You were afraid a lot when you were growing up, weren't you?" she asked softly, her words pinpointing the most vulnerable target possible.

Without hesitation he nodded. "Yeah. I was." It wasn't until after he'd confirmed it that he wondered how she'd known.

She leaned down and brushed her lips across his cheek. "Whatever it was didn't stop you from becoming a hell of a man, Ashville Coye. A hero, in my book. My hero."

He shook his head. "Poor princess, waiting for a knight on a charger to show up, and instead you got a frog on a lily pad."

She started to say something, but they emerged into the waiting room then, and Caroline came to meet them. Brittany looked a good deal better, and Bethany's face glowed with joy.

Both girls lunged for Ash's legs, hugging him fiercely.

"Can I ride next?" Bethany shouted.

"No, me," Brittany said. "I'm the one that almost got drowneded."

"Your Aunt Joey is the one who hurt her leg, so I guess she has you both beat. But when we get back to the house I'll give you both a turn."

Squeals preceded them into an elevator, and then out to Caroline's minivan. Caroline lowered the third row seats, and Ash lowered Joey in through the open hatch door, so she could keep her leg stretched out. And when they reached the house, he scooped her up again and carried her inside. He saw the suitcases near the door and glanced at Caroline.

"They're ours. I took them out of the car before I left for the hospital."

Joey's face was tight when Ash lowered her to the sofa. "You should have locked the door, Caroline."

"Sorry, little sister. I was too busy wondering if you'd survive the trip. Sheesh, at least I thought to toss the groceries into the fridge. Bags and all, but what the heck?"

Joey's frown deepened. Ash leaned closer to her. "What is it?"

"I don't know." She shook her head slightly. "Something..."

"Rides now, Uncle Ash!"

He turned Joey sideways on the couch, lifting her injured leg onto a pair of throw pillows. "I'm going to make you my super deluxe subs for lunch, you lucky kids."

"Go change your clothes first, Ash. I can start the subs," Caroline offered.

"I'll help—"

"*You* will sit there and rest," Ash told Joey. "Doctor's orders." He turned to Caro. "Five minutes." Then he ran upstairs to put on clean clothes. He returned and approached the girls. "Bethany, for courage above and beyond the call of duty, for remembering what you learned in school and calling 911 for your sister, I award you the first ride." He hunkered down and a giggling Bethany climbed onto his back, wrapping her small arms around his neck. "Careful not to choke the old guy now." Ash straightened and began a mock gallop around the living room, into the kitchen and out the other side. All the time, though, as he gave each child a turn, he watched the worry on Joey's face increase. It scared him.

The subs were made and devoured in record time. When they finished, Caroline stood. "We have to go."

"Go where?" Joey sat straighter on the couch.

"Airport. I told you, Joey, the girls and I are going to Miami."

"You didn't say today!"

"Well, I was going to, but..." Caroline didn't finish the sentence. A car pulled in, and seconds later the back door thudded open and footsteps came pounding up the stairs.

Ted stopped in the doorway, his gaze jumping from Caroline to the two girls who were still munching potato chips in the kitchen. His eyes fell closed in apparent relief, and he moved toward Brittany, dropping to his knees and gathering her into his arms.

"You okay, Brittany? Huh?"

She nodded hard. "I fell in the river, but Aunt Joey and Uncle Ash swimmed out and got me."

Ted's arms tightened. He kissed Brit's cheek and put her back in the chair.

"And I called 911," Bethany put in proudly.

Ted ruffled her hair. "You're a good girl, Beth." He looked up, met Caroline's gaze. "Were you even going to tell me?"

"I was going to call—"

"I should have been there, Caroline. I'm her father."

"Did you bring your suitcase, Daddy?"

"Course he did," Bethany told her sister. "See, Mommy, I told you Daddy would come to Grandpa's house with us."

Caroline bit her lip as Ted's gaze widened. He opened

his mouth to speak, but Joey was quicker. "Look, you two obviously need to talk." She slanted a meaningful glance toward the girls. "Alone."

Ted didn't seem to hear her. He stepped into the living room toward Caroline, shaking his head. "You're *leaving*?"

She only nodded, her eyes filling.

"Caro, this is crazy. I know what you've been thinking, but you're wrong—"

"Am I?"

He looked as if he'd been punched. Then his face hardened. He turned on his heel and rushed back down the stairs. Ash wasn't sure why, but he followed. Something about the sudden pain on the guy's face hit him hard, and his instincts read it as real.

He stopped Ted at the door. "You're just letting her go?"

Ted's hand tightened on the doorknob. "For now, yes." His voice was choked, and his eyes narrowed in apparent pain when they fell on the suitcases on the floor. "Doesn't look like she's giving me much of a choice."

Ash sighed hard, pushing a hand through his hair. "You could talk to her. Tell her—"

"Look, Coye, this really isn't any of your damn business. And with you and Joey up to your elbows in this Slasher thing, I'm beginning to think it isn't a bad idea for Caro to get the hell out of Dodge for a while. At least she'll be safe." He thumped a fist on the door.

"I wasn't trying to butt in." Ash opened his mouth to say more, then threw his hands in the air. "You're right, it's none of my damn business."

Ted gripped the door, jerking it open. He started to step through it, then stopped with his back to Ash. "There is no other woman, but Caroline isn't going to believe that. It's her father... Sometimes I'd like to slit that bastard's throat for messing those two up the way he did."

Then he left, slamming the door behind him. And Ash couldn't help but ponder his parting words. Slit that bastard's throat. Not break his neck, or blow his head off, but slit his throat. Did it mean anything?

He went back upstairs to see Caroline gathering the girls, apparently ready to leave. "Caroline," he said, sure he was still overstepping and unable to stop himself. "Are you sure this is what you want to do?" Why did he want so badly to fix this mess? He was letting himself get carried away with his role as a member of this family. Caroline only nodded. "Because you *can* stay here, you know. I'd hate to think you were going south because of me—"

"It's better if she goes," Joey announced loudly. Ash frowned. She'd done a complete turnaround since he'd been downstairs with Ted. A few minutes ago, she'd hated the idea of Caroline and the girls leaving.

Joey glanced at the clock on the wall. "You'd better hurry, or you'll miss your flight."

"She's right, Ash. But thanks for the offer." Caroline hugged her sister, and the girls flung themselves at Ash's legs.

He picked them up, one in either arm. "All right, then, how about one last ride out to the car?" He spun in a circle as the girls giggled.

The Slasher had been in her house.

The sickening sensation had settled in the pit of Joey's stomach from the second they'd arrived home, but she hadn't been able to pinpoint the source. Then it had hit her all at once. What she was feeling was a presence. Someone was in the house, or had been very recently. Someone with evil intentions.

And somewhere in the darkest dungeons of her soul, she knew who. And she'd had to get Caroline and the girls away from there.

As soon as Ash went outside with the girls, she retrieved her gun from its newest hiding place atop a kitchen cabinet, checked to be sure it was loaded and started up the stairs, wincing with every excruciating step. The feeling grew stronger with each second that passed. Before she reached the top she was breathless. Moisture stood on her brow. She held the gun in a two-fisted grip, muzzle up, and glanced around at four closed doors.

Directly ahead was the guest room she'd designated as the girls' when they visited, filled with toys and coloring books and dolls. To her left was the guest room she'd offered to Ash that first night. To her right, side by side, were the doors to her bedroom and the bath.

She stood frozen at the top of the stairs, concentrating on those doors, sending out invisible feelers. If she chose poorly, and the killer was still here, she might get caught from behind.

"Joey?"

She whirled, gun first. Ash stood on the bottom step. Why did he have to be so quick? She pressed a finger to her lips to silence him and held a palm outward to tell him to stay where he was.

He came up the stairs, anyway, but he kept his voice low.

"What the hell is going on?"

"Someone...has been here. May still be here. I don't know."

He frowned. "Where?"

"It's strongest near our room." The words came out that way before she thought to rephrase them. She lifted the gun again, taking a step nearer.

Ash's hand on her shoulder stopped her. He took the gun from her hands and pushed her back to the wall. "Wait here."

"Ash, no. You shouldn't even be here. You could get killed." Panic gripped her. She didn't want him anywhere near this dark menace.

Ash ignored her, stepped forward and shoved the bedroom door open. As he stepped in and looked around, Joey threw the bathroom door wide, afraid the Slasher might have slipped through the adjoining door from the bedroom. No one was there. The tub's sliding door was open, no one lurked behind it.

"Joey."

She hurried to the bedroom at Ash's call and froze in the doorway, half expecting to come face-to-face with evil incarnate. But there was no one there. She stood, trembling while Ash checked the other rooms. When he came back to her, he didn't speak. He just looked at her, waiting.

"You think I'm crazy."

He shook his head. "No. I think you're nervous, jumping at shadows, terrified for your sister and, for some reason, for me, too. What I don't know is why." She said nothing. "Joey, talk to me, tell me what made you think someone was—"

"I don't think it, I *know* it. Someone was in this house while we were gone."

His voice became placating. He moved closer, stroked her hair. "Honey, you've been through a rough day.

There's no one here. There's nothing missing. Look around, everything is just as we—"

He stopped there, his muscles slowly tensing under the skin where her hands rested. She turned, followed his gaze and saw the laptop opened on the dresser. The flash drive that had been in the USB port was gone.

Joey drew a sharp breath, feeling, for just an instant, the distinct sensation of an ice-cold blade tearing across her back.

What was *that?*

Then Ash was touching her, his hands on her shoulders. "We won't touch anything. There might be prints."

"No." She leaned back against him, letting his warmth chase the cold, tearing feeling from her shoulder blades. "There were gloves. Black, kid-leather gloves, with two little buttons..." She held up a hand and touched the back of her wrist. "Right here." She could feel the gloves, too tight on her hands. Only they were *not* her hands at all.

Her eyes flew wide. "Where is Caroline?"

"On her way to the airport. Safe and sound. Now dammit, Joey, tell me what the hell is going on. Who wears gloves? Who is it you think was in here?"

She sniffed, trying frantically to control the fit of violent shaking that began at her fingertips and raced its way up her arms to her shoulders, down her spine to her legs. She couldn't say it. She couldn't tell him that his murderer was getting closer. God, she didn't want to lose him. It was so much more important now. More than just a means to stop the Slasher before Caroline became a victim.

She turned into Ash's arms, clung to him. "We have to get out of this house."

CHAPTER 8

Radley Ketchum's office at the *Chronicle* was little more than four stark walls, every one of them sporting a photo of his wife in better days, surrounding a paper explosion. He paced toward the closed door, then back again, and handed the coral-frost lipstick back to Ash. Ash took it and shoved an overflowing ashtray aside before sitting on the edge of the desk.

"You could get your ass tossed behind bars for evidence tampering, Coye." It was little more than a harsh whisper, delivered as Rad glanced over his shoulder. "You know better than this crap."

Ash dropped the small cylinder back into his pocket, trying not to think about what the lipstick's presence in Joey's makeup bag might mean. He was guilty of more than evidence tampering. He was obstructing an investigation, and he knew it. He glanced beyond Rad, through the glass in the office door, and saw Joey on the other side. She clutched a ceramic mug with steam rolling off the top and sat on the edge of the little chair in front of Ash's desk. One foot tapped rapidly on the floor. One hand, the one that wasn't holding the mug, kept flexing and relaxing on her wounded thigh. She'd have been pacing if she could have managed it

"Look at her, Rad."

Radley turned his head slowly and stared for a moment. "Yeah. I get it. She doesn't look like a killer, but—"

"Not that. Look at her face. Her eyes. That's one scared woman sitting out there." Ash shook his head. "She won't go back to her house, wouldn't even stick around and wait for the police to show up."

Rad shook his head slowly, facing Ash once more. "Yeah, but scared of *what?*"

"Of the Slasher, I think."

"Or maybe scared of getting caught. Maybe she's scared you're close to finding out *she's* the Slasher." Rad shook his head, crossed the room slowly and straightened a photograph of his wife.

"How's Amelia doing, Rad?"

Radley lowered his head, shook it slowly. "It's just a matter of making what time she has left as easy on her as I can."

"Dammit, I'm sorry."

Rad shook his head hard, turning away from the photo. "Let's stay focused here. I understand you wanting to protect this woman. It's pretty clear to me you've got feelings for her." Ash opened his mouth to argue, but no words emerged. "Use your brain, Ash. Why would *she* be afraid of the Slasher? All five victims have been men."

"Four, Rad."

"What?"

"Four victims. You said five, but there's only been—"

"Four, five—what difference does it make? There'll

be more. The police haven't got much to go on, and you're hiding anything they might *get* to go on. They're getting desperate."

"That's what I'm afraid of." Ash jumped down from the desk and walked closer to the door. "They need a suspect even if it's just to take the heat off for a while, and I'll be damned if it's going to be Joey. They could ruin her life, Rad, all on the basis of one tube of lipstick."

"The same brand, even the same shade of lipstick that ringed every one of those cigarette butts at the crime scenes. And no trace of DNA on any of them."

"It's coincidence. Look, I can't stand by and let her get railroaded."

"Why the hell not?" That Rad's patience was reaching its limit was evidenced by the deep color rising in his face and the tightening of his jaw. "It's due process. If she's innocent she'll be cleared, and if not she'll pay. That's the way the system works, isn't it? You can't cover up her crimes just because you're sleeping with her."

Ash had him by the collar before he could finish the sentence. Two fists bunched Rad's dingy white shirt at the front and drew him forward.

"See what I mean, Ash?" Rad ground the words out between clenched teeth as Ash glared at him, wanting to knock out a few of his teeth. "You're not objective anymore. You're messing around with evidence, protecting a suspect, risking your job...." He glanced pointedly down at the fists that held his shirt, and Ash sighed hard, releasing him.

"You're wrong." Ash turned and paced away slowly. "Not that it's any of your business, Rad, but I haven't slept with her. And I'm on top of this story. Objectivity intact."

Rad was silent a long moment, then, "I don't think so, Ash. I'm going to put Harris on the Slasher case."

Ash whirled. "The hell you are!"

"You aren't yourself. You're—"

"Quitting."

Rad's mouth fell open, the rest of his sentence left hanging unfinished in the air, silenced by a single word.

"That's it. Your choice. Give the story to Harris, and I walk. And if I walk, you'll probably be behind me in the unemployment line, because the paper will fire you for losing their star reporter. Now what's it gonna be, Rad?"

Radley's eyes conveyed his anger. He didn't like being backed up to the wall, but Ash was saying no more than the truth, and Rad knew it. "What are you planning, besides trailing along after her like a hungry pup and hoping she drops you a crumb?"

Ash glared right back at him. "Go to hell, Rad."

"Damn you, Coye—"

"All right." Ash held up one hand. "Truce, okay?"

Rad stuffed both hands deep into his pockets and nodded. "What are you planning?"

"To talk to a psychiatrist, an expert on serial killers. Try and get a profile of our suspect. And I want to see some of these executive types Joey's worked for, find out what they have to say about her...abilities."

It was Rad's turn to stare through the window at Joey. "You still think she's a fake, right?"

Ash hesitated before answering. "I'm beginning to wonder."

"Why? You're a dyed-in-the-wool skeptic about that kind of crap, Ash. What's she done, read your mind or something?"

"Or something."

Rad's face seemed to relax all of a sudden, all the tension going out of it. He turned again toward the door and looked through it, eyes speculative. "Well, now. Isn't that interesting?"

Ash shook his head slowly, reaching for the doorknob. "Don't go asking her about it. She thinks I don't know. And treat her right, Rad. She's my wife, don't forget."

"As long as *you* don't forget that she *isn't.*"

Joey stiffened when she saw them coming toward her. She'd tried to concentrate on their conversation in Mr. Ketchum's office, but as usual, the harder she tried to focus, the less she picked up. In a newsroom that was bursting with wall-to-wall desks, rushing people and the constant clicking of keyboards, it was tough to hear herself think, let alone pick up what someone else might be thinking. She sensed, though, that a lot of the time they'd been talking about her. Not knowing what was said made her uncomfortable and self-conscious.

"Mrs. Coye." Radley Ketchum nodded toward her. "Feeling better now?"

She nodded politely. "Yes. Thanks for the coffee."

Ash stood in front of her, putting both hands on her shoulders. "Bev called while I was in Rad's office."

Bev. Detective Lady Atlas, he meant

"They've finished at the house."

"Did they find anything?"

Ash squeezed her shoulders. "A few prints, they're being analyzed but—"

"They're ours. I told you, the person wore gloves." She stopped, blinking. Ash would have her committed if she didn't stop going on about the gloves. She glanced up to see if his boss found her as nutty as Ash must, but he only stared at her, his gaze dark and probing.

"Anyway, we can go back now—"

"No."

He shook her so slightly she barely felt it. "Joey, we can still stay at my apartment. But don't you think you ought to pick up a few clothes? Your toothbrush?"

"I'm not going back there."

Ash shook his head, and she knew he thought she must still be distraught over the intruder, stressed out from all that had happened. The truth was, she was calm, and thinking as clearly as she ever had in her life. She simply did not want Ash in that house. A sense of danger loomed larger in her mind at the very thought of it.

"Okay. All right, if that's what you want." He nodded toward his boss, who still stared hard at her. "I'll be in touch."

"Good." Mr. Ketchum smiled gently at Joey, the way you smile at a crazy person. Humoring her. "Hope to see you again soon, Mrs. Coye." Then he turned and walked away.

Ash drove to his apartment, a few short minutes from the offices of *The Chronicle*. He unlocked the door, and Joey preceded him in, limping slowly, senses on alert. She was more wary than she could ever remember being. She stepped into the short, dark hallway and felt the wall for a light switch.

Ash beat her to it, and as soon as he flicked it on Joey stepped farther inside. Still, she was careful. She poked her head through the archway on her right, into the kitchenette, leaning heavily on the doorframe and fumbling for that light switch. When she saw nothing there, aside from the gleaming white cupboards and checkerboard tiles, she returned to the hall and hobbled through the door on its other side, into the small bathroom. She turned that light on, as well.

She knew Ash stood in the hallway, leaning against the wall, just watching her peculiar behavior. Stubbornly, she glanced around the little bathroom, even going so far as to open the frosted-glass doors on the three-sided shower stall in the corner to peek inside.

Sighing her relief, she stepped back into the short hall. Ash put an arm around her. "You'd better relax, Joey. You're jumping at shadows. No one's here but us."

"Better safe than sorry. And I'm not jumping. Just checking." The hall opened into the large living room of Ash's corner apartment. At the far end, glass doors led out to a balcony. Darkness gathered beyond, dotted by Syracuse's lights, only visible in the slits between the vertical blinds. The bedroom was on her right. She checked both before she sank onto the brown modular sofa.

"Feel safe now?" There was worry, as well as a hint of amusement, glinting in his eyes.

She smiled at him. "It isn't *me* I'm—" She stopped herself. "Yes. Perfectly safe."

"You're sure?"

She squinted at him. "Why so interested?"

"Just checking. Thought I'd go out for some supplies."

"Like what?" She was no longer relaxed on the sofa, but leaning forward, tense.

Ash shook his head and sat down beside her. "Like food. I haven't been here in a while. The place isn't exactly well stocked."

She turned to face him, wanting to beg him not to leave her side—not for an instant—but knowing how insane that might sound to him. "I'm not all that hungry, anyway."

"Well, I am. Look, I know you're still shaken. Just stay here, okay? Take a hot shower, watch some TV, drink a glass of wine. I'll be back in thirty minutes, I promise."

She shook her head slowly. "We can order in."

"Joey—"

"Don't go, Ash." He frowned, searching her eyes for a long moment. "Just...don't go."

He lowered his head until his chin touched his chest. When he lifted it again she saw the impatience in his face, the frustration. "You want me to stay, then you're going to have to tell me why. What is it you're so afraid of, Joey?"

She blinked, turning her face away. "I—I'm not afraid, just—"

"Bull." He caught her face in his hands and brought it around, then stared deep into her eyes. "Stop keeping things from me. Joey, I want to help you, but I can't if you won't tell me what's wrong. Can't you trust me even that much?"

She said nothing, and after a second he dropped his hands, sighed in anger and rose from the sofa. "Dammit, Joey, I'm not your father or your stepfather, and I'm not Ted. I'm not going to betray you. But I guess it's too much to ask you to believe that."

He started toward the hall, then down it, and Joey lunged off the sofa after him. The pain in her thigh screamed, but she forced herself to run, and she gripped his arm just as he reached for the doorknob. She jerked him back.

"Don't! Don't leave, Ash, you can't...."

He stood motionless, not even turning to face her. "Give me one good reason, Joey. And if it's another lie—"

"The Slasher is going to kill you."

There was utter silence after she said it. He was going to laugh at her, call her crazy. But it would be better than letting him go out and end up dead.

He turned slowly and looked down at her. "How do you know that?"

He was watching her face so damned closely she knew he'd see through any lie she concocted. She caught her lower lip between her teeth and took a single step backward. "I just do."

"How?" he demanded, advancing. "Do you know the Slasher, Joey? Is that it?"

She shook her head from side to side, and when he reached for her she took another hasty step backward. But she'd forgotten her injury, and she put too much weight on the leg too suddenly, and yelped as white-hot pain shot through her leg.

Ash swore as he reached for her, caught her around the waist and kept her from falling. He hauled her up and forward, hesitated for an immeasurable instant, then pulled her closer, tight to his chest. His arms closed around her, and Joey pressed her face against the cool fabric of his shirt, inhaling his scent.

"It's not firsthand information." He murmured the words into her hair and slowly began to rock just slightly back and forth. "It's not that you're a part of this insanity. I know that, Joey. But for God's sake, you have to tell me what it is."

She nodded, moving her head against his chest as her

arms crept up around his neck and tightened there.

He turned her slightly and then scooped her up and carried her down the hall, but didn't stop in the living room this time. He took her into his bedroom instead.

As he lowered her onto his oversize bed, Ash studied her face in the too-bright lights of the bedroom. *Tell me the truth this time, Joey. I'm trying to believe in you, but, God, you're making it tough.*

He propped pillows behind her and eased her onto them, then pulled the extra blanket from the foot of the bed, shook it out and covered her, tucking it around her shoulders. The apartment was chilly. He hadn't thought to adjust the thermostat when they'd come in. He hadn't been thinking about much at all lately, except the mystery that was Joey Bradshaw and how he might solve it.

He looked at her huddled on his bed like a frightened child, at the way her hair tumbled over her shoulders, and the way her lips were slightly parted and moist and full.

He'd been thinking about those lips, too, and how they tasted. And those thoughts led to others, until he was surprised he could remember how to breathe, let alone investigate a string of murders. Maybe Radley had been right about that.

He pushed a hand through his hair and turned away, went to the living room and heard the anxiety, the raw fear, in her voice as she called his name.

"I'm not going anywhere," he called back. "Just stay put." He stalked to the kitchenette and found a bottle of white zinfandel in the fridge. For a minute he just looked at it, sitting there, unopened, waiting for the notorious Ashville Coye to introduce it to his latest conquest. There was an instant when he was disgusted with himself and his endless search for the perfect woman. Who did he think he was, anyway, that the perfect woman would be interested in him? And where did he get off, listing the standards she had to meet? What did he know?

Nothing. Not one damn thing. Joey Bradshaw was proof of that. He'd written her off the day he'd met her, and as it turned out, she was probably the closest thing to perfect he'd ever seen.

He slammed the fridge closed and fumbled in a drawer for a corkscrew. He felt things for Joey. Things he didn't want to feel. Hell, in all his big plans involving the wife of his dreams and the perfect nuclear family, he'd never given much thought to actual *emotions* being involved. He guessed he'd just assumed some deep, abiding fondness would come with the package.

What an idiot.

So he meets a woman who's as far from what he thinks he wants as was humanly possible, and starts wishing he can have her—wishing he can *always* have her. And it has to be a woman who's lying to him every time she opens her mouth. A woman who can't trust him. A woman who gives every indication of being mixed up in murder.

The cork popped and Ash threw it, corkscrew and all, onto the shiny white counter. "And she thinks she can read minds, to boot. It's crazy." He reached into the cupboard above for two wineglasses and filled them both. Then he set the bottle aside and just stared into the pinkish liquid, remembering the way she'd known little Brittany had fallen into the river, the way she'd known a lot of things she shouldn't have. Those thoughts made him uneasy. He gripped one glass and tipped it to his lips, draining it, then set it down and filled it again.

"Maybe I'm the one who's crazy."

"Ash?"

God, she was so afraid to let him out of her sight.

"Right here. I'm right here." Maybe now she'd come clean with him, tell him why she'd started this game, why she was pretending to be his wife, and what she knew about the Slasher.

He carried the two glasses back to the bedroom, sat on the edge of the bed and handed her one.

She gave him a wary look and took a sip. Then another. "This is good."

"Talk to me, Joey."

She nodded, taking a bigger gulp of wine. "You won't believe me. You'll think I'm a flake." He watched her, waiting. She cleared her throat. "Sometimes I *know* things."

"What kinds of things?" He wasn't going to help her. He needed to know if she would be honest on her own.

She averted her eyes. "Like when Brit fell in the river."

"You said you heard the splash."

"I wasn't...being honest. I didn't hear anything. I just... *felt* it. In my mind, I saw Brit fall in, and I knew." She took a breath, then rushed on. "That's how I help the companies that hire me as a consultant. If I'm around people, I sometimes sense their dishonesty and I..." Her voice trailed off.

"So you're a psychic."

She closed her eyes. "Don't laugh at me, Ash."

He took the wine glass from her hand and set it on the bedside stand, placing his beside it. "I wouldn't do that."

"I can't control it. I'm not sure I want to."

He wasn't sure he believed it, even now. "Is that how you knew someone had been in the house? You just *felt* it?"

She lifted her head and nodded

"And what you said about the gloves—"

"I saw the hands...the gloves."

"And what else have you...seen?"

Her eyes widened and took on an intensity he hadn't witnessed before. "Ash, you're in danger. You have to believe that. The Slasher wants you dead, and I can't let it happen."

"Because I'm your husband?"

Tears gathered until her emerald eyes glittered. "Because... I care about you. I don't want to lose you, and that's nothing but the truth."

It was some kind of pain that twisted inside him when she said that. Some kind of excruciating, wonderful pain. She was telling part of the truth, at least. Or what she believed to be the truth. But it was difficult to swallow. He'd never put much stock in farfetched claims of extraterrestrials, or Elvis sightings, or ESP.

"You don't believe any of it, do you?"

He reached out, brushing a single tear from her cheek with his thumb. "I believe you care." He shook his head. "Can't imagine why, but you do. And I think you're convinced of this...this mind-reading thing. I just..." His hand fell away from her face. He got up and reached for his wine, then paced the room, carrying it. "It's damned hard to buy into, Joey." He took a huge gulp and went on. "Maybe if you could *show* me—"

"I'm not a magician, Ash, and this isn't some parlor trick."

He turned to face her, seeing the anger rising in red blotches on her cheeks. "I didn't mean—"

"Yes, you did. You were going to ask me to read your

mind, tell you what you were thinking while you evoked some unlikely image. It doesn't work that way. I told you, I can't control it. I can't just look inside your head and read your thoughts as if I was reading a book. God knows I've tried."

He felt his brows shoot up as her anger ran its course. "You have?"

She nodded, looking miserable.

"And you couldn't read me, huh?"

She shook her head, then paused. "Well, except..." She bit her lip and didn't finish the thought.

"Except what?" Why did his voice sound so eager? Was he actually hoping she could prove her claims?

She sighed, reaching for her wine and finishing it in one big gulp. "You had a nightmare one night. A bad one. One you have a lot."

He stiffened, suddenly feeling as if someone was invading his most private hell. But it was silly. He'd probably tossed and turned, broken into a sweat, maybe muttered in his sleep. Anyone would know he'd been dreaming.

"I did, huh? I don't remember."

She looked at him, her anger vanishing. "You were alone in a very small, very dark place. You felt like you were suffocating, you couldn't breathe, and you were afraid you'd be left in there forever."

"All right." He didn't mean to snap, but she was picking at an old wound. More gently he said, "All right, I believe you."

"I'm sorry." She got out of the bed and limped toward him. "I know it still hurts—"

"Well, your ESP is flawed, then, because it doesn't."

She stopped two feet from him. "You can tell me

about it, talk it out—"

"It's not something I talk about." He finished his wine and looked down into the empty glass.

"Maybe that's the problem."

"My only problem is that my wife won't let me out of the apartment to buy food, and my stomach is empty."

She lowered her head and he knew that she would let the topic slide.

"Help yourself to the bathroom, Joey, and something to wear to bed. I'm gonna call a deli that delivers." He turned to go, then turned back. "Hey, you wouldn't happen to be *sensing* any great hoagie joints that are still open, would you?"

His attempt at humor worked, he thought. She smiled, reaching back to the bed for the pillow and throwing it at him. "I suppose I'll be pummeled with ESP jokes for the rest of the night now?"

"You read my mind."

CHAPTER 9

She couldn't eat. But he didn't seem to have any trouble. Nor was his sleep disturbed in any visible way. He'd been snoring loudly when she'd slipped out of his bed. He knew she was lying, keeping things from him. It was in his eyes whenever he looked at her. But she'd told him as much as she could. If he knew she wasn't his wife, he'd probably send her packing...and she couldn't protect him if she wasn't with him.

She stood on the balcony and stared down at the city lights below. The warm summer breeze played with the shirt she wore. His shirt. Though fresh from the dryer, it still held his scent. It wrapped it all around her, and she found she liked that sensation. Maybe too much.

She drank more wine and told herself she was stupid to get so attached to him. It wouldn't last. It couldn't, because his memory was coming back.

It hadn't hit her at first. Only as she lay in the bed beside him, watching him as he slept, wishing she had the nerve to reach for him, to kiss him, had the suspicion taken root. He remembered his nightmare, remembered its source. And he hadn't seemed at all unfamiliar with his apartment. His memory was returning, and when it did he would know she was lying about their marriage.

And then she would lose him. Even if she managed to keep up the charade long enough to save him from the Slasher, in the end she would lose him to her own lies.

Why did it hurt so much to know that? Why was she standing on a balcony, in the dark, sipping wine and silently crying?

"Couldn't sleep, huh?"

She stiffened, but didn't turn around. She didn't want him to see her foolish tears. "No."

"Neither could I." He moved up to the railing beside her, slipping an arm around her shoulders. He wore a short terry robe, untied, over the briefs he'd slept in.

"Liar. You were sawing timbers when I left."

"*Until* you left." He turned her to face him and looked down at her. "What's this?" He wiped the moisture from her cheeks with his fingertips.

"Stress, I suppose." She reached for the wineglass. He did, too, bumping her hand with his and sloshing the wine onto her wrist. She drew her hand away, but he caught and lifted it. He brought it close to his face, his lips. Then he kissed it, drinking the wine from her skin, his mouth moving slowly over her wrist and forearm.

She trembled, and he straightened.

"Cold?"

She shook her head, unable to speak. She wanted him so much, wanted this make-believe marriage to be real... just for tonight And she knew he wanted it too. His eyes glimmered with desire for her.

She averted her gaze. This was insane. "The shirt will

stain," she said to break the tension.

Then his fingertips were at her neck, and she realized he was undoing the buttons. And she stood there, not moving, with neither the will nor the desire to stop him.

He reached the lowest button and stopped. He looked into her eyes, not touching her, waiting for her to say no. She didn't. Instead she caught the front of the shirt in her trembling hands, parted it and let it slide down her shoulders to fall at her feet.

And there, in the moonlight, he looked at her...the way a lover of art must look at the work of a master. Awe and adoration glowed from his face, as he looked at her from head to toe. Then he blinked and met her gaze again, lifting a hand to caress her cheek.

"Ah, God, Joey." It was a whisper, hoarse, as if he was in some kind of pain. His hand drifted downward, over her chin, her throat. His fingertips skimmed her breast, then his palm closed over it.

She closed her eyes and let her head fall back in reaction to his touch. His hand slid over the curve of her waist, around to the small of her back, and he pulled her to him. His free hand buried itself in her hair, and he brought her face level again, and then he kissed her.

It was slow, almost reverent in its tenderness, that kiss. As if it was the first one, as if he wanted to learn the shape and taste of her mouth, memorize it, savor it. She felt the roughness of a day's growth of whiskers razing her skin. She tasted the wine on his lips. His fingers kneaded at the base of her spine, hypnotic and wonderful.

She brought her hands up between them and pushed his robe open, wanting more, needing the brush of his chest over her breasts and the feel of his taut skin under her hands. He released her with only one hand at a time to shrug the robe off, never breaking the sweet, erotic rhythm of his kiss.

His head angled. His lips slid over her face, and he nibbled at her jaw, then moved lower, the damp warmth of his mouth bathing her neck and the hollow below her ear. Her heart raced, drowning out the sounds of traffic below. Her senses filled with him, with wanting him, needing him.

"Ash...we should go...inside," she managed, her voice sounding weak and shaky.

He kissed a trail back to her mouth, pausing in between as he spoke, not lifting his mouth from her skin, so that his words were warm caresses against it. "No, Joey. There have...been others...in there." His fingers tangled in her hair and he lifted his face slightly from hers, staring into her eyes. "This is different. *You're* different. I want you here, where there's never been anyone else."

Tears burned her eyes as she twined her arms around his neck to bring his lips to hers. He lowered her to the floor on a rumpled bed made by the shirt she'd worn and his robe. And he came down with her, his arm pillowing her head as his lips moved over her body. His mouth moistened her throat and chest, her breasts and her belly. His free hand roamed downward and her hips rose of their own will. She was trembling, and her desire encompassed her mind and soul.

When she felt his hardness touch her softness, she closed her eyes and pulled him closer.

Over and over his steely strength caressed her from within, and all the while he kissed her and whispered softly against her skin. Words that had no meaning for her then. Words like "You're safe, Joey...always safe with me."

Time stood still. There was nothing but the two of them, entwined like one being, rising together until they broke through the clouds and into space.

And then they slowly drifted back to earth together, coiled muscles began to relax into blissful fulfillment. Lying close to her, he wrapped her in his strong arms and let his chest be her pillow.

Ash held her there, snuggled against him. Not that she tried to move away. She wrapped her arm around his waist and she nestled even closer. Which was good, because he hadn't yet managed to blink all the moisture away from his eyes, and he sure as hell didn't want her to see it there. He hoped her mind-reading talents were as undependable as she'd said they were. His thoughts, his feelings, right then were something he had no desire to share with her. He wasn't even sure he understood them himself. He'd never been moved near to tears by making love to a woman before.

Hell, he'd never thought of it as *making love* before. But damned if there was anything else to describe what had just happened with Joey. Until tonight, he hadn't been aware of the difference, hadn't thought there could be more than physical pleasure, mutual satisfaction, two adults sharing a few minutes of passion with the connection broken as soon as it was over. He'd never *expected* there to be anything more.

He almost laughed at his naiveté. Then he justified his ignorance. How could he have known it could be like this? He'd never seen it firsthand, never known a man and a woman to share anything deeper. No, wait, that wasn't true, was it. Radley and Amelia had that kind of connection. There wasn't anything his editor wouldn't do for his beloved bride.

He looked down at Joey, cuddled against him, and wished he was the one with ESP. He'd kill to know if she felt anything like what he was feeling. As if she belonged to him now, and he to her. As if there was no one else in the world he could feel this way with. As if he'd never let her go...not now, not if it meant he had to battle an army to keep her.

The power of his feelings scared the hell out of him. Especially knowing she'd been lying to him from the start, and still not knowing why. But he would find out. He would dig until he knew everything about Joey, and he would find a way to make her trust him.

He rose to his feet, smiling when she looked up at him with her delicate brows arched. He bent and scooped her into his arms, carried her inside and lowered her onto the bed. Then he got in beside her and held her close. And somehow he knew that as long as he did, the nightmares of his childhood would be powerless to haunt his dreams.

She was in the shower when the phone bleated the next morning and Ash snatched it up, growling a greeting. He hated the interruption, since he'd been about to slip into the bathroom to join her.

"Okay, Coye, you owe me big time for this one."

Rad sounded smug, and his opening line caught Ash's attention. "What have you got for me, pal?"

"Nothing you wouldn't have got on your own, just saved you some legwork. A lot of it. I figure the sooner we get this asshole caught, the safer you'll be. You were planning to sift all the information from the Vegas murders, but I did it for you, and two tidbits came up that I think you'll find pretty juicy."

"What're you, longing to get back into the action? Tired of sitting behind a desk?"

"Only when my star reporter's—my good friend's—life is on the line."

Ash tried to avoid getting choked up. What the hell was going on with his emotions anyway? "Admit it, Rad. You don't trust me to check the facts with an unbiased eye."

"Hell, what're friends for?"

Ash sighed into the mouthpiece, but he was still smiling. Come to think of it, he'd been smiling ever since he woke up all wrapped around Joey. He might've even been smiling in his sleep, for all he knew. "All right, Rad. What've you got?"

Rad chuckled. "I knew you'd come around." Then he cleared his throat, and his tone turned serious. "This might go down hard, Ash. Joey Bradshaw was in Vegas during the summer the Slasher killings went down."

Ash felt his spine pull tight, as if it might snap in two at the base of his neck. "How do you know?"

"Hotel records. I still have a few connections from my reporting days, you know."

Ash released his breath in a rush, not bothering to ask how Rad had known which hotels to check. He'd either checked them all, or he'd had a tip. "What else?"

"Your Christmas present. Like I said, you owe me one. I kind of like that little mind reader of yours. She's cute. And she's spunky. I like spunk."

"Yeah, so do I," he said.

"I know you don't want to see the girl do time for this. Frankly, I don't either. I'd rather find evidence that clears

146 | MAGGIE SHAYNE

her. She's good for you, Ash."

Aw, hell, his throat was getting all tight again.

"Turns out there's a far more likely suspect," Rad went on.

"Who?"

"A cop. A cop who was fully involved in the Vegas investigation. The same cop who's heading up the local one."

Ash frowned. "Bev Issacs?"

"The same. She worked on the Vegas PD when the murders were committed. And she smokes the right kind of cigarettes."

Ash swore softly, his mind working full speed. "I can't believe Bev's a killer."

"No one believed Ted Bundy could be one either, Ash. I'm just giving you the facts."

"Are the police aware of this?"

"I don't know. If they are, they aren't talking. But Ash, I got a tip. The cops finally got lucky. Found a little DNA on a cigarette butt from the most recent scene."

Ash's heartbeat sped up, his reporter instincts kicking into high gear. The sensation was familiar, and a welcome relief from the chaotic emotional windstorm in his mind. "We need to get our hands on a sample of Bev's DNA and compare it," he said. "That's the only way we'll know for sure."

Rad was silent for a long moment, then, "Look, Ash, don't get mad, but if we're checking DNA, don't you think we ought to have a sample of Joey's, as well?"

"Hell, no." He answered too fast, and automatically. "It wouldn't match anyway."

"Then it would clear her," Rad argued logically. "I'll get an independent lab to do the testing and work on getting my hands on a copy of the DNA profile the cops have on the killer for comparison."

Ash hesitated, chewing his lip.

"Look, Coye, we won't tell the cops anything until we have the results. If this will clear her, you have to go for it. The evidence against her is getting dangerous. If you want to protect her, then—"

"All right, all right. I'll get a sample. How long will the test take?"

"A few days."

"That's too long."

"Nothing to be done about that, Ash. Can you get me a sample from Joey?"

Ash looked around the room, his gaze settling on the wad of bandages she'd taken from her thigh before going to the shower. There were traces of blood marring the white gauze. "Yeah. I can get it. What about Bev?"

"I'm on it already." He didn't elaborate and Ash didn't ask. "I think you ought to sit tight on this until we have some answers. No more digging. It's too dangerous for you, Ash. And for the mind reader too."

"Okay. I mean, except that I already have an appointment to talk with that shrink I told you about. I want to see it through."

"Waste of time," Rad said.

"My time to waste. I'm still on leave, remember?"

"Pigheaded son of a—"

"It can't hurt, Rad. The more we know about who we're dealing with, the better."

"No shrink's gonna tell you anything you don't already know. They're quacks, all of 'em."

Rad's feelings about psychiatry and profiling were well known around the office. Ash thought it was a generational thing. Radley cut his journalism teeth in the days when legwork, brains and instinct solved crimes. Not psychology.

"This one might be different, though. Benjamin Kramer has been studying serial killers for twenty-odd years. I've only been at it for a few weeks, myself, so no matter how little he has to tell me, it's liable to be more than I already know."

"Kramer, eh? Never heard of him."

"He's from Ithaca. I'm heading down there this afternoon."

His boss sighed and said, "Might not be a bad idea for you to get out of town anyway. Wild goose chase or not. Taking Joey along?"

"Well, I'm sure as hell not leaving her alone here until I get to the bottom of this. Not that she'd let me." Ash glanced toward the bathroom and smiled slightly.

"Probably safer for her that way too. Wait, why wouldn't she let you?"

"Because she thinks the Slasher's added my name to the hit list. And now that you mention it, while you're checking on Bev, keep your eyes open for a pair of black gloves, kid leather, two small buttons at the wrist. Joey says that's what the killer wears."

Rad was quiet for a beat or two, and Ash didn't blame him. He might as well have told him he believed in unicorns. Finally, he said, "Gee, Ash, why don't you just ask her who the killer is? If she's that good, she ought to be able to figure it out. Save us all a lot of time and effort."

"She doesn't know, says she can't control what she, you know, what she *sees*." He sounded crazy even to his own ears. "I know how this sounds. But when she does get something, it's so damned accurate, it's scary."

"Never thought I'd hear you talking like that about an alleged psychic."

"No less than I did." Ash heard the shower stop running. "I gotta go. Later, Rad."

"Be careful, Ash. Just in case we're...." He stopped before he finished the sentence, and said again, "Just in case."

Ash hung up just as Joey stepped out of the bathroom, wrapped in a towel. He got up, stark naked, and met her halfway across the room, pulling her towel away. She squeaked in surprise, but he silenced her with a kiss. God, she tasted good. Then he picked her up, carried her into the bathroom and turned the shower back on.

Dr. Benjamin Kramer's office seemed more like a living room, and Joey was glad of the comfort after the hour-plus drive down from Syracuse. Her leg was still sore, but a million times better than it had been the day before. They'd stopped at her house and Ash had made coffee and filled a Thermos he said would keep it hot all day, while Joey had packed a few things. He didn't see her stuff her two caving helmets with headlamps into her duffel bag, and she was glad. She wasn't sure her attempts to get him into a cave would be successful and she was sure they wouldn't if he had time to think about it. She wasn't even sure today would be the best time to try, but she wanted to have equipment on hand, just in case.

Ash, she sensed, was a little bit claustrophobic. Maybe a lot. She wanted to help him get over it.

Shivers of dread had rippled up her spine when she'd entered her bedroom, but the sense of a menacing presence had faded a bit overnight. Still, she packed quickly, wanting to get out of the house as soon as possible.

Now she reclined in an armchair, extending her aching leg in front of her. Dr. Kramer frowned at her, his bushy gray brows bunching behind round tortoiseshell glasses. Then he pushed a footstool in front of her. She smiled gratefully and propped her leg on it.

"Recent injury?" He settled himself into a rocker, his paunch protruding slightly over the waistband of cream-colored trousers.

"Very recent," she replied.

"Can I get you anything? Aspirin?"

"No, thank you. It's not that bad."

He nodded and turned his attention to Ash. "Now then, the reason for this visit. You're interested in serial killers. No doubt due to the string of murders you're investigating for *The Chronicle*?"

Ash said, "You know about that?"

"Of course I do."

Of course he did, Joey thought. He was a serial killer expert. He'd probably been following the crimes as closely as she had.

Ash said, "I'm hoping you can give me an idea of the kind of person we're looking for."

"Perhaps. The press hasn't been very forthcoming with details. It's difficult to judge without knowing more. Have the murders been particularly grisly?"

Ash glanced at Joey. "A single slash to the throat, Doctor. The victims bled to death. And there were..." He frowned a little. "Of course, I'm counting on your discretion. None of this is public knowledge."

"You have my word, Mr. Coye. Believe me, I'd do

nothing to jeopardize the investigation. Please, go on."

Ash bit his lip. "There were cigarette butts found at three of the four scenes."

Joey stiffened. He hadn't told her that.

"Any blood on them?"

"No. And there would be if the killer smoked while killing or if he smoked beforehand, say, while waiting for the victim, and tossed the butt aside. The butts would've had blood spatter."

Dr. Kramer rubbed his naked chin as if he had a goatee. "A man who slashes, then steps out of the way and calmly smokes while the victim lies bleeding to death." He shook his head. "He's a predator. A hunter. But then, they all are."

Ash shook his head. "*She*, Doctor."

"Ben, please," the doctor admonished with a wave of his hand. "Do go on. What makes you think the killer is a woman?"

"The butts were ringed with lipstick."

Kramer smiled slowly and shook his head. "Well, now I see why the police are stumped. They're taking too much for granted."

Joey blinked. "Are you saying it *isn't* a woman, Dr. Kramer?"

He tilted his head to one side. "No, no I can't say that for certain. There are female serial killers, of course, but the latest studies indicate only about fifteen percent of serial killers are women."

"But they aren't nonexistent?" Ash stood, obviously agitated.

"They exist. Although, those few I've studied have been far less violent in their methods. Poisoning is the most common. And usually their victims are helpless individuals, children, the weak, the infirm, the elderly. The Slasher's victims have all been men, correct?" The doctor's gaze slid toward Joey. "I'm sorry. It disturbs you to hear all of this. You're pale."

"I'm fine."

Ash sent her a worried glance. She nodded to assure him she could handle whatever was said, and he returned his attention to Dr. Kramer.

"Have they *all* been males, Mr. Coye?"

Ash had been pacing, but he stopped. "No. I don't think so." Joey frowned at him. He watched her face as he went on. "I think this killer may be the same one who committed a series of murders in Las Vegas six years ago. One of those victims was a woman."

"Ah, yes. I'm familiar with the case."

"OhmyGod," Joey whispered. Her eyes widened as she searched Ash's steady gaze.

Dr. Kramer rose from his chair and went to the window, pushing aside the curtains to look outside. "We're dealing with a rare one, Mr. Coye. One who doesn't wish to be caught. Sometimes they do, you know. And this one kills not in passion, but calmly...coldly. It's not the act of killing that is the payoff. It's watching them die. The victims might well be people that the killer firmly believes deserve to die, which is a secondary reason for him to stay around and make sure the deed is done. That, and of course, the pleasure he gets from watching the life force leave his victims. He or she, but far more likely he, might be acting in vengeance against a real man in his past, perhaps a man who is no longer around for him to kill. And I don't believe he'll stop until he feels that man has died by his hand, which will never happen. The ghosts that haunt these tormented souls rise up again and again no matter how often they try to exorcise them through murder." He turned away from the window and let the curtain fall back into place. "Your killer will not stop until he's caught. I'm not sure of the significance of the single female victim. There are hundreds of possibilities there. I wouldn't presume to hazard a guess."

"You really believe the killer is a man?" Ash asked, his voice incredulous.

"The odds are that it is a man, though it is not impossible that it's a woman. Perhaps the lipstick on the cigarettes is a deliberate attempt to mislead police. Perhaps he dresses as a woman only when he kills as a precaution in case he's seen. Both of those things are far more likely than it being an actual female killer."

Ash pushed a hand through his hair. "You're not giving me much to go on."

Ben Kramer said, "I'm not a psychic, Mr. Coye. I can give you a bit more, though. I believe you're looking for someone who was horribly hurt by an adult male, or witnessed someone they loved being hurt by him, probably in early childhood."

"Physically hurt?"

"Not necessarily, but that's likely. The killer believes this man deserves to die for whatever he did."

Ash looked at Joey, and she cringed, knowing he must be thinking about her feelings for her father. God, did he suspect *she* was the Slasher?

He didn't give her a clue as they left the office, and he remained silent when he slid behind the wheel of her car.

She got in, fastened her seatbelt and turned to face him. "You think it was me, don't you?"

CHAPTER 10

He looked at her. Just looked at her, his eyes probing so deeply she felt their touch. "No, Joey. I don't think it's you." He started the car and pulled into traffic.

"I despise my stepfather. I blame him for my mother's death. You know that."

He nodded. "I know that."

She closed her eyes, wishing she could tell him everything, wishing she could believe he trusted her, even knowing about her lies. "Ash, I was *in* Vegas when those killings happened. I was there with Caro and Ted. I was—"

"I know that, too."

She felt her eyes widen. "And you told me not to tell the police I smoke. Which I don't, really. I mean I quit, years ago, and even then I didn't—but then all this started and now...the cigarette butts they found—"

"Same brand you have tucked away in your kitchen. And before you ask, so was the lipstick. Same brand. Same shade. Coral frost."

She pressed her fingertips to her temples. "Oh my God." She felt her stomach heave. "OhmyGod."

Ash pulled the car onto the shoulder, gripped her shoulders and turned her toward him: "How long have you been smoking that brand, Joey?" She didn't answer and he gave her a little shake. "How long? Tell me."

She bit her lip and tears filled her eyes. "A month, I guess. I never liked menthols before. Then I quit for a while, and when I got the craving again I bought those. I...God, I don't know why." She was crying silently, big fat tears rolling slow and hot down her cheeks. He thought she was a killer and she felt sicker by the minute. "I didn't kill those people, Ash. I swear—"

"I know you didn't."

She blinked and looked up at him.

"I believe you, Joey."

She shook her head, confused, bewildered. "Why?"

He pulled her across the space that separated them and kissed her hard and long and deep. And when he finally lifted his mouth from hers she saw the passion and the caring in his eyes.

"That's why."

He let her go, pulled back onto the highway and drove a short distance in silence. "The lipstick is new too, isn't it?"

She nodded.

"I thought so. Never bought that color before, did you, Joey?"

She frowned. "How did you know?" He said nothing, so she went on. "No. I haven't even used it more than once or twice. The shade's all wrong for me. And I never liked frosts, anyway. I bought it on impulse."

"When?"

Searching her memory, she said, "About a month ago."

"You bought it because the killer bought it."

She frowned hard. "What do you mean?"

"I have a theory. And I want you to hear me out before you shoot it down. I think you're more connected to this person than you realize. You're picking things up from him...or her, and you're not even aware of it."

She thought about that "Ash, do you hear yourself? You don't even believe in psychics." She shook her head, looking at her hands folded in her lap. "I'm not even sure I do. At least, I didn't. Before all this."

Ash frowned at her, then shifted his gaze quickly back to the highway. It was smooth, and the blacktop smelled new. The yellow lines were still glow-in-the-dark brilliant.

"How could *you* not believe in it? You've made a business out of it."

"But I never saw myself as being...*psychic*. Just intuitive. Maybe more sensitive than other people. I never...never had visions or dreams or anything like that. Not until... these murders started."

Ash tipped his head to one side and took a gentle curve too slowly, deep in thought she presumed. "Maybe there's a reason for that," he said at last. "Maybe...maybe there's a connection between you and the killer that you just aren't aware of. Maybe it's someone you know."

She sighed hard, shaking her head at the ridiculous idea. "Like who?"

"Like Ted." He sent her a quick, curious glance. "You said it yourself, Joey—he was in Vegas with you when those murders went down. And he's been acting odd lately. Oddly enough that your sister thinks he's having an affair."

Joey closed her eyes and tried to picture Ted as a killer.

Ted dressing as a woman to hide his identity, or putting on coral-frost lipstick and.... Her eyes flew wide. "Caro has the same lipstick, Ash. We were together when I bought mine, and she decided to try it too."

"So we know Ted has access to it. Does he smoke, Joey?"

She shook her head, almost going limp with relief. "Not in years. He quit right after Brit was born. Said he had to be a good example for his girls."

"You remember his brand?"

Joey shook her head. "I don't think I ever knew it." She concentrated hard, trying to find the answers in her mind, but they simply weren't there. And she knew too well there were other reasons for her to feel connected to this killer, to feel like the bastard had invaded her mind. Compelling reasons. Her own sister was on the hit list. And so was Ash. Those two things alone might have some bearing on her uncanny abilities in this. It didn't have to mean the killer was someone she knew.

But she couldn't tell Ash about her sister, because he was going to get his memory back soon. And if he knew the truth—that she'd only come to him in order to save her sister, that she'd played cruel, wicked games with his already-fragile mind—he would hate her. And she couldn't bear that.

"What kind of background does Ted have? What kind of childhood? Is he close to his family?"

She jerked herself out of her misery and tried to focus on Ash's questions. "His parents still live in Nevada. He doesn't see them much anymore, but it's not because of any discord. Just the distance. They all seemed to get along fine whenever I saw them together." Images danced at the fringes of her consciousness. Images she'd seen before, in the nightmare. Her sister, Caroline, lying facedown on the floor, her regulation sweats and baggy shirt stained with blood, her long blond hair tipped in red. And the hands, those leather-gloved hands, reaching for her.

Joey pressed her fingers to her temples and sucked air through her teeth. God, she just wanted it to stop!

"Joey?"

She glanced at Ash and bit her lip. "You're right. There's some kind of connection, but I don't think it's Ted. Whatever it is, it's getting stronger. I can hardly close my eyes anymore without feeling...that blackness...closing in."

Ash reached out, stroked her hair. "We won't talk about it anymore today, okay? We'll just..."

She looked at him, smiled softly. He really seemed concerned. "Just what?"

"Whatever you want. Dinner in the most elegant restaurant in town. Syracuse Stage for the latest play. Ballroom dancing. You name it, lady. You need a night off from all this, and to tell you the truth, so do I."

She didn't think she'd be able to forget, even for a minute, the sense of danger all around her. Around all of them. But she was more than willing to try.

Ash couldn't get over it. And he couldn't quit looking at her, lying back with her head pillowed on a backpack. She wore faded jeans that were a little too big with their legs rolled up, and a pair of black army boots. The flannel shirt she'd pulled on over her tank top was worn-blanket soft, and its plaid pattern was fading. Her hair was long and loose, falling over her shoulders from under the most ridiculous-looking hat he'd ever seen in his life. Her fishing hat, she called it, and it dangled with hooks and lures of every imaginable description. The white light from a Coleman lantern bathed her face, shimmered in her hair, and her green eyes darted every few seconds to the fishing pole propped in the crotch of a forked branch she'd stuck into the ground.

Still, baggy clothes, ridiculous hat and all, she was the most irresistible woman he'd ever seen. It made no sense, but she looked better to him than any swimsuit model ever could.

And she was relaxing. The tightness had eased from her jaw, and the worry that had clouded her eyes earlier was all but gone. He would sit outside with the mosquitos all night if it would ease her mind.

She tensed up all of a sudden, eyes on the water. "Ash!"

"Hm?"

"You have a bite."

He dragged his eyes from her to the fishing pole and saw its end twitching sporadically. He'd much rather continue watching Joey, but he leaned forward, carefully picked up his pole and waited. When it jerked in his hands, he yanked it once, felt his success in the frenzied tugging on the other end, and began to reel it in.

Joey stood, weight mostly on her good leg, and reached for the line when it was in the shallows. "Oooh, it's a nice one, too." She grabbed the slick black bullhead and worked the hook free. Ash shook his head slowly. Squeamish, she wasn't. She dropped the fish into the waiting pail, grinning from ear to ear.

"You really like this, don't you?"

She handed him a can of worms and settled back

down in her spot beside him. "What's not to like?" She extended her wounded leg carefully and drew the other knee up to her chest, wrapping her arms around it and gazing out over the calm blue. Crickets chirped madly, and once in a while the deep croak of a bullfrog floated like a foghorn on the breeze. The night wind stirred her hair.

Ash baited his hook and, with a less-than-expert cast, sent his line sailing out over the small lake. "So how did you know about this place?"

He balanced his pole in his own forked branch and sat down, closer to her than before. But when he glanced at her face, it was troubled. "Joey?"

She swallowed, sighed softly. "My dad used to bring us here when I was a kid. Back when I thought he *was* my dad. I didn't know he was my stepfather until two years ago."

"Did you like it this much then?"

She didn't look at him, just kept staring out at the water. "Mom would pack more food than an army could eat. We'd build a fire, toast marshmallows." She laughed, just a little. "Caroline would never bait her own hook. She hated touching worms, and she never caught a thing because she'd insist on holding her pole. She wiggled it so much a fish would have to be nuts to try and bite. But Dad would hook one on his, and he'd let Caro reel it in."

Ash felt a twinge inside. Jealousy, maybe, for the childhood he'd never had. And then he felt something else, something sad, when her smile slowly died. "That was before I knew what he was really like. I thought he was Superman back then."

"Tough image to live up to."

She said nothing, just looked away, up toward the

starry sky. Her eyes shone a little too much, and she blinked quickly.

"Joey, have you ever sat down and talked to him, heard his side of things?"

"There's no excuse for what he put my mother through, so why bother asking him to explain?" She shook her head. "No, Ash, I don't want to talk to my stepfather."

"But maybe if you—"

"Or *about* him." She shook her head. "It hurts too much."

"If you didn't still care, it wouldn't hurt at all."

She looked him square in the eye. "Sounds like the voice of experience."

He clamped his jaw. He was certain what he'd said was true, in her case. But not in his. He didn't care at all. Never had. It was different

"Were you close to your father, Ash?"

"I never knew my father."

"Neither did I. Not my birth father, I mean. He died before I ever knew he existed. Turns out he was a skunk, too. Although…."

"Although…?" he prompted.

She shrugged one shoulder. "Toni adored him. Even after she knew he'd cheated on her mom and fathered kids by other women, she still adored him."

Ash got to his feet. "You know, that campfire idea isn't bad." He looked around, spotted some twigs and dried leaves and began gathering them.

"What about your mother?" Joey asked.

Ash deposited the kindling atop the charred remains of other fires, old ones. "You didn't happen to bring any marshmallows, did you?"

He felt her gaze on him for a long moment. Then she released her breath all at once. "Afraid not."

He looked at her and saw the knowledge in her eyes. He knew she was feeling his emotions just then, experiencing his private hell right along with him. And for some reason, it didn't feel like an invasion. More like a mental hug. When their eyes met, those fingers of horror from his past released their brief grip on his mind. Warmth and light took their place.

She got up and limped toward him, stopping right in front of him, and he straightened from his task of arranging kindling. Her hands slid up his chest, around his neck, and she stood on tiptoe to press her lips to his. His arms encircled her waist and pulled her closer, and then he opened his mouth over hers, kissing her deeply, slowly, savoring her taste and her scent and her sweetness.

God, what was this thing that filled him when he was with her? Not lust, though he wanted her more every time he looked at her. No, it was more than that, deeper, fuller, bigger than that. It seemed to ooze from his every pore and press in around him from without at the same time. It enveloped them both, he thought, trying to fuse them into one being.

He felt her fingers threading into his hair, and her body pressing to his. He felt the cool, damp breeze bathing them both with its marshy scent. He lifted his head, staring down at those glittering green gems.

She blinked at him, her eyes wide and wonder filled. "I'm so afraid of this," she whispered.

"Of wanting me?" He slipped his hands beneath her shirt and ran his palms over the warm, smooth curve of her back.

"Of...of *needing* you."

He closed his eyes at the impact of her words. "I know."

"It's overpowering. It's getting worse all the time, and I—"

"And I can't do anything to stop it," he finished for her. "I'm not sure I *want* to stop it." He took her hat off and tossed it aside. Then he kissed her cheek, her jaw.

She let her head fall back and he trailed his mouth over her neck. "It's out of my hands," she said softly, her voice wavering like the breeze skipping over the water's surface.

"Then just let it go." His lips moved over her throat as he spoke. "Let it go, Joey."

He brought his hands around between them and pushed the soft flannel from her shoulders. As it fell to the ground, he pushed the tank top up, wrestled it over her head and tossed it aside. They fell to the ground wrapped in each other's arms, melding into one, just like before. It was intense, supernatural, he thought, the way he felt when they made love. It felt as if she was the part of his soul he'd been missing, and when they joined, he was perfect, and whole.

He made love to her, and she to him, as the isolated lake's water lapped softly against the shore, and the stars twinkled overhead, and the crickets sang like a holy choir as he savored their sweet oneness. And afterward, he closed his eyes and relaxed on top of her, supporting most of his weight on his knees so he wouldn't crush her. Her small hands stroked his back, and her lips moved over his face and neck. He smiled, smoothing her hair and lifting his head enough to look into her eyes. They sparkled, searching his.

"No one's ever made me feel the way you do, Ash."

His ego launched skyward. She had that effect on him a lot. "I was thinking the same thing about you."

"Faint praise from a man with no memory." She laughed softly, but her smile died seconds later. "But that won't be the case much longer, will it?"

Ash frowned, immediately alert. Was she onto him? "What does that mean?"

"Your memory. It's starting to come back." She averted her eyes.

"What makes you think so?"

"You wouldn't be having that nightmare if you didn't remember something about your childhood. And you said you never knew your father."

She was too perceptive. He hadn't even considered the possibility that she would...read him so well. "The doctors said that my oldest memories would most likely come back first. To tell you the truth, I'd just as soon forget those for good."

She ran one hand over his hair. "It was pretty terrible, wasn't it?"

He nodded, not wanting to talk about the hell of his past. She must have read that, too, because she went on. "And then there's the apartment. You seemed to know where everything was. Didn't seem disoriented or anything."

"Oh, that." He said nothing for a moment, kicking himself mentally for slipping. "It felt sort of automatic."

She smiled, but her eyes seemed so sad it tugged at him.

"You're getting better and you don't even realize it. Soon you'll remember everything."

"You don't sound happy about that."

"I *want* you to get better, Ash. Don't doubt that."

"But?"

She closed her eyes, shook her head. "It doesn't matter."

"I think it does."

"Let's not talk about it, Ash."

He sighed hard, rolling off her and reaching for his clothes. For just a second there, he'd thought she might come clean, tell him everything, explain her lies. She had disappointed him.

When they got back, Detective Beverly Issacs was pacing the hallway in front of Ash's apartment door, looking fit to bite nails in half. She looked at Joey briefly, then focused her attention on Ash.

"I've been trying to get in touch with you for hours." It had the ring of an accusation.

Ash's arm fell slowly from Joey's shoulders, and she wished he'd left it there. She disliked this woman instinctively, felt the hairs on her nape stand upright in warning.

"Why?" Ash stepped forward, frowning hard.

Bev's face hardened. "We found another one."

CHAPTER 11

Joey's blood ran cold. Her fingertips felt like ice and tingled. Another one. Another of the Slasher's victims. She closed her eyes. God would the killing ever end?

"When?" Ash hurried past Bev to unlock his door. He shoved it wide and stood aside while the tall woman preceded him through.

"Three hours ago, in a run-down house up in Central Square." She spoke as she walked.

Joey saw Ash glance back at her. She stiffened her spine and made herself move forward. She didn't want to hear this, but she supposed she had to. At least this time no one could suspect her. She'd been with Ash all day, all night. Never once out of his sight.

"Victim number five," Ash quoted as Joey passed him. He closed the door, and they walked into the living room.

"Two," Beverly Issacs corrected. Ash only frowned at her. "Number two, near as we can tell. This one had been dead a while. Older man, lived alone, no close neighbors. Probably still wouldn't have been found if some kid hawking magazine subscriptions hadn't noticed the smell."

Joey turned away from them, her hand going over her mouth.

"Dammit, Bev, can you get any more graphic?" Ash stood behind Joey, his hands closing on her shoulders, squeezing.

"Sorry. Didn't know she was squeamish."

Joey stiffened, and slowly she turned to face the woman. She was *not* squeamish. She'd just cleaned and skinned a half-dozen bullhead. Her hand tightened on the paper-wrapped fish. She'd forgotten she still held them. She didn't say a word, just walked into the kitchen, dumped the package into the sink and turned on the water. As she washed the filets, she could still hear Ash and Beverly talking.

"So why were you so frantic to reach me?"

"I wasn't, until I couldn't find you. Then I got to thinking our friend might've decided to make you his evening's entertainment"

"That's a leap of logic, even for you, Bev."

"Yeah, well it's damn near two a.m. Who's out at this time of night? And then there's your new wife, who hangs out at murder scenes for fun. Add in all the information you have about the case—you know, the stuff you aren't telling me—and it isn't so farfetched."

"You know everything I do," he said, but even Joey could tell by the slight smugness in his tone that he was lying. Joey sprinkled the fish with salt, wrapped them in clean, white paper and set them in the fridge. Then she washed her hands, letting the warm wet flow and soapsuds sooth her.

"Oh, yeah? Well I don't know why a guy named

Harris, from the paper, would come to see me about a routine burglary investigation, snatch a few butts from my ashtray and slip 'em into his pocket. Can you explain that to me?"

Joey could picture the way Ash would shrug, his face all innocence. "Beats me. Nicotine fit, maybe?"

"So you're not talking?"

"Bev, will you relax? If I find anything solid, you'll be the first to know. You think I want this creep to go on killing?"

"If I find out you're withholding evidence—"

"You know me better than that."

"Stubborn son of a—" Beverly broke off, eyeing Joey suspiciously as she reentered the living room, then shook her head hard and started for the door. "God, I hate men!" The door slammed behind her when she left.

Ash gave Joey a careful look. "You okay?"

She nodded. "Is Bev a suspect, too?"

Ash shrugged and slipped an arm around her. "What, just because she hates men?"

He was being evasive. "What does the *Chronicle* plan to do with her cigarette butts?"

"Rad's having them DNA tested at an independent lab...just to be on the safe side. Turns out Bev was working in Vegas when those other murders went down. I don't really believe she was involved, but—"

"Did you give him something of mine to have tested, as well?" He didn't answer. Joey stared up at his face, and he didn't have to. She closed her eyes. "God, you really do think it was me."

"Joey, that's not true and you know it. I expect the test to clear you."

"But you're not sure, are you?" She looked away,

speaking before he could answer. "No, don't say anything. There are already too many lies between us, Ash."

"Maybe if there weren't, I could give you the answer you want to hear." He held her shoulders, staring down at her, searching her eyes. "Talk to me, Joey."

Tears burned her eyes and she blinked them away. Telling him would mean losing him, and maybe getting him killed. "I can't." She pulled free of him, shaking her head sadly, and went into the bathroom.

He didn't try to stop her.

Joey woke from her makeshift bed on the sofa to the smell of hot oil, and the sound of the shrilling telephone. She sat up, still groggy, feeling a dull ache of emptiness she knew was due to sleeping alone. She hadn't realized how comforting she found being wrapped in Ash's arms all night until she'd spent a night without it. But she'd been unable to sleep with him, knowing he could suspect her of something so heinous. It only brought home to her how little they really knew about each other, and made her feel cheap and easy. So she'd told him she would be more comfortable on the sofa, where there'd be no chance of his rolling over and jarring her sore and tender leg. And he had gone along with it, knowing it was just an excuse.

He poked his head out of the kitchen, breaking into her thoughts. "Oh, you're awake." She heard sizzling, snapping sounds and then the phone jingled again. "You want to get that? My hands are kinda full."

She nodded as he ducked back into the kitchen. She reached for the phone. There was a lengthy silence after her hello, and she repeated it twice before she got a response.

"Sorry, Mrs. Coye. I'm...not used to calling Ash and having a woman answer. How are you?"

She recognized Radley Ketchum's voice. "Fine." She was distinctly uncomfortable, knowing this man shared Ash's uncertainty about her, perhaps was even convinced of her guilt by now. "And you?"

"All right, I suppose."

"I'll get Ash. Just a—"

"I'd like to talk to you for a minute if you don't mind."

She swallowed hard, tensing, wondering if he would come right out and accuse her.

"I don't mind."

"It's...well, it's a strange question on the surface. But I'm aware of your...your gift"

She felt the blood drain from her face. "Ash told you?"

"I found out on my own. The point is, I need you to tell me if you...if you begin to, you know, *sense* anything about this case."

She cleared her throat. "I see."

"I don't think you do. I know you'll confide in Ash if anything...comes to you, so to speak. But you've probably guessed by now that Ash could be a target. He doesn't always know what's best for him, Mrs. Coye, and even when he does, he doesn't always *do* it. It would be just like him to ignore serious personal risk to get a story. Especially *this* story. So if you come up with anything, it might be best if you tell me first."

She lowered her voice so Ash wouldn't overhear. "You really think he's in danger?"

"I've worked with Ash for three years now. We're friends. Good friends. I don't want to see anything happen to him."

She closed her eyes. "Neither do I."

"Then I can count on you to keep me posted?"

She hesitated, then sighed. The more people working to protect Ash, the better. "Yes."

His relief was evident in his tone. "Thank you. Now can I talk to him?"

"Just a sec." She put the receiver on the end table, threw off her covers and walked barefoot to the kitchen, limping a little less than yesterday. Ash was just piling aromatic, golden brown fish onto a platter. She saw another dish, heaped with home fries on the table, beside a stack of pancakes and a bottle of blueberry syrup. She shook her head in awe.

"Peace offering," he said softly. "Forgive me?"

Forgive him? She was the one keeping the secrets, telling the lies. But she smiled at him. She hated the tension between them, wanted it to end, even though she knew it couldn't. Not entirely. Not until she told him everything. "Your boss is on the phone."

"I missed you last night, Joey." He came closer, ran one hand through her hair.

She lowered her head. "Radley's waiting, Ash." When she looked up, he was still staring at her, waiting. She knew what he wanted. "I missed you, too."

He nodded, as if satisfied with her answer, and left the room, calling behind him, "Don't start without me."

"Where the hell were you all night?"

Ash shook his head, scowling at the mouthpiece before bringing it back to his ear. "Some greeting. What're you, my parole officer?"

"I won't go into the five calls I had from your lady

cop friend, or the number of messages I left on your worthless voicemail, or the gray hairs I got wondering if the Slasher finally caught up with you."

"I think you just did."

"From now on, Ash, let me know where you are, when you're coming back and what the hell you're up to."

"Or what?"

"Or you're off the story."

Ash swore fluently into the receiver.

"Dammit, Ash, I want this scoop as bad as you do, but it isn't worth getting yourself killed. Keep me posted. That's an order. Understood?"

"Fine." Ash agreed, but he didn't like it

"Good, so the next time I can't reach you, I assume the worst and send the police."

As threats went, it wasn't half bad. "Right."

"Okay. So what'd you find out from the shrink?"

"He's of the opinion that our killer is a man. Says it's rare to find a female serial killer."

"That's nuts."

"That's what I said, but he was adamant."

"What else?"

"Probably abused in childhood, or saw someone he loved being hurt, maybe by a trusted adult male."

Rad cussed softly. "Sounds to me like you're more apt to learn who it is from your wife than from this quack."

Ash glanced toward the kitchen. He could hear plates clacking together, silverware jangling. She must be setting the table. "Maybe."

"What's that mean? Has she said anything?"

"I just have a feeling she's close." Ash frowned. "And it scares the hell out of her."

Rad was quiet for a moment. "You think there's a

chance she already knows and just isn't saying?"

"Why the hell would she keep it from me?"

"Why do women do anything?" Rad sighed. "Ah, hell, it was just a thought."

"It was a stupid thought. She'd tell me if she knew."

"Like she's been so honest up til now, right?"

"Dammit, Rad—"

"Okay. I'm sorry, I know you two are...close. And I'm no good with pistols at twenty paces."

"You're not even in the ballpark. And by the way, don't send Harris to do any more snooping. The guy's about as subtle as a sledgehammer."

"Bev saw him take the butts?"

"You got it. Maybe you'd better come up with some plausible explanation before you run into her again. Look, is there anything else? My breakfast is getting cold."

"Go eat. But don't forget—"

"Yeah, Rad. I'll fax you a written itinerary before I leave the apartment again, okay? You want it notarized?" He hung up while Rad was still swearing at him.

When he walked into the kitchen, Joey was pouring coffee. He stopped in the doorway, because the sight of her there slammed him in the chest. For a second, he just looked at her. She wore one of her own nightgowns. Not one of the slinky ones, just a plain white one with ruffled straps for sleeves, and a hemline that hovered around her ankles. Her hair was loose, fluffing around her shoulders like a cloud.

He liked looking at her, fresh from sleep with her eyes still puffy and her hair unbrushed, standing barefoot in his kitchen, pouring their coffee. He'd like to look at her that way a lot.

She carried two cups to the table and sat down. "So

how's the boss?"

"Like a mother hen. He was worried about me." Ash took a seat across from her and helped himself to a piece of fish and a scoop of potatoes.

"So was Beverly Issacs."

He met her gaze across the table. "She's only worried I'm keeping evidence to myself."

"No, she was worried about you. I think...I think she cares."

Joey was jealous. It was in those transparent eyes of hers. He would have been idiotically glad to know it, if he wasn't aware of her mistrust of men in general, thanks to her father figures. "Joey, I am not interested in having a fling with Bev."

She nodded, averting her eyes, filling her plate. "You told me once you don't believe in cheating."

"It was the truth. I don't." That should end her worry, he thought, and stabbed three pancakes with his fork, dropping them onto his plate.

"But what if...we weren't married? Would you be interested then?"

"If we weren't married, all I'd be interested in would be getting us that way."

He blinked and only shook himself. What in God's name had made him blurt *that* hunk of baloney? Frowning, he picked up the fork he'd dropped and stuffed a piece of fish into his mouth to prevent any more absurdities from coming out of it.

The doorbell buzzed. "Damn. Seems the whole world is conspiring to keep me from having breakfast." He chanced a look at her, but she was just staring at him with those big green eyes, looking as if he'd just told her aliens had landed on the roof.

He pushed away from the table and went to get the door.

Ted Dryer stood there looking like a wrung-out rag. His shoulders slumped, his shirt was rumpled and his eyes had dark circles ringing them.

"I need to talk to Joey." There was no preamble, no greeting.

Ash swung the door wider and stepped aside, waving one arm with a flourish. "In the kitchen. Join us for breakfast?"

Ted didn't answer, he just walked in, his hands stuffed into his pockets. Ash followed in time to see him pull out a chair, turn it backward and straddle it. Ash took his own seat and resumed eating.

"Have you talked to Caroline?" Ted asked.

"Of course I have. Haven't you?" Joey finished her food and got up to carry her plate to the sink. She took out another cup, filled it with coffee and set it down in front of Ted.

"No." His voice was dead.

"Well, you could try calling her."

He closed both hands around the mug. "I have. She won't talk to me."

Joey shook her head and Ash could see she felt sorry for him, even though she probably believed the same thing her sister did. "She's upset, Ted. Give her some time."

He nodded and lifted the mug, closing his eyes as he sipped from it. "How is she?"

"Fine. And so are the girls." Joey reached out to touch his shoulder. "They don't know anything's wrong. She hasn't told them. They think it's one big vacation, and they're having a ball."

Ted looked at Joey and smiled just a little. It was the saddest thing Ash thought he'd ever seen. "Thanks for that." He glanced across at Ash, then looked pointedly at his plate. "You almost through?"

Ash shook his head and shoved the half-finished breakfast away, thinking it just wasn't meant to be eaten. "Tactless, but to the point. I take it this is going to be a private conversation."

Ted nodded.

"Well, hell, I *always* shower right after not eating. Knock yourselves out."

He left to go into the bathroom, and he turned the shower on. But then he slipped back out to the living room, where he could listen in. It wasn't that he didn't trust Joey. He did, in spite of everything. It was Ted that worried him.

"You guys were out late last night."

"We went to the lake."

"Ah...the fish."

"Bit like crazy. I'd like to go back today, but—"

"Tell me the truth, Joey."

God, he'd heard that one before. Ash tensed, waiting for her reply.

"I don't know what you're talking—"

"Don't give me that. This marriage to Coye is a sham, isn't it? There's no record of it in Vegas, or here or anywhere else."

Silence. Then, "How do you know?"

"I checked is how I know. This whole thing has smelled like bad meat from the start. Does Coye even know, or have you got the poor guy completely buffaloed?"

He heard her sigh, long and hard. "He doesn't know. And you can't tell him."

A chair scraped the floor. Heavy steps seemed to pace. "It's this Slasher thing, isn't it? It's all wrapped up in these murders. Dammit, Joey, you've been obsessed with this thing from the first day it hit the papers. What in hell's going on with you?"

Another chair moved, more gently. "Ted, I'll explain it all to you. I promise. But not now. Not yet."

Silence again. A longer one this time, and Ash could feel the tension in the air.

"You know who it is, don't you?"

"Not yet. But...I think I will. Soon. And then this nightmare will be over."

"Or maybe it'll just begin. Joey, if you keep sticking your nose into places it doesn't belong, you're going to get yourself killed."

Ash stiffened. Was that menace in Ted's voice? A threat? Or just genuine worry? Either way, enough was enough. Ash stripped off his shirt, dropped it on the floor and sauntered back into the kitchen. Both sets of eyes turned toward him, startled, guilty.

"Sorry to interrupt. I forgot my coffee."

Ted's gaze turned skeptical. "You always take coffee into the shower with you?"

"Old habits die hard."

"So do cockroaches." Ted sent Joey a warning look, then shook his head and left them alone.

Ash watched him go, then faced Joey. "He seemed upset."

"Just like your editor. He's worried."

"About you?"

She nodded. "He's sees himself as some sort of father figure—has ever since he and Caro got married. It drives me nuts, but it's kind of endearing." She sighed and started clearing the table. "At least it was, before he hurt my sister the way he has."

"Fell off his pedestal, did he? Just like your old man?"

She picked up the platter of leftover fish. "You ought to have a cat."

But her face had tightened at his words, and anger had flashed in her eyes.

She felt it all day, crushing in on her. *Danger.* No longer a subtle tingling sensation up her spine, but a big, suffocating hand slowly closing around her. Its grip tightened until she felt like her brain was in a vise and someone was turning the screw. She knew the threat to Ash was drawing nearer all the time.

The Slasher was somewhere close, watching, waiting.

Ash spent the morning on the phone, talking to everyone involved with the old crimes in Vegas. Not witnesses—no one had ever seen the Slasher strike—but people who had known the victims, or who had been unfortunate enough to discover one of their bodies. He was milking them for every crumb of information, hoping something would click into place, giving him a clue to the killer's identity. But it was apparent from the increasing tension in his face and in his voice that he was getting nowhere.

He hung up the phone and stared hard at the filled pages of notes in his hand as if waiting for a line to jump out and grab him.

"We have to get out of here," Joey said.

He looked up fast and frowned at her. "What's wrong?"

"We just have to get out of here. Ash, something's

going to happen. I feel it. Let's just leave."

He crossed the room to where she stood, pulled her into his arms and hugged her hard. "Relax, Joey. We're going to be fine, I promise."

"I should have brought the gun. God, why did I leave it locked up at home? I must be insane." She wrapped her arms around his neck and squeezed. "Please, let's go somewhere."

She knew he could feel her trembling, but there was nothing she could do to stop it. "Where, Joey?"

"Anywhere. The lake. There wasn't this tension there. It felt safe."

He pulled slightly away from her, looked down at her face, then glanced once toward the phone. "This isn't getting me much, anyway. Okay. A picnic lunch at the lake, but you owe me."

She sighed her relief and grabbed his hand, starting for the door.

"Aren't we packing sandwiches?"

"We'll pick some up on the way." She tugged again, but he stayed where he was.

"I'd better call Rad first, or I'm liable to be out of a job."

"Call him on the way."

He made the call short and sweet, but the whole time he was driving out of the city, he kept looking at her as if he was afraid she might be cracking up. She let him drive, wanting to be free to watch all around them. All the way out of the city her gaze was darting to the cars around them, the pedestrians, even the traffic cops.

It was only when they'd left Syracuse far behind, and exited 81 to take winding, narrow roads of Cortland County, that she began to relax. Ash smiled at her and squeezed her hand. "Better?"

"Yeah." She let her head rest against the back of the seat, closing her eyes. "I wish we never had to go back."

The car passed over sun-dappled pavement, beneath leafy green bows and needled limbs. They bounced through dips and potholes, and Ash slowed down.

"The lake is off that road, isn't it?"

She nodded as he approached a narrow dirt track and turned the car onto it. He drove a little farther. The track simply ended at a copse of maple saplings. Coming to a stop, he twisted the key, and they both got out. He came around the car to meet her, put his arm around her shoulders and walked toward the barely discernable footpath through the trees. A short distance later, they emerged onto a mat of green rolling gently down to the shore of the lake. It was small, and tucked away amid state forest. She wasn't even sure it had a name.

Ash held her closer. "We forgot the fishing poles this time. What are we gonna do to pass the time?"

Joey tipped her head back, inhaling to experience the full impact of the place—the pines, the lake water, the wild-flowers. "We could swim," she suggested.

"That wasn't exactly what I was thinking."

"I know." She smiled up at him, the relief she felt in being away from that sense of menace making her feel playful. "But we could still swim."

"We didn't bring—" he slanted her a mischievous glance "—swimsuits. But I don't see that as a problem."

She lifted her eyebrows and looked at the lake. "Could be snapping turtles."

"Trying to back out, are you?"

He lunged for her, catching her up in his arms and striding toward the water as if to throw her in, clothes and all. She laughed, and struggled with him, and they wound up on the ground in a tangle of limbs and laughter. She was on top of him, and he caught her face between his palms and kissed her thoroughly. Then he rolled her off him and rose to his feet. He reached one hand down to help her stand. She took it and let him pull her upright

"Let's do something," he said. "Before I lose my head."

She lowered her gaze. "I like it when you lose your head, Ash."

He growled playfully and drew her to him for one more scorching kiss. "It's broad daylight, honey, and I'd never forgive myself if some hunter or hiker came along." He looked at her with mock severity. "No one sees my wife naked but me. Got that?"

Her brows shot up. "Well, I guess I'll have to start wearing clothes to the supermarket, then." When he stopped laughing, she slipped an arm around his waist. "Let's walk a little."

"You sure you're up to it?"

She nodded. "It only aches a little today. Besides, if it gets too painful you'll have to be chivalrous and carry me."

He chuckled, put an arm around her and began moving along the lake's curved shore. "So what are you going to wear to the market? Leather pants and a biker jacket?"

"Of course not. I'm saving those for the PTA meetings I'll attend with our kids."

He stopped walking and turned to look into her eyes, his own filled with some unrecognizable emotion. She saw his throat move as he swallowed hard, but then he began walking again.

God, was she going to keep letting herself forget that this marriage wasn't real? Why was that so easy to do?

"Come on," she said, changing the subject. "I'll show you some of the most private spots you'll ever find anywhere."

His brows lifted. "Oh, yeah? And just who showed them to you?"

She elbowed him in the side playfully. "You've heard of Lewis and Clark? Well, these woods were explored and mapped by the great team of Bradshaw and Bradshaw. Caro and I left no stone unturned, even though at twelve and fourteen our map-making skills left room for improvement."

Ash let Joey lead the way, enjoying just being with her, watching her as she walked, her limp very slight, her pace slow, relaxed. He liked watching her eyes dart around, taking in everything.

When she'd mentioned having kids with him, something very fragile had taken root in him. Something that made his stomach feel queasy and threw his equilibrium out of whack. He tried to ignore it and pay attention to the things she pointed out as they picked their way silently through the dense woods—a deer track, a pair of chipmunks chasing each other and chattering madly, a hawk circling above, a bare, green spot on a sapling where a buck had rubbed his antlers, scraping away the bark. But he found himself more interested in looking at her. More intrigued by her scent, than that of the pines. More impressed by her grace as she practically danced through the trees, than by that of the hawk gliding above them in perfect circles. He felt good about himself, filled with satisfaction. And all because she'd relaxed. He'd eased her mind, had taken away some of her turmoil. He couldn't think of a higher cause to strive for.

Until she stiffened and stopped walking. Her eyes went wide, her jaw tight. Her lips trembled slightly. She spun around, staring back the way they'd come. "No..." It was a bare whisper.

"Joey?" He gripped her shoulders, brought her around to face him. The fear in her green eyes made his heart flip over. "What is it?"

"The Slasher...is here!" She pulled free of his grasp, gripped one of his hands in hers and veered off the path, pulling him. "Come on. Run!"

CHAPTER 12

She was frantic. Her palm against his hand was too warm and damp. She pulled him off the marked trail into the dense trees, running like a scared rabbit with one lame leg. He knew that every step sent pain through her thigh. She grunted softly with the impacts, and her face twisted into a tormented grimace. He had little choice but to go along with her, though he had to wonder if she had finally succumbed to all the pressure she'd been under. He hadn't heard a thing, and he was damned sure no one had followed them.

Still, she limped up a steep incline, dragged him behind a cluster of brush and pulled him down until he squatted on his haunches beside her.

He scanned her panic-stricken face, his worry increasing with her every hoarse breath, every shift of her wide eyes. One palm rubbed up and down over her injury. Damn, she could have ripped the stitches out with that little performance. "Joey, take it easy. It's probably nothing. You've been under a lot of—" Her hand shot out to press over his mouth. Her other one rose, pointing down the wooded bank they'd just climbed.

He frowned as she moved her hand away and looked where she was pointing. And then he heard it. Brush crackling loudly beneath hurried steps. He squinted, trying to see through the dense growth. A shadow took shape beyond the branches, moving a few steps, then stopping, waiting, then moving some more.

The form finally stepped into a clear spot and Ash felt Joey go ice-cold. A tall woman, her long legs in black nylons. He couldn't see her feet, but there was a tight black skirt and a loose-fitting knit sweater. Red. He waited for her to step farther forward, so he could see her head, her face, but she didn't. She just stood there, silent, as if listening. And then her hand lifted, and he saw that she wore a black glove and held a blade that glinted in the sun.

He felt Joey's death grip on his forearm and looked at her. She was pulling him, but her wide eyes remained riveted on the form lurking below. Ash followed, moving with softly placed steps. Joey carefully pushed a tangle of berry briars to one side, tearing her eyes from the woman to look at him, and then she nodded toward whatever she'd uncovered. Ash looked and saw the black hole the briars had concealed. His gaze met Joey's, and he shook his head once.

"We have to," she whispered. "Ash..."

He heard the rustle of brush below them and glanced down once more. The killer was climbing upward. Personally he'd rather stay right here and face the bitch, blade or not, than go into that well of darkness Joey had exposed. But he couldn't risk Joey's life that way. She could be hurt. Killed, even.

He looked again at the cave.

"Trust me." She mouthed the words with trembling lips. He braced his spine against the tremors that were trying to shake it apart and nodded. Joey bent double and crawled under the briars, disappearing into the darkness. Ash got down on all fours and backed in, so he could check the ground to be sure they'd left no telltale signs. As soon as he was completely surrounded in inky blackness, Joey reached past him, tugging the briars back into place to conceal the entrance. Then she reached out, felt for his hand, found it and gripped it.

"You can stand," she whispered. "There's room."

He straightened slowly. She led him forward, deeper into the darkness, and he went, telling himself over and over that it was necessary. That the danger was outside in the sunshine, not here in this dank, black well. He didn't need to reach out to feel the narrow walls of stone on either side of him, or reach up to know the cold ceiling was inches above his head. He hated the closeness, hated the sensation of there being no air, hated that his breaths came short and quick as she pulled him behind her at a slow, uneven pace.

He steadied himself, clenching his hand around hers, trying to concentrate on her pain instead of his own. She was hurting. She must be, after that uphill run. He couldn't let her see what this place did to him. He prayed she wouldn't feel his hand shake or sweat. It was the damned darkness! If only there was a light, even a faint glimmer, to break the pitch. He thought of his cellphone--there was a flashlight app. But that might reveal their hiding place to the menace outside. So there was no light, and the memory began swirling in the pit of his mind.

There had been darkness then, too. And the feeling

of four close walls looming around him, closing in as he crouched on the floor with his knees pulled tight to his chest. No silence, though. His little cell's walls had been thin, and he could hear the sounds that came through them. His mother's sounds. Animal sounds. As if she was hurting, dying. And if she died, he would remain in the closet forever, behind the locked door, a prisoner of the darkness.

He stopped walking. Joey's hand tugged at his, but his feet refused to move. He fought the misery, the sudden certainty that Joey and the Slasher and the cave were just a dream and that he was still that little boy. He turned as if to look around him, but saw nothing. He took a step backward, retreating from the horror, only to come up against a cold stone wall. He closed his eyes and sank to the floor.

"Ash?"

"No." He didn't want her to see him this way, didn't want her to touch him, didn't want her anywhere near him right now.

She knelt in front of him, her hands running over his face, over the dampness of sweat and, if he was honest with himself, perhaps a few tears on his skin.

"It's all right." Her breath warmed his face, dried it. Her arms encircled his shoulders and she held him.

Get away from me, dammit.

But his head obeyed when she urged it onto her shoulder. His body surrendered to the feel of her warmth, her fingers moving through his hair in soothing rhythm. God, he didn't want her to know....

"I already know." She shifted position, sitting down and pulling him down with her, holding him with a strength that surprised him. Her arms were silken steel and they wouldn't let go. "There are no locked doors here, Ash. We can walk out any time we want to. We're in a big section of cave, here. There's plenty of room. You could park a car in here. And you're not alone. Not anymore."

His head came up and he faced her, not seeing her at all, only feeling her there. He stroked her arm, her shoulder, squeezed it. "I'm sorry."

"You're hurting." Her lips touched his face. "So am I. You don't want to let me in, Ash, but I'm already there."

His breathing had calmed. In her arms, the old terror had evaporated. The little boy inside still cried, but this time someone was listening. He relaxed slightly, leaning back against the wall. He felt her turn to sit tight beside him, her body touching his. She gripped his hand.

"It was your mother who locked you in the little room."

He nodded, though he knew she couldn't see. "She was a whore. I was bad for business."

Her hand clenched. "You were afraid for her."

"I hated her."

"How old were you, Ash?"

He tensed. Bitterness coated the inside of his mouth and his voice came out thick with it. "Four, the first time."

She settled her head on his shoulder. "Four-year-olds don't know how to hate."

The child inside him cried harder. Ash ignored it, focusing instead on his anger. "This one did."

She shook her head. "I don't think so."

From somewhere deep inside him, the cries became words, pleas. *I just wanted her to love me. Why couldn't she love me?*

Ash went rigid, shaking himself. "Maybe we'd better

move on."

But her hands cupped his face and held it close to hers. Her lips touched his, and he tasted her salty tears on them. Her arms crept around his neck. "You're not alone anymore." Her lips moved and she kissed his face, his neck, his ear. "I won't let you be...not ever again."

He snagged her waist and pulled her closer, kissing her with an urgency that surprised him. Then he brought her head to his chest and held her there, against his thundering heart. God, he wished he could believe her. It would be so easy to let her in, let her warmth, her love, heal the old wounds.

But he was all too aware that none of it was true. There was no love between them. It was all a farce, one he still didn't understand. And for a moment he wished his pretend amnesia was real, so he could relish this moment, believe in it. It would be easy. It *felt* real.

He pushed her away and got to his feet, gripping her hands and pulling her with him. He shouldn't have talked about his past with her. It made him feel vulnerable, weak. He'd deal with his own problems in his own way. Alone. He would piece together the puzzle of Joey Bradshaw, and he would see the Slasher pay the price. And then he would go his way, resume his search for a life, a family of his own. He would find a woman, one he could build something with, one he could trust. He would have children and give them everything he'd longed for as a child. Everything he'd been denied.

But there would never be love. He hadn't realized that until now. There was a big hole inside him where love should have been. It had never been filled, so there was none there to give.

He cleared his throat and his mind. "Let's go back to

the entrance. Maybe the Slasher gave up and left by now."

She stepped nearer, her hands on his shoulders. "Ash, I—"

"No, Joey. No more. It was a brief lapse. I'm fine now."

He thought she nodded. He was glad he couldn't see her face, read whatever was in her eyes, or misread it. He turned the way they'd come, but her hand caught his again.

"There's another exit. This way."

It was as if he'd slammed a door in her face. Joey wished she could understand why, but she couldn't. She'd felt his thoughts so clearly only moments ago—his anguish, the rush of memories that had engulfed him. But now there was nothing.

She consoled herself that it was good he'd stopped her when he had. She had been about to tell him that she loved him, just to ease his aching heart. Where the impulse had come from, she had no idea. She'd just been overcome with the need to take away his pain, and the words had bubbled up in her throat like some living thing inside her, desperate to escape. She'd let herself get so caught up in wanting to help him that she'd forgotten to protect herself. If she'd blurted out something so blatantly false, he'd have known, or he would find out, as soon as his memory was restored. And then he'd have all the more reason to hate her.

She ignored the recurring urge to hold him close again. She focused on finding the right passages. She knew the cave well, but always before, she'd had a light to guide her. This time all she had was her memory, and it had been a long time. She'd avoided this place and its happy memories after her stepfather had let her down. She hadn't thought she could ever enjoy coming here again...until she'd come with Ash.

He didn't say a word as they walked. His palms were dry, his breathing normal. Maybe she had helped him, then, just a little.

Finally she saw daylight filtering through an opening ahead. She walked slowly, careful not to make a sound. Ash did the same without her warning, just in case the Slasher knew about this cave and was waiting. She honed her senses, opened her mind, sought the prickling sense of danger she feared would come. But she felt only fresh air bathing her face, brilliant sunlight warming it as they drew nearer.

They emerged on a grassy hillside overlooking a farmhouse, a red barn, a cluster of cows. Ash pulled out his phone, held it up, moved it left and right. "No bars."

"We'll go down there. They'll have a phone."

She didn't take her hand from Ash's and he didn't release it until they started down the hill. But then he stopped her, turned her and then scooped her into his arms. "I couldn't help you in there. Too dark not to bash you into something. But I'll be damned if you're walking on that leg anymore today."

She leaned forward and kissed him. He stared at her for a second, and she saw her own confused feelings mirrored in his dark eyes. Then he started off, carrying her down the hill to the farmhouse.

While Joey spoke to the farmer's wife, Ash used their phone to call the police.

"This proves Joey isn't the Slasher." Ash said it for the fourth time as he paced Radley's office. It had been three hours since they'd been in the cave. Between talking to the police, filing a report, and then making the drive back, the day was about shot.

"It only proves that," Rad said, "if you can be sure the woman you saw *was*."

"Well, who the hell else would have been slinking through the woods with a knife in her fist?"

Rad's hands came up in front of him. "I didn't say I doubted you, I'm just asking if you're sure."

"I'm sure." Ash stopped pacing and stared at his friend. "What I'm not sure of is how the hell she knew where to find us. You're the only one I told, Rad."

"Whoa, whoa. Are you saying you think *I* had something—"

"Of course not. Jeeze, Radley. I'm asking if you told anyone else."

Rad shook his head as he rose from his chair. "What do you think, I'm an idiot? Of course I didn't tell..." His words trailed off. He pushed a hand over his graying hair and swore under his breath.

"What?"

Rad sighed. "Bev Issacs. She was in my office when you called to tell me you were going down there. Freaking grilling me about that cigarette butt Harris lifted from her ashtray." He grimaced. "Dammit, Ash, I jotted the location down in case I needed to reach you." He turned, searching his desk, moving file folders aside. "The note's gone. She could've taken it. I'm an idiot."

As he said it, Joey reentered the office. He'd tried to get her to stay off the leg, but she couldn't seem to sit still. Her wide eyes met Ash's. He answered her unspoken question as she handed him a mug of coffee. "There's a chance Bev Issacs knew where we were."

Joey's tongue darted out to moisten her lips. She obviously wanted to say something, but hesitated.

"Go on, Joey. What is it?"

"I think...I think Ted might've known, too. I mentioned this morning that we'd been there fishing last night, and that we might go back there." She crossed the room, putting her back to both men, and stared out the window between the white slats of the blinds. "I don't think it was him, though. I really don't. Not Ted."

"I thought you said it was a woman?" Radley's voice conveyed confusion.

"She—the *person*—was wearing a skirt. I never got a look at the face. It could've been a man in drag, I guess." Ash stepped up behind Joey, placing his hands on her shoulders. "It would explain a lot. Ted's late-night calls, the things he's been keeping from your sister. And he was in Vegas during that other string of murders."

She whirled to face him, and his stomach tightened when he saw the dampness in her eyes. "It wasn't Ted. And suspecting only the people who could have known where we were is a mistake. There's always a chance we were followed."

"She has a point there, Ash."

Ash heard Rad's words, but kept his eyes on Joey's face. He suddenly understood what she'd meant in that cave, when she'd said she felt his pain. Because he felt hers now. It would tear her up if Ted turned out to be the Slasher. And it would tear Ash up to see it. He felt close to her, too damn close.

He blinked at the unexpectedness of that thought. Sure, he was growing fond of her. But he knew they'd go their separate ways in the end, and he knew he wouldn't wither and die because of it. Even if he might wish he could. Damn, there he went again, exaggerating his feelings. What was wrong with him, anyway?

She looked up at him, her eyes so intense he wondered if she'd been reading his mind again. "I want to go home, Ash." She closed her eyes, shook her head slowly. "It's been a long day. I just want it to end."

He nodded, turned her toward the door and slipped an arm around her shoulders, holding her close to his side. It had been a long day. They'd gone back to the lake with the police, answered endless questions, waited restlessly while the area was scoured for evidence. All for nothing. Not a single clue had been left behind. Whoever he or she was, the Slasher was good. Careful. Cunning. Sooner or later, though, there would be a slip. And then the killer would land behind bars. And then....

He stared down at the top of Joey's head. Seemingly sensing his gaze, she looked up, met his eyes. And then *what?* he wondered.

The closer the car got to her house, the better Joey felt. She had to put all of this out of her mind, just for one night. She wanted to relax in a steaming bath, drink a glass of wine and spend the night wrapped in Ash's strong arms, feeling safe from the world.

She tensed, though, when Ash drove the car over the graveled driveway and the house came into view. Lights glowed in the windows. Shadows moved behind them. Dread ran in her veins like ice water, and she shot Ash a glance, seeing the same alarm clouding his beautiful face. Then it eased, and he pointed.

"Look. It's Caroline's. She's back."

Joey glanced in the direction he pointed, seeing her sister's station wagon parked in its usual spot on the paved strip. But instead of relief, Joey felt an even deeper fear take root inside her. Caro shouldn't be here. She was in danger. God, she'd only been in Florida for a couple of days. Why did she have to come back now?

Ash pulled the car to a stop beside Caroline's, and Joey was out like a shot, limping around the house as fast as she could manage, flinging the back door open. "Caro? Caroline! Where are—?"

Her words were forcibly stopped by two small bodies hurling themselves into her arms and hugging the breath out of her. She returned the girls' hugs, but didn't hear their giggling greetings. She focused beyond them, to the foot of the stairs, flooded with relief at seeing Caroline there.

She released her pent-up breath all at once, smiling. But the smile died on her lips when a tall, straight form stepped from the bottom stair into her range of vision. Her arms fell limply to her sides, and she gaped.

"Hello, Joey."

Ash was at her side. She felt his strong presence there, felt his eyes on her. But she couldn't look away from the man.

"Isn't it great, Aunt Joey? Grandpa came back with us. He's gonna take us to the zoo and..."

The stream of high-pitched words faded. A dull roar filled Joey's ears instead. Clenching her teeth she forced herself to speak. "Hello, Father."

"Joey." He came forward, smiling, stretching out a hand to clasp Ash's. "You must be my new son-in-law."

Joey watched Ash shake her stepdad's hand. "Ash

Coye," he said. "Good to meet you, Mr. Bradshaw." As he spoke, Ash glanced her way.

"Matthew to you," he replied. "I had to come. Had to meet the man who managed to lure my Joey to the altar."

"I am not *your* Joey. I'm not your anything."

Caroline bustled her way between them, gathering the girls away from Joey's legs and chattering loudly in an effort to break the tension that filled the room to bursting. "Let's all go upstairs. I made us supper, and if it stays in the oven any longer, it'll be dry as a chip. Come on."

Joey opened her mouth to say she was leaving, but clamped it shut before the words escaped. She couldn't leave Caroline alone, not when the Slasher was so close, so perceptive, always seeming to know where she was, what she was doing.

"Go on ahead, girls, and finish setting the table," Caroline instructed.

They groaned, but obeyed. When they'd left the room, Joey glared at her sister. "What is he doing here?"

"You can address me directly, Joey. I'm standing right in front of you."

Her gaze shifted to him. She hadn't seen him in a year, not since her mother's death. He looked older. His skin had lost its tightness and some of its color. His hair was grayer than she remembered. "I have nothing to say to you."

"Well, that's good, because I have a lot to say to you. Maybe you'll be quiet and listen for a change, hm?"

She shook her head quickly, her hair flying over her face. Ash's arm came around her and squeezed, infusing her with strength when she thought her knees would buckle.

"Come on, Dad," Caroline said softly. "Come on upstairs. Just give her a minute." She tugged on their father's arm and, reluctantly, he turned and went with her.

The second they were out of sight, Joey turned into Ash's arms, burying her face against his hard chest. Her arms twined around his neck and she clung to him as if she would never let go, battling tears that fell anyway.

He held her tightly, nearly crushing her to him. One hand stroked her hair. "It's okay. I'm here, just hold onto me. You can get through this."

"I don't want him here."

"I know."

"Make him leave, Ash. Throw him out, tell him—"

"Joey..." He cupped her face in his palms and tilted it up to his. "*You* have to tell him. Whatever it is that's burning inside you, you have to let it out, say it to his face. And maybe hear whatever it is he feels he has to tell you."

She blinked the tears away. "I don't want to do this. I can't."

One hand left her cheek to brush the hair away from her face. "Sure you can. I'll be here for you. I'll help you."

As she stared into his eyes, Joey saw the pain in their velvet brown depths. Pain for her. And steely strength, as well. If he would stay beside her, hold her close to him, maybe she could get through this night. With Ash at her side, she felt all of a sudden, she could get through anything. Anything at all. My God, how had she let herself fall so hopelessly in love with him?

Oh my God, she thought. I am. I'm in love with him!

He lowered his head and caught her lips with his, still cupping her face with one hand, while the other threaded through her hair. He tasted her, sipped from her mouth. A tender kiss, but one packed with emotion. He slanted his lips over her face, kissing away her tears, then lifted his head, staring into her eyes.

"I need you, Ash." Her voice was choked, hoarse. The words came of their own volition.

"You've got me, Joey."

She closed her eyes, knowing all too well that she didn't have him. Not really. Not for much longer. But at least for tonight.

CHAPTER 13

The doors were locked, the gun loaded and within his reach. Brittany and Bethany were finally asleep upstairs, but only after insisting Ash tell them a half-dozen fractured fairy tales. Ash had Beverly Issacs's word, for what it was worth, that a squad car would cruise the neighborhood all night, just in case.

Joey stood stiffly, watching him. Her sister occupied the rocking chair, and her stepfather Matthew Bradshaw sat in the recliner. Ash took a seat on the sofa, and Joey immediately sat down beside him, her body tight to his. He put an arm around her, bent to kiss her cheek. Why he felt like a lion protecting its mate, he didn't know. He wished he could take every ounce of her pain and suffer it himself. But he couldn't. The best he could do was help her through this as he'd promised he would. She'd seemed to take strength from that promise. He vowed to live up to it.

"Does Ted know you're back?" Joey's voice was as tense as her body.

Caroline shook her head. "I'm going to call him later, before I go to bed."

Joey glanced at Ash, worry in her eyes, then looked back at her sister. "Why don't you wait until tomorrow, Caro?"

"Why?" Caroline stopped rocking, her brows furrowed. "Do you know something, Joey? Is he out meeting some–"

"Of course not!" Joey's eyes widened in surprise. "God, you think I'd keep something like that from you? I just thought you could use tonight to unwind, get your head together. That's all."

Caroline still looked skeptical, but she settled back in the chair and began rocking again.

"My God," Matthew Bradshaw said in a gruff voice. "My God, just look what I've done to my daughters." He addressed Ash, and his eyes were brimming. "It's all because of me, you know. They can't trust any man now, because the father they thought was perfect had a flaw."

"A *flaw*?" Joey turned her icy stare on him, and he seemed to shrink back into his seat. "Is that what you call it? You broke our mother's heart, and it's nothing to you but a flaw? She died alone while you were in bed with another woman, and it's a *flaw*?"

Ash squeezed her closer, hearing the tears that choked her voice, but she pulled free and shot to her feet, immediately adjusting her stance to take most of her weight on the good leg, then turning as if to leave the room.

Her father stood, as well, gripped her shoulders and forced her to face him. "Your mother didn't die alone, dammit. She died with her lover right beside her."

Joey slapped him so hard he rocked back on his heels.

"How dare you!"

He lifted a hand to his face, running his palm over the red mark she'd left there. "You're going to hear some harsh truths tonight, Joey." He glanced at Caroline, who had gone still and white. "Both of you are. And you're going to sit there and listen to what I have to say. After that, you never have to see me again if that's the way you want it. But no one is leaving this room until I've said what I came here to say."

"No. I won't listen to you spew lies about my mother!"

Again she turned from him, and again he caught her shoulders. Roughly. Too roughly. Ash got to his feet and shouldered between them, folding Joey into his arms. Her entire body shook, and he held her tighter. He looked over her, at her father, and saw the man's distress. Matthew spun away, pacing a small circle, pushing his hands through his hair. Ash was glad the girls were playing upstairs, out of earshot.

"Look, I'm not trying to tarnish your mother's memory. I'm not saying she wasn't the most wonderful woman on this planet, because she was. But, Joey...Caroline, she never loved me. I never loved her. We married because she was pregnant. We were both too young to know anything about love."

Joey turned in Ash's arms, but held them around her waist and kept her back pressed to him. "I don't care why you married her. She was your *wife*. She gave her life to you, and to Caroline and me. She didn't deserve...." Her voice trailed off. Her head lowered and a sob wrenched her body.

"We were honest with each other from the start, your mother and I," he said. "Our feelings were out in the open. We decided to stay together, raise Caroline in a stable environment. That's why we didn't split up when she had the affair with Tito del Rio, and got pregnant with you, Joey. I didn't blame her. We were very clear about what we were to each other, and what we were not."

Joey stared at him, frowning. "You always knew you weren't my birth father?"

He nodded slowly. "I just couldn't bring myself to tell you sooner. Your mom and I planned to go our separate ways when you two girls grew up. As time went on, she fell in love with someone else. Not Tito, that was just a fling. But she did fall in love, deeply in love with another man. And I fell in love with another woman. It wasn't a secret dirty liaison. It was all right on the table. When we moved to Florida, we lived separate lives. We only kept up the pretense for the sake of you two girls. Your mother couldn't bring herself to tell you the truth. Not even after she'd admitted to you, Joey, that I was not your father."

"I don't believe it. She loved you and you broke her heart," Joey whispered.

"It was George Prentiss, wasn't it?" Caroline spoke for the first time, her voice soft, wounded. "He was always coming around, bringing presents for us...and for Mom. Sometimes he'd be there when we came home from school...."

"Uncle George was just a friend!" Joey shouted. "God, Caro, how can you believe this garbage?"

Ash reached down to close his hands around her clenched, trembling fists. "Easy. Hold on to me, remember?"

She opened her hands, laced her fingers through his and held on tightly.

"Yes, it was George."

"Liar," Joey spat.

"I don't expect you to take my word for it." He stared at Joey, his eyes filled with pain. "I brought your mother's diary. It's all there, written in her own hand. I know she wanted you both to know the truth after she was gone. She wanted you to have it sooner, but I just...I hoped you'd never have to know." He shook his head, his shoulders slumping. He looked like a beaten man. "You're adults, women, with families of your own. It's time you understand...and forgive. If you can."

Joey shook her head rapidly. "Get out, damn you. Just go, I don't want to hear any more of this."

He nodded. His feet scuffed the floor as he walked into the kitchen and through the door, down the stairs to the back entrance. Caroline ran after him. "Daddy, wait!" Her footsteps pattered down the stairs, and their muffled voices floated up from below.

A few minutes later, the back door slammed. Then the sound of an engine came, and Caroline's car headlights moved slowly away from the house.

Joey stiffened, then pulled free of Ash's arms and limped to the top of the stairs they'd descended. "Caro?"

Her sister came up slowly, her face tear-stained. "I let him take the minivan. He's going to a hotel." She clutched a small satin-bound book in both hands, bit her lip and handed it to her sister.

Joey stared at it and shook her head slowly from side to side. "It isn't true. None of what he said is true."

Caroline pressed the book into Joey's hands. "I don't know what to believe anymore. Was our entire childhood just one big lie?" She closed her eyes and turned toward the stairs, starting up them. "It would explain a lot. I mean, I never could understand our mother having an affair with your birth father."

"My birth father was a real player, according to Toni." She sighed, lowered her head.

"Read it, Joey. I can't"

"No. I won't read it."

Caroline stopped halfway up the stairs. "You've always been the strong one. I can't do it. You have to." She moved the rest of the way upstairs and disappeared into one of the extra bedrooms, closing the door behind her.

Ash stood in the center of the living room, watching. Joey looked at the diary. She stared hard at its cover, and he knew she was trying to work up the courage to open it. But at last she seemed to decide against it. She crossed the room and set it down on the coffee table. Then she lifted her gaze to meet his.

"What can I do, Joey? What do you need?"

She took a deep, shuddering breath and let her head tip back until she faced the ceiling before releasing it. When she looked down again, there were fresh tears in her eyes. "Just hold me, Ash." As he moved forward to wrap her in his arms, she went on. "Yes, hold me. The only time I feel right anymore is when you hold me." She melted against him, her bones going limp.

Ash shifted his stance, scooped her up and held her tightly as he mounted the stairs. She wasn't faking the emotions that racked her body. She wasn't faking the tears that burned red trails into her cheeks, or the tremors that passed through her, or the desperation he felt in her arms. She clung to him as if he was the last life preserver on the *Titanic*.

No, he decided as he reached the top of the stairs and turned toward the bedroom, she definitely was not faking any of this. What, then?

He nudged the door open with one foot and carried her inside. Was she really turning to him for support and comfort in the most confusing time of her life? Why, for God's sake? It was almost as if *she* were beginning to believe this phony marriage was for real.

He heeled the door shut, crossed the room and lowered her to the bed as gently as if she were a fragile bird with a broken wing. He caught himself brushing the spun-honey hair away from her cheek, where tears had glued it in place, then stroking the tears away, as well. And even knowing this was all a sham, her feelings for him, and his for her, he leaned over her and pressed his lips to her quivering mouth.

Whatever delusions she was suffering, he was showing symptoms of the same—the way his throat tightened until it hurt to swallow, the way his eyes stung, the way his stomach clenched. He reacted to her pain as if he really was her husband, as if he really was in...in love with her.

In love with her? God, what a harebrained notion that is!

He pushed the errant thought aside and went into the bathroom to start a hot bath. He sifted through the cabinet there, sniffing one bottle after another until he found a scent that seemed soothing, then sprinkled the water with perfume. He draped a thin towel over the light fixture on the wall, taking care that the material didn't touch the bulb.

The effect was a softer, slightly pink hue rather than the harsh white glare. He pulled the thickest, softest towels from the shelf and stacked them near the tub.

Without even asking himself why a man who was only passingly fond of a woman would go to so much trouble, Ash slipped out the bathroom's other door and trotted down the stairs to search for wine and glasses. He found both, and returned without pouring, carrying the full bottle of white zinfandel, which he already knew was her favorite wine. He left the bottle and glasses beside the tub, shut the water off and returned to the bedroom.

She lay just as he'd left her, eyes red rimmed and wide, staring at the ceiling, looking shaken and vulnerable. The surge of emotion that flooded him was ridiculous and silly and inexplicable. But that didn't stop him from feeling it, and he decided to stop trying to figure this out and just go with it.

"Joey?"

She blinked, but didn't face him. "I'm all right. I can handle this."

"Never doubted it." He moved around the foot of the bed and sat down close to her.

"Caroline was right about that, you know." Her voice was as coarse as cherry bark, but no longer wavering or weak. "I *am* the strong one. I'm the one Mom leaned on when things went bad. And now Caro's doing the same thing, turning to me when she can't turn to Ted."

"You're right." He reached up and began freeing the buttons down her shirt. "But you know something, Joey?"

She shook her head, finally meeting his eyes.

"You have someone to lean on now."

Her lips trembled, turning upward at the corners, but it wasn't quite a smile. "If I lean on you any harder, I'll break your back." She closed her eyes briefly. "I'm not usually like this, you know."

He finished unbuttoning the shirt and moved his hands to the fly of her jeans, deftly releasing the snap, sliding the zipper down. "Like what?"

"Weak. Dependent. Weepy. I usually hate women who act the way I'm acting right now."

He tilted his head to one side, giving that some thought. "Look at it this way, kid. A man wants his woman to lean on him once in a while. Just so he knows she still needs him." He turned away from her, taking her foot in his hands and removing her shoe, then her sock. He repeated the process with the other foot.

She took a deep breath. "I do, you know."

"Do what?"

"Need you."

He turned fast, catching her gaze in time to see the anxiety in her eyes before she averted them.

"It scares the hell out of me. I hate it, and God knows I never meant for it to happen. But all of a sudden I don't..." She bit her lip and squeezed her eyes closed tightly. The act didn't stop the tears from seeping through to dampen her lashes. She swallowed loudly and rushed on. "I don't know what the hell I'm going to do without you."

"Hey..." A fist gripped his heart as Ash gathered her into his arms, held her to his chest, stroked her hair. The words that leapt into his throat and danced on his tongue were reassurances, promises that she'd never have to be without him. He bit them back, just barely restraining himself from blurting outright lies. Of course she'd have to get along without him. They weren't married. She'd lied and schemed to get him here with her, though he still didn't know exactly why. And no matter how comfortable or how *right* it felt, it was just a game. They were two grown-ups playing house, and nothing more.

She pretended they were married, he pretended to believe it. He couldn't tell her of his deception—no matter how powerful the urge to do just that had suddenly become— until she told him about hers. He had to know the reason for her lies. She'd started this and only she could end it.

He held her close and pushed the blouse down her arms. She remained still, not objecting when he unhooked the bra and stripped that away, as well. He ignored the warm skin of her back beneath his hands, and the gentle curve of her spine, and the soft swell of her breasts pressing to his chest. He'd have to be heartless to try to make love to her now, when she was an emotional basket case. But that was exactly what he would do if he looked down at her naked, beautiful body.

Instead, he rose, lifting her into his arms and carrying her to the bathroom. There he lowered her to her feet "Lose the jeans, fair lady. Your frog-prince hath deduced ye be in need of a relaxing bath and some fruit of the vine to ease your weary mind."

She smiled, just a little, then glanced around the bathroom. Ash turned away from her on the pretense of filling the glasses. In truth, he didn't think his chivalrous mood would last two seconds if he had to stand there and watch her slide out of those jeans. He heard the brush of the denim over her legs, her hopping steps as she kicked out of them. He closed his eyes in agony and waited for the gentle lapping of the water to tell him she'd sunk into the tub before he faced her again.

She lay in water to her chin, her knees poking up. Her bandages were soaking off, but he thought the water would sooth the partly healed wound. Her head rested on the white porcelain; her lashes caressed her cheeks. "Mmm, smells heavenly."

Ash put a glass of wine close to her face, touched its

cool rim to her cheek. Her eyes opened, then she lifted a dripping hand to take the glass from him. She sipped. Ash's gaze stubbornly fixed itself to her lips, loosely pressed to the rim of the glass, slightly parted as the pink liquid flowed through them. She lowered the glass to the side of the tub. Her tongue swept over her lips, sweeping up the traces of wine there. Ash swore under his breath.

"What's wrong?"

He met her gaze head on. Not much sense in lying about it, was there? It must be written all over his face. "I'm an insensitive clod, driven by a one-hundred-eighty-proof libido, and sadly lacking in princely chivalry, no matter how I try to fake it."

She frowned at him. "In English, Your Highness?"

"Okay, in English. I want you, Joey. Here I am, blown away that you'd even think about leaning on me in your hour of need, that you'd trust me to help you through this crisis. And all I can think about is stripping naked and climbing in that tub with you." Her green eyes rounded, but he held up two hands before she could speak. "Don't say it. I'm a rutting buck, a pig. I know."

She looked to be deep in thought for a moment, took a slow sip of wine, then another, while Ash awaited her condemnation. Then she stood. Graceful as a swan taking flight from the glistening surface of a lake, she rose out of the water. Rivulets streamed down her body. Droplets clung to her belly, glistened on her breasts. She reached out, caught the front of his shirt in two hands and pulled him closer. Her lips pressed to his as her hands worked the buttons of his shirt. A second later she pushed the material down over his arms and the shirt pooled at his feet.

"Do me a favor, Ash?"

"Name it." His voice croaked as if he really was a frog. His hands skimmed over her wet skin and he found it hard to breathe.

"Leave the mind reading to me. You're no good at it."

"No?"

She shook her head, shoved at his jeans. "No. I want you, too. I want you to hold me and make this crazy world disappear, just for a little while."

Ash glanced at the bathroom door to be sure it was locked, then kicked away his remaining clothes and stepped into the tub with her. Joey's arms slipped around his waist and her body pressed tight to his. He groaned under his breath, bending over her, catching her mouth beneath his and kissing her deeply. His hands slid up and down over her back, tracing its contours, then lower, to cup and squeeze her perfect buttocks, and lower still to the backs of her thighs. He lifted her legs, wrapped them around his waist and then anchored them atop his hips, slowly lowering himself into the water.

They made love tenderly, so slowly it was torture, but bliss too. Trying to be quiet, not to splash or moan, they clung and rocked until they both lost themselves to feeling. And then as his muscles uncoiled, Ash stretched out, lying back in the tub and pulling her down atop him, her chest pressed to his. He massaged her shoulders, rubbed her back.

"Mmm. Nice."

He smiled, glad he could give her something "nice" to counterbalance all the not-so-nice things in her life right now. "Feel better?"

"Yes." She relaxed against him, and her voice was drowsy.

"Think you'll be able to sleep now?"

"Umm-hmm."

"Right here in the tub?"

"What?" She lifted her head, but her eyes were heavy lidded.

"The water's getting cold, fair lady."

"I thought frogs liked cold water."

"Not this one."

She settled her head on his chest again. "Well, I guess that proves it. You're no frog."

"Oh, no?" He gripped her tight and held her as he rose. He reached for a towel, wrapped it around her and saw goose bumps rising on her thighs.

"No. You've evolved."

He smiled as she tucked her head down on his shoulder and closed her eyes. Stark naked and dripping wet, he carried her back into the adjoining bedroom, tugging down the covers on the bed. He stood her on wobbly legs and rubbed her vigorously with the towel, then urged her to lie down and pulled the covers over her. "How's the leg?"

"A little sore. No problem." She burrowed deep, hugging the comforter around her shoulders, her head sinking into the soft pillow. Closing her eyes, she released a long sigh. "Maybe you were a prince all along and I just couldn't see it."

"I'm no prince, Joey."

Her lips thinned, but she said nothing. Ash used her towel to dry off, then went back to the bathroom to drain the tub and swipe up the water they'd splashed all over the floor. He unlocked the door into the hallway, so the kids could use the bathroom during the night if need be. Then he poured himself some wine, refilled Joey's glass and took them back to the bedroom with him.

She lay very still, and he would have thought her asleep except that her breathing wasn't deep or regular. He set the wine on the nightstand.

"What am I going to do about that damned diary, Ash?"

He shrugged, facing her. Her eyes were open now and searching his. "Read it?"

She licked her lips. "You think?"

"That's what I'd do."

She nodded. "Okay. I'll read it. Only...only not now. I've got enough to deal with right now, with the Slasher, and Caroline and Ted breaking up, and this thing with you—"

"Thing with me?"

She averted her face, closing her eyes again. "No, I have too much to deal with now. I'll read it later. When all this is settled."

He wanted to ask what she'd meant by that remark, but realized a second later that he didn't have to. He knew. Hadn't he been wondering about this *thing* with her? This feeling of being too close? Of caring too much? Was he to assume, then, that she was having similar concerns? Maybe she'd never intended to care about him when she'd concocted this insane plot of hers. And maybe now she found herself caring in spite of herself, just like he was.

Right. And maybe I'm spinning straw into gold, thanks to an overactive imagination and a case of wishful thinking.

Wishful thinking? Then he did care about her? And he wanted her to care back?

Not. Why would I care for a woman I know is lying to me with every breath she draws? A woman I can't even trust? No way.

He glanced down at her again and knew without a doubt she was sleeping this time. She looked relaxed, peaceful, innocent.

Gorgeous.

Shut up.

He went to the dresser and quietly pulled open the drawer she'd cleared out for him. He found clean clothes and pulled them on. He had to go out. Alone. He had to get to the bottom of all of this. He'd never be able to sort out his feelings for Joey until he knew why she'd lied to him. And he wouldn't know that until the Slasher was stopped, once and for all. It was time to start doing some serious digging and he couldn't risk dragging Joey along. She'd be safer here. He would make sure of it.

CHAPTER 14

She'd drifted off to sleep wrapped in the comforting warmth of her make believe husband. And she woke with a chilled start, as she realized that warmth had gone missing.

Shaking the grogginess of sleep from her mind, she focused on what she was feeling. Blackness. An ugly, bloodstained soul eclipsing hers. Cold. Violence. Death. She ran a hand over her brow and felt cold sweat beading there.

God, no!

She lunged naked from the bed, tore clothes from the dresser and slung them on at record speed. She pulled on shoes with no socks and ran from the room, wincing every time she landed on the injured leg, but refusing to slow her pace because of it. Ash was gone. Nowhere in the house; she was sure of it without even looking for him. She turned, raced crookedly down the stairs and skidded to a halt, then turned to look toward the guest room door.

"Caroline," she whispered. Then she glanced down the stairs. "Ash." God, to protect one of them was to leave the other alone, vulnerable.

The sound of a car out front snapped her out of the quandary. She hobbled through the living room to the sliding-glass doors.

The car was Caroline's minivan. Her father got out of it and stood there, staring at Joey through the glass. For the first time ever, Joey wrenched the broom handle from the tracks, flicked up the lock and tugged the door open.

"Dad. What are you—?"

"Ash called me, asked me to come over."

Joey shook her head in bewilderment.

"He said you could be in some kind of danger, Joey. Why on earth didn't you tell me about this? What's been going on in your life that's got you in trouble? What—?"

"Not now." The tone of her voice seemed to get through to him. "Look, I'll explain later. Right now I have to find Ash. He's the one who's in danger, not me. Did he say where—?"

"He's in danger?"

"Where is he, Dad?"

Her father stepped forward, ran one hand over her hair as if soothing a child's headache. "You saw it, this danger he's in?"

She nodded hard. Her stepfather had never doubted her visions. He was the only one who had never questioned them.

"But you're safe? You're sure?"

"Yes, Dad. But I'm not so sure about Caro. I want you to stay here with her. Watch the house. Don't let anyone in. No one, not even the cops. Especially not a tall blond female cop. My gun is in the nightstand beside my bed.

Go and get it, and then stand watch over Caroline and the girls."

"You're going to try and find Ash?"

She nodded. "I have to."

"You love him, don't you Joey?"

She swallowed a huge lump in her throat. "God, yes."

"He said he needed to ask someone some questions. I thought he sounded like he suspected them of something."

One of the people Ash suspected could be the Slasher, she thought grimly. Ted, or Beverly Issacs?

She'd have to check both. She gripped her father's arm, looked him in the eyes. "This is no joke, Dad. Watch out for Caro. Don't let me down...again." She drew him inside and turned to grab her leather jacket from the back of the chair where she'd left it. Then she exited the door he'd just entered. "Lock this behind me. And put mom's broom handle back."

He did, and turned on the outside light. Joey trotted to the garage, swung one leg over her big bike, since Ash had taken her car, and painfully kicked it to a start. Her trusty Harley always started on the first try. The rear wheel spun as she took off into the night.

The message Ash spoke was simple. "Meet me to talk about the Slasher." He had only needed to utter those seven words to get Bev Issacs' full attention. She still had an answering machine. Didn't trust voicemail stored off site on some computer, she said. But as soon as he said those words, she had picked up her phone.

"Ash, what is this?"

"Screening your calls, Bev?"

"What have you got on the Slasher?" she demanded.

"Meet me. We'll talk."

"Where?"

"Someplace quiet. How about the last crime scene?"

"You're one morbid son of a—"

"You afraid I'm the Slasher, Bev? Afraid your throat'll get cut?"

"Try it and I'll break you up in little pieces and feed you to the glow-in-the-dark bass in Onondaga Lake, Coye."

"Funny."

He hung up and then eased Joey's car out of the driveway as quietly as possible. He'd already put in a call to Joey's father, explaining as much as he could and asking him to come and stand watch over the girls while he checked this out. If Bev was guilty, then he'd be able to get her to slip up and reveal something. The woman had a temper like nitro and it wouldn't take much to set it off. If she got mad, she'd slip and then he'd know for sure.

Or at least he hoped so. It was worth a shot.

Anyway, he'd made it there, to the old man's house in Central Square. It was empty, ghostly, and the sickening aroma of decay still lingered. It was a simple house, a shoebox kind of a place with a sickly sweet smell clinging to everything—tobacco mingled with liniment mingled with mothballs. It almost overshadowed the scent of death.

He walked back and forth in the living room, past the worn plaid sofa and the tilted recliner and the magazine rack that spilled over with junk mail, past the flooded ashtrays with their stale butts, and a half-dozen brown pill bottles huddled together as if for warmth on a folding tray table nearby.

The damned door hadn't been locked. Then again, he saw little worth stealing there. The TV was so old it still had a knob to turn the channels with. He stiffened as a sound came from behind him.

Turning slowly, Ash scanned the dim room. He'd only turned on one light, a low-watt bulb in a big lamp with a yellowed shade. The front door, the one through which he'd entered, was just to his left. But the sound hadn't come from there. It had come from the rear of the house. Maybe from inside the house.

He strained his eyes in that direction. A set of steep, narrow stairs ascended into blackness and the second floor. Another black hole led to what must be the kitchen. There would be a back door in there, wouldn't there? And maybe a basement. And the front door hadn't been locked, so why the hell would the back door be? Someone could have come in. Hell, someone could have been there waiting.

The Slasher?

Ash swore the skin around his jugular retracted just a little as he moved slowly forward to investigate the sound. He stopped, going rigid for an instant when someone's fist thumped the wooden door behind him, then spun around. The door swung open and Bev stepped inside. She pulled a restless hand through her David Bowie haircut, then gave it a shake, as if she was worried the night wind had messed it up. There wasn't enough there to mess.

"I'm glad you came," he said.

"This better be good, Ash. My last experience in this shack was a little too memorable."

He shrugged and crossed the room toward her, the

noise from the kitchen momentarily forgotten. "Have a seat?"

She glanced down at the faded brown couch, then shook her head. "No thanks."

Ash wondered if he'd been tactless. "That isn't where they found the guy, is it?"

"Hell, no. You've seen the Slasher's work."

She was right, he realized. There was no blood anywhere. His curiosity was piqued. This was the one crime scene he hadn't taken a good look at. He glanced at her, brows raised.

"The kitchen. You been in there yet?"

He shook his head, the sound he'd heard out there leaping to the front of his mind again.

Bev glanced toward the darkened doorway, her face going tight. "Bloodbath."

"Worse than the others?"

Her gaze came back to his, but it was unfocused, as if she was seeing the crime, instead of him. "He struggled."

Ash closed his eyes, trying to block out the image those two words painted in his mind. He was unsuccessful.

"So what did you want to talk to me about?"

He blinked at the way she shifted gears without warning. It took him just a second to catch up. Then he said, "Vegas."

She stared at him. Hard, as if she was trying to read him. "What *about* Vegas?"

"Come on, Bev. You know what I'm talking about. A string of murders, just like what's happening here. You were a rookie cop with a Vegas beat when they went down."

She averted her eyes, shrugged. "Four murders. I wouldn't call that a string. And they *weren't just* like these.

One of the victims was a woman."

"I see you've been giving this some thought."

Her head came up fast, chin jutting. "Damn straight I have, Coye. Wouldn't you? There are similarities, but just as many differences. I've reached the conclusion that we're dealing with two separate killers."

"You're sure?"

She stabbed holes through him with her eyes. "Positive."

He nodded, rubbing his chin. "Because the only other answer is that it's the same lunatic. And if that's the case, we'd have to start wondering about the connection between the Vegas murders and our own. So far you're the only connection I see."

She leaned forward, glaring at him, her eyes narrowing to ice blue slits. "What are you getting at? You saying I have something to do with these killings?"

"Just asking, Bev."

She was on her feet before he finished the sentence. "Damn you to hell, Ashville Coye. You dare even hint at this bull in that rag you call a paper and I'll have you wrapped up in so many lawsuits—"

"Easy, Bev. Come on, you know I wouldn't print anything without facts to back it up. And *The Chronicle* is no rag. Rad wouldn't let anything libelous slip by him."

"You can take Rad Ketchum and his paper and..." She stopped, mid-sentence. "Is that what that fiasco was all about? That clod you call a reporter sifting through my ashtray?"

"It's just a precaution. I'm planning to use a DNA profile to rule people out."

"Well, why didn't you just ask? We've already run DNA analysis on the butts found at the crime scenes."

He shrugged.

Bev's eyes widened. "You thought I'd get access to the results, didn't you? God, you really think I had something to do with this. I can't believe it."

"Look, I'm just trying to cover all the bases."

"You're trying to cover any base that would take attention away from your little wife, Coye."

"Joey's not a suspect. She was with me the last time the Slasher tried anything, remember?"

"Doesn't mean she might not know more than she's saying. She was at the crime scenes, don't forget. You ought to be grilling her, not me."

Ash sighed and shook his head.

"Don't think I'm not aware of the way you've been covering for her, Coye. The times you claimed to be with her while murders were committed, and God knows what else. If I can prove it, I'll have you up on charges."

"Knock yourself out, Bev."

She paced away from him, her strides long, forceful. "So do you have anything useful to tell me, or was this whole meeting just supposed to shake me up?"

"I was hoping *you'd* have something useful to tell *me.*"

"Like what?"

"Like details about those Vegas murders. The things they left out of the official reports. The things that might help me piece this crap together."

She stopped walking, faced him, her expression like chiseled stone. "There *is* no connection between those deaths and these. None."

"How can you be so sure?"

She rolled her eyes, then heaving a tremendous sigh, said, "Fine. I'll give you something we never released. The Vegas killer was right handed." She lifted her right arm, bent at the elbow and drew an invisible blade across the front of her neck. "The throat was cut left to right. But the Slasher—"

"Is left-handed," he said.

"That's right. Every neck out here was cut right to left. Can't be the same killer Ash. You're barking up the wrong tree, and I have better things to do than stand here and listen while you do."

She started for the door. Ash lunged after her, gripping her arm. She stopped, but refused to face him. "There is a connection and you know it. If it isn't you, then I have to find out what it is, or this lunatic will go on killing. Is that what you want?"

Her spine was rigid as she twisted her arm from his grasp. "I thought you knew me better. We dated, for God's sake. We were friends. You know, you're obsessed with this case. You were objective before *she* came into it. Now it's like nothing else exists. She's involved up to her neck, Ash, and you're scrambling to get her out. But it's not gonna work."

"She's not involved in anything."

"Tell it to a cop without instincts, pal. She's hiding something, and I'm going to find out what it is before you manage to pin this whole thing on me just to clear her."

He started to argue, but she whirled on him. "Don't deny you're trying to protect her."

"I wasn't going to." He pushed a hand through his hair. "But you can hardly blame me for wanting to look out for my wife."

"I can if she's guilty."

"I *know* she had nothing to do with the murders. I know it as sure as I know my own name, Bev. I wouldn't cover for her if I thought—"

"Hell, Coye, you're so head over heels in love with her you don't know what you're doing. But I'll tell you what you're *not* doing. You're not setting me up to take a fall, just to clear her." She shook her head slowly, turning again toward the door. "Must be nice to have somebody care enough to put their own head on the block for you. Does she know how much risk you're taking for her? Your career could be in the toilet, Ash. Is she aware of that?" She gripped the doorknob, yanked the door open. "Call me when you get your precious test results back. Then you'll know I'm not moonlighting as a crazed killer and maybe listen to what I have to say."

She stalked out into the night, slamming the door behind her. Ash heard her car start and move away a second later. He paced, rubbing one palm over his nape in a vain effort to ease the knot of tension coiled there. This was like beating his head against a brick wall, and he was beginning to doubt his skull could outlast the bricks. There was a kernel of truth to what Bev had said. If Joey turned out to be guilty and it came out that he'd lied for her, his career would be over. He might even end up serving time.

But it was a moot point since she wasn't guilty and had nothing whatsoever to do with the murders. Nothing.

He stopped pacing, sighed and felt his gaze drawn again toward the darkened doorway that must lead to the kitchen. Well, he was here. He might as well get a firsthand look at the crime scene, much as that thought disagreed with his stomach.

He approached the doorway with caution and reached through it to pat the wall in search of a light switch.

Joey had found Ted alone, watching television. She didn't even bother to knock. As soon as she saw him through the window, and her car nowhere in sight, she got out of there, found a quiet spot and called Radley Ketchum. The man had given her his home number when he'd asked her to keep tabs on Ash for him, and she was glad now that he had.

Rad answered in a sleepy voice, but came alert as soon as she explained the situation and asked for Beverly Issacs's home address. He recited it, and Joey hung up while he was still barking questions. Bev's house was only five minutes away. Joey skidded into the driveway in under three and a half.

The lights were on inside, but the house was silent. No car sat in the driveway, dammit. Joey walked around the small Cape Cod, peering through windows, searching for any sign of Ash or Beverly. Her heart plummeted...and then a tiny red light, flashing insistently, caught her eye. She did a double take. An answering machine? Seriously? Hell, it was worth a shot

She continued around the house until she found an unlatched window, pushed it up and climbed inside. Then she went directly to the machine and depressed the Playback button....

Bev's recorded message played, and then there was a beep followed by Ash's voice. The machine had still been recording when Bev picked up the phone to talk to him. It had recorded their entire conversation.

Twenty minutes later, Joey lurked outside the small house in Central Square. She'd shut the bike off and coasted down the last stretch of road, parking in the shadows behind a huge oak tree. No one would notice it there. She saw Beverly go inside, and knew Ash was already there because her car was parked by the curb. Silently, she crept closer to listen in.

Something in the center of her chest throbbed when she heard Ash defending her, and heard Beverly say he was too in love to know what he was doing. God, she wished it could be true. She knew too well, though, that it wasn't. Ash might be protecting her, but only because he thought she was his wife and saw it as his duty. When he learned the truth...

At least she knew he wasn't seriously jeopardizing his career by covering for her. She wasn't guilty, and she'd make damned sure no one else ever learned that he'd lied to protect her.

Beverly exited the front door, and Joey ducked lower in the shrubs. She breathed the scent of green leaves and night air as she waited. When Bev's car left, she waited some more, thinking Ash would come out a moment later, then worrying anew when he didn't.

She slipped out of the shrubs and peered through the window into the living room. Ash wasn't there, but a light glowed from another room. Shadows in there moved. She went around to the back of the house slowly, peeking through one window after another, her fear for him growing. The dark, clawed hand that had a grip on her mind tightened. She felt an instinctive panic bubbling up inside her and fought to keep herself rational, calm, ready. But her pulse accelerated and her heart throbbed.

Ash stood in the center of a small kitchen, his face twisted into a grimace. One hand rose to cover his nose and mouth, as he turned slowly, examining the room. Joey moved to the next window to see what he was looking at, then finally stepped right up to the glass panel in the back door.

Her breath caught in her throat. Dark stains marred the kitchen floor. Ugly spatters dotted the walls, and the fridge, taking odd, grotesque shapes, even seeming to move....

Wait, that one stain *was* moving.

No, not a stain, a shadow! An arm lifting, a slender pointed blade clutched in its fist as it came flying downward toward Ash's throat.

Joey threw the door open, slamming it into the dark form. "Ash!"

There was a thud as the person hit the wall. Joey hurled herself at Ash, knocking him backward right through the doorway into the living room. They both crashed to the floor, Joey landing on top of Ash. Terrified, she scrambled to her feet spun around and faced the darkened kitchen. She saw nothing, only a darker shape amid the blackness. She stepped closer, put herself squarely in between Ash and that darkness.

"Come on, you son of a bitch," she said. He chin came up, and her shoulders squared.

Ash got to his feet behind her. His hands closed on her shoulders, but Joey stiffened her stance, refusing to be moved aside. She focused her full attention on the dark form moving closer. One hesitant step, then two.

"Come on," Joey said. "Yeah, that's it. Closer." She spread her arms as if to shield Ash. She was panting, and her heart thudded so hard in her chest that it made her entire body pulse with every beat. "You want him, you're gonna have to go through me. But the minute you touch me, I'll know who you are. I almost know now. I can feel it. That's why we're so connected, you and I. You're sick and evil, and I'm the one who's gonna stop you. I'm the only one who can. So come on, if you think you have time. Let's wrap this up right here, tonight."

The figure froze in the middle of the dark room, but only briefly. Then it turned, and in a burst of dark motion, it was gone, through the back door and into the night.

Ash lunged to go after it, but Joey, gripped his upper arm and held on for all she was worth. She shook with reaction, every bit of that unexpected steely strength draining from her in a rush.

Finally, he gathered her to his chest and held her there. "You're insane, you know that?" He held her away from him, searching her face. "You okay?"

She nodded, then stiffened as something warm and wet touched her palm when she slid her hands around his neck. Her blooded rush to her feet. Dizziness swamped her, and she drew her hand away, staring first at it, then at the red stain on his throat.

"My God! Ash, you're cut!"

He touched his throat, gave his head a shake. "It's just a scratch. You pummeled that maniac with the door just in time." His eyes darkened, and a frown furrowed his brows. "You could have got yourself killed, Joey."

"So could you. Are you nuts, coming here alone in the middle of the night to meet a suspect?"

Headlights bounced through the front windows. Tires skidded, and a second later Radley Ketchum surged through the front door. "What the—?" He swore a blue streak when he saw the blood on Ash's neck and rushed forward.

"It's nothing, Rad."

"I saw her, Coye! I actually saw her, running down the street. Tall woman. Still had the knife in her hand. I thought you'd be dead by the time I got here."

"I would've been if it hadn't been for Joey." He slipped an arm around her and held her closer. "Which way was our Slasher going?"

"East, but she veered off into a backyard and could've changed direction. I called the cops from the cell."

Rad rushed into the kitchen, flicked on the light and ran cold water over a clean white hanky he took from his pocket. He returned, and Ash flinched when Rad pressed the cloth to his throat. He took the cloth out of Rad's hand and held it to the wound himself. "So what are you doing here, Rad? How'd you know—?"

"I called him." Joey seemed to think it was her turn with the wet cloth. She shoved Ash's hand aside and held the hanky in her own. "I knew you'd gone to meet someone you suspected. I checked Ted's and found him home alone, so I called Radley to get Beverly Issacs's address."

Ash looked down at her. She kept her gaze on his neck. "And?"

She scrunched her eyebrows together, chewed her lip. "You're not going to like it, but then I didn't much like you slipping out and leaving my father to watch me." She drew a deep breath. "I sort of broke into Beverly's—"

"Sort of broke in?"

"Well, the window was unlocked. I listened to your conversation on her answering machine. That's how I knew to find you here."

Ash shook his head, visibly upset. "And how did you know, Rad?"

"She sounded so upset on the phone, I decided to

meet her at Bev's place and see if I could help. But by the time I got there, she was shooting off like a rocket on that Harley of hers."

"If you followed her, then what took you so long to get here?"

Joey started at the sound of suspicion in Ash's voice. She glanced up at him, worried that he was beginning to mistrust everyone he knew.

"Your lady love is hell on wheels. She lost me two miles back. I drove around for a while trying to catch sight of her, and then it hit me that I was near one of the crime scenes, so I figured I'd check it out."

Joey lifted the cloth from Ash's neck and shivered. The nick was small, not deep. But right above the jugular. If that blade had cut just a bit deeper...

"Can we just go home?" she asked. "I hate the idea of Caroline and the girls there with no one but my father watching over them."

Sirens sounded and grew louder as she finished the sentence. "You can go ahead if you want, Joey." Ash stroked her hair. "I'm gonna have to stick around and answer questions."

She gripped the hand that stroked her hair and held it still. "Dammit, Ash, don't you get it? There's a serial killer after you. I don't want you out of my sight again, not even for a second."

She bristled when he smiled. "My little bodyguard, right?"

"This is no laughing matter."

"Who's laughing? You just saved my skin." His smile faded, and his eyes took on a serious gleam. "You did, you know. But if you'd been hurt doing it, I'd never have forgiven you. Or myself." He pulled her close, surrounding her with his arms.

"Hell of a woman, you got there, Ash," Radley said. "You were that close, huh Joey?"

She nodded. "So close. I am so close to knowing who it is. It's right there, it's just...just barely out of reach."

Ash held her tighter. "You were too close. Dammit, Joey, don't risk so much for me. I don't know what I'd do if anything happened to you."

The police came in, Bev Issacs leading the way. "I heard the address dispatched on the radio in my car before I got five miles away. What the hell happened?"

Joey and Ash exchanged glances, and she knew he was wondering the same thing she was. Had Beverly ever *really* left?

CHAPTER 15

Joey sat on the dock in a wooden chair long past its prime, trying not to feel a killer's heart lurking inside her. She felt it invading her again and again, growing stronger with each attack. She felt its evil, its darkness and its rage. She felt its hatred. And she battled it with the love she felt for Ash, for her sister, for her nieces.

She was going to sit in a corner somewhere and go quietly insane.

He could have died last night by the Slasher's blade. God, what if he had? What would she have done if he had?

Quiet. Peace. She needed it in megadoses right now. She still shook all over when she thought of last night. That blade. The killer. So close. That blinding explosion in her mind when she'd stood face-to-face with the embodiment of the shadow of death. When she'd understood, at last, why her fate was entwined with that of a murderer. She had to stop the Slasher. Maybe it was the entire purpose in her having this "gift." Maybe this was what fate had intended by bestowing it. It was a daunting prospect. She wasn't sure she could live up to it.

"You're not relaxing."

Ash massaged her neck and shoulders. His warm breath stirred her hair and his body heat warmed her back. She stared out over the muddy river, her eyes tracing the current and the dapples of orange fire on the water ignited by the rising sun. "Sorry. I'm trying."

"You didn't sleep last night."

"You did," she told him. "I don't know how you could, when you'd just come within an inch of—"

"Don't think about that."

She turned to face him, head tilted up. "Ash, I can't *not* think about it. I almost lost you—"

"But you didn't." He slid his arms around her waist, crossing them at the small of her back and pulling her tight to him. "And you're not going to."

Tears swam in her vision. "Yes, I am. I am, and it's killing me. When you remember...when you know..."

"Go on." He searched her face, his gaze intense. "When I know what?"

She bit her lip and closed her eyes, willing herself to screw up enough courage to be honest with him for once, even as she realized she couldn't. She couldn't let him storm out of her life. Not yet. Not until he was safe from the wrath of the Slasher. Maybe he'd hate her in the end, but it was worth that price to save his life.

Damn, but fate was asking a lot of her.

"I know there's something you've been keeping from me, Joey. Something big, important."

She opened her eyes and let his probe them as she battled inwardly with her urge to be honest and her need to protect him.

"Tell me, Joey. Trust me."

His melted-chocolate eyes were darker than she'd ever seen them. She felt trapped in their depths and felt them pulling her deeper. Like quicksand. She could drown in those eyes and not regret it. God, how she loved him. And it went against everything she believed to love a man this much and still lie to him. Maybe he would understand. Maybe he would find a way to forgive.

"Ash...I'm not really—"

She broke off as her name was shouted. Blinking away her surprise at how close she'd just come to ruining everything, she got up and turned to see Ted loping down the lawn toward the river. For just an instant, she'd thought it was her father. The tall, long-limbed build, the straight-backed stance. She had never realized how much Ted resembled her stepdad. Maybe that was why Caroline had chosen him.

She heard Ash's frustrated sigh, but kept her eyes on Ted as he came to a stop on the dock. He was not in a good mood.

"Caroline up yet?"

Joey frowned. How could he know Caro was here? Dad had taken her minivan back to his hotel last night, so Ted couldn't have seen it parked out front "Ted, I don't—"

"You've always been a lousy liar, Joey. So don't bother. Your father called me last night. I know Caroline and the girls are here."

"She was still sleeping last time I checked, Ted." Ash stepped off the dock, one arm slung around Joey's shoulders to propel her along beside him, and to support some of her weight. "Come on up to the house and have some coffee. Brit and Beth will have her awake any time now, if they don't already."

Joey planted her feet and glared up at Ash, then turned her gaze on Ted. "Look, if my sister wants to see you, she'll let you know."

Ted shook his head. "Not this time, Joey. I have to see her. We've got to talk this out, her and I." He opened his mouth to say more, then snapped it shut again. "How is she? Did she read the diary yet?"

Joey frowned. "I can't believe that bastard told you—"

"What, Joey? The precious family secret? I'm family, too, don't forget."

Ash's arm tightened on her. "He had a right to know, Joey. What's going on between Caroline and your father is having a direct impact on their marriage. You can't deny that."

She tugged free. "The only thing hurting Ted's marriage to my sister is Ted." She took a step closer to her brother in law, tipping her head up to look at him, her breaths coming faster in her anger. "Sneaking out nights, lying about where you were going, spending huge sums of money on God knows what, mysterious phone calls and meetings at all hours. You think she's an idiot? You think she doesn't know what you've been up to?"

"The only thing I've been *up* to is looking out for my wife's hellion sister!"

"Looking out for me? What in hell is that supposed to mean? Dammit, Ted, don't spin me some fairy tale. I trusted you. I loved you like a brother, for God's sake, and you let me down. You let my sister down. You broke both our hearts when you were unfaithful."

He gaped as if searching for words. But it was Ash's deep voice that broke the strained silence. "Just like your stepfather did, right, Joey?"

She closed her eyes at the pain of those words hitting home like well aimed arrows. Then she opened them slowly and met Ted's tortured stare.

He looked drained. "I was afraid it was you, Joey," he said slowly. "I couldn't tell Caroline. She'd have hated me for thinking it. God knows I couldn't go to the police. I wanted to protect you from them, get you some help..."

Joey puckered her face and shook her head. "What help? What are you talking about?"

"The murders. You've been so obsessed with them, and since the beginning you've been...different. Strange, preoccupied. I knew your feelings for your father."

She felt her eyes widen in horror. "You thought *I* was the Slasher?"

He looked at the ground between them. "Not at first. At first I just wanted to know why you were so involved in the crimes. But once I hired the P.I. and started getting his reports..." He shook his head. "There were the cigarette butts, the way you were seen at the crime scenes...and then this thing with Ash. Hell, Joey, what was I supposed to think?"

"You hired a private investigator?"

Ted nodded. "That's where the money went. Those were the secret meetings and phone calls. I didn't want Caroline to know."

Joey felt like she'd been hit with a hammer. She couldn't even justify feeling angry with Ted for suspecting her. Hadn't she been on the verge of suspecting *he* was the Slasher? She lowered her head, released all her breath in a rush. "God, you're an idiot, Ted." When she looked at him again she asked, "So do you still think I'm a crazed murderess?"

"My P.I. says the Slasher has made two attempts

on Ash, both while you were with him. I guess you're exonerated."

"Your faith in me is astonishing." She turned, and the three of them began walking again, toward the house. "So what if your P.I. had found out I *was* the Slasher, Ted? What were you going to do then?"

Ted's brow furrowed. "I have a stack of information on various mental hospitals in the shop."

"So you were gonna lock me away in a psych ward?"

"I figured it would be better than prison."

When they walked inside, Ted was assaulted by his daughters, still in their matching purple nightgowns with a well-known little girl explorer on the front. They leapt into his arms and he caught them with practiced ease, one on each side. He kissed them both, then his gaze moved past them to Caroline. She stood at the foot of the stairs in her pajamas, her long wavy hair pulled into a ponytail.

"I've missed you, Caroline."

She nodded. "Me, too."

"We need to talk."

Ash heaved a sigh of relief when the four of them left for an overnight getaway. God, the look of bliss on Caroline's face after she and Ted had spent an hour talking alone had almost had Ash choking back tears. He no longer suspected Ted had anything to do with the murders. Partly due to instinct, but mainly because he had proof. While Caroline and Joey were packing the girls' things upstairs, Ash had had a heart-to-heart with Ted. Not only had Ted produced the name of the P.I. he'd hired, but he had also shown Ash some of the reports he'd had from the man. It was obvious the P.I. *had* been investigating the Slasher killings and trying to find evidence of Joey's involvement, or lack thereof. Ted would hardly hire someone to find out if Joey was the Slasher, if he were the Slasher himself.

Cross one more suspect off the list, he thought glumly. He hated to think Beverly Issacs was a killer. But it was looking more and more like that was the case.

At least Caroline and the girls would be out of harm's way tonight and tomorrow. They'd all packed into the wagon to head up north to a popular theme park, where the girls could raise hell to their hearts' content, and Ted would have time to romance his wife.

The lucky bastard.

Ash looked to the sofa, where Joey had collapsed as if exhausted. She sat there now, and her gaze kept straying to the diary on the coffee table.

"There's time now," he said softly. "You can read it if you want."

She met his gaze, shook her head. "I don't know if I can."

"I'll leave, give you some privacy—"

"No. If you go, I know I won't be strong enough to do it."

"Then..."

"Read it with me?"

Ash tilted his head slightly.

"Sit beside me, and hold me close, and read it with me, Ash."

There was so much in her eyes. Pain, fear and something else, reaching out to him with a magnetic pull. There was some sticky, invisible substance that seemed to want to meld him to her—soul to soul, pain to pain.

It was an intensely private thing she was asking him to share. And he couldn't have refused her even if he'd wanted to.

He sat beside her, and she curled close to him. He put an arm around her shoulders, and she pressed her head into the crook beneath his chin. She lifted a hand, reaching for the little book, but the hand stopped in midair and began to tremble.

He kissed the top of her head and picked up the diary. He opened it to the first entry and held it low, so they both could read.

Clouds roiled outside, dark black masses blotted out the sun, and thunder reverberated in the distance. Joey sobbed as she hadn't done since she was a child. Violent, racking, uncontrollable spasms that tried to snap her diaphragm in two. And Ash held her tighter all the time. He kissed her. He made love to her with tender caresses and gentle touches and seemed to absorb part of her pain into himself. And later he bathed her face with a cool cloth.

Her life had been a lie. Everything she'd ever believed about her parents, her family, had been make-believe. Everything her father had told her was true. They'd never been in love. Her mother had been the first to indulge in an affair, with Joey's biological father. But her stepdad had forgiven her. He'd understood, her mother had written. He was truly the best man she'd ever known. And later, they'd both fallen in love with someone else. They'd only remained together for their daughters, and neither could bring themselves to tell the truth.

Her father had, last night. She hadn't believed him

then. She still didn't want to believe any of this, but it was unavoidable now. All the proof she'd needed had been shown to her, in her mother's own hand.

And there was more. Tito del Rio, the man who had fathered her, Toni's dad, had fathered other children. And her mom and dad had found the names of two of them. Caitlin Rossi, a billionaire heiress from Maine, and Alexandra Holt, who was a doctor in Manhattan. Toni had lived in New York City and never known she had a sister so nearby.

"You okay, Joey?"

Ash was pulling a big, soft brush through her hair, his strokes soothing her aching head as he worked. God, he was going to a lot of trouble to make her feel better.

She'd worshiped her parents once. Then she'd grieved for her mother and despised her father. And now... now....

"I don't know how to feel, Ash."

"Give it some time. It'll come to you. I promise."

She shook her head. "I don't know."

"It will. You're still reeling from the shock. In a day or two that will fade, and you'll know how to deal with this."

She closed her eyes as he pulled the brush through her hair. Then he set the brush aside and replaced it with his fingers. "I couldn't have done this without you. You took away the pain, Ash, and I wish..."

He moved around in front of her, knelt down and stared up into her eyes. "You wish?"

"I wish I could do the same for you. I wish I could take away the hurt your mother caused." She saw his face tighten, but she caught it between her palms gently and she lowered her head to kiss him. "If I could go back in time, I would. I'd be with you in that closet every time.

And I'd hold you, love you, until the door opened again."

She saw his eyes widen in wonder, just before the telephone shrilled and broke the fragile bond she'd felt forming between them. Ash rose, averting his gaze. He reached for the phone as Joey searched her mind for some way to heal his oldest, deepest wound.

He spoke softly, then hung up. "Ted," he told her, his eyes still not quite meeting hers.

"Problem?"

"They're worried about Felix. He was outside when they left for the park. They couldn't find him to put him inside, and they just heard it's going to storm tonight. We've been elected to drive over there, find the cat and put him in. Ted says you have a key."

She nodded, glancing toward the the window. "We'd better hurry. Looks like it's going to pour any minute."

Her prediction proved all too accurate. Ash drove Joey's car through the deluge, wipers swashing back and forth in a frantic attempt to clear the windshield. She hoped it would let up a little by the time they got to Caro's house, but it rained all the harder as they pulled to a stop in the driveway, huge droplets ricocheting off the car's hood like tiny explosions.

After exchanging one long do-or-die glance, they both leapt out of the car and went in opposite directions, calling "Kitty, kitty" at the tops of their lungs just to be heard over the rain.

Joey finally heard an answering pathetic yowl and followed the sound. Felix sat in the tree house on the back lawn, peering down at her and crying over and over.

"Ash, he's out here!"

Ash joined her. His hair was plastered to his head, rivulets of water running down his nose. She laughed. He lifted his arms from his sides in a helpless gesture, then squinted at her. "Don't knock it, princess, you're pretty soggy yourself." He hugged her hard, gave her a long, wet kiss, then strode purposefully toward the tree and mounted the ladder. "If this doesn't elevate me to prince status, then nothing will."

He climbed the tree, picked up Felix and then struggled to hold on to the frightened eighteen-pound cat all the way back down. They ran around the house again, and Joey quickly unlocked the door.

Inside, Ash put the cat down. He looked down at his dripping wet clothes, and at the puddles forming around their feet. "Now what?"

Felix tilted his head up and yowled plaintively.

"We get dry. Come on up. I'll find us something of Caro and Ted's to wear home. They won't mind. Especially since we saved Felix from a fate worse than death."

"You sure?"

She nodded, reached down to scoop up the cat and led the way up the stairs. She pointed Ash toward the bedroom, while she carried Felix into the bathroom to rub him down with a towel. A few minutes later, Ash joined her, wearing a pair of Ted's jeans and a sweater. He reached for another towel and rubbed his hair dry.

"Hurry and change, Joey."

"Felix could catch pneumonia."

"So could you."

Their eyes met, and Joey's hands stilled on the cat. Felix twisted from her grip and jumped gracelessly to the floor, his fur sticking up in odd patterns, a black patch laying one way, a white patch another, some sticking straight up. Ash swallowed and cleared his throat. "Might as well hang out here until the rain stops."

Joey nodded. "Looks like it might be a while."

"Yeah. I'd better let Rad know where to reach us."

"There's a phone in the kitchen. Why don't you see if you can scare up a hot drink while you're at it. Caroline usually has cocoa mix in the cupboard."

"Okay." Ash started to turn away. Then he looked back at her. There was a longing in his eyes, a glow of something she didn't recognize. "Joey, I..." He bit his lip, then shook his head. "Later. Change now, your lips are turning blue."

I love you. That was what she'd thought he was going to say. *Joey, I love you.* So was that her psychic receptor picking up on a phrase that was practically screaming from his mind? Or was it wishful thinking rearing its persistent head yet again? She watched him go, then shivered and hurried into Caroline's bedroom to find some dry clothes.

It didn't take long. She pulled out a pair of warm, comfy gray sweats and an oversized T-shirt. She found some thick socks and even borrowed a pair of tennis shoes from Caro's closet. Brushing her hair and wielding the blow-dryer, she took out most of the moisture.

As she worked she realized that she hadn't been hurting over the diary's revelations. It seemed the shock had been what rocked her at first, and now the knowledge seemed to be settling in her mind and in her heart, rather than eating away at them. When she'd first learned she had another sister, she'd looked Toni up and and arranged a meeting. They'd become very close very quickly. She wouldn't trade that relationship for the world. And now there were two more half-sisters whose names she knew. Maybe two more chances for relationships just as special, just as precious. She glanced toward the phone and thought about calling her father at the hotel, at least just to tell him she'd read the diary. She recalled the pain in his face when she'd spoken to him, called him a liar. She'd branded him a cheat, a heartless bastard. She'd been wrong. She was still angry, or perhaps just hurt, that her parents had lied to her. But she'd convicted an innocent man of the wrong crime. Didn't he deserve this? Just one, brief call?

Ash ought to be finished with the phone by now. She reached for it, still undecided, but when she brought it to her ear, she heard voices. Ash's and Rad's. She shook her head and started to replace the receiver.

"Then she's still lying to you," Radley grumbled.

Joey frowned at the earpiece and slowly pressed the phone back to her ear.

"She almost told me the truth today, Rad. I know she wants to. It's only a matter of time—"

"You don't *have* time, Ash. Look, I like her. I do. But maybe it's time to just tell her the damned amnesia was a ruse all along, and that you've known she was lying about the marriage from the start. Force her to come clean so we can get to the bottom of this."

"Rad, I can't—"

The receiver fell from her suddenly numb hand and clattered to the floor. She heard a male voice ask, "What was that?" but ignored it. She turned, stricken, and sank onto her sister's bed, staring into space, seeing nothing, feeling her heart begin to bleed.

She heard Ash swear, then silence from the fallen receiver. Hurried footsteps came next. He stood in the doorway, and she knew he was staring at her, at the receiver on the floor, at her again.

"Joey?"

She didn't look at him. She couldn't, or she'd break down. "You knew. You knew all along."

"Joey, it isn't—"

"Didn't you?"

He was silent for a long moment. Then, "Yes."

"And yet you deceived me. You never had amnesia."

"*I* deceived *you?* Joey, you told me you were my *wife.*"

"And you pretended to believe me. Why?"

He came closer, reached out to touch her face, but she ducked away and he let his hand fall to his side. "Because I needed to find out what you were up to. I thought it might have something to do with the murders, and I had to know for sure."

She nodded stiffly. "For a story. You turned me inside out for a story."

"You're twisting this whole thing inside out, Joey. *You're* the one who started this deception, not me. You going to tell me you had a better reason than I did?"

Finally she lifted her chin and met his eyes. The tears in her own prevented her from reading whatever emotions might be there. "I know that bastard is going to kill my sister. I saw it. She was lying on the floor, facedown, the back of her T-shirt covered in blood, the ends of her beautiful hair tinged crimson, that dagger on the floor near her. The Slasher standing over her. And I saw you. *You* are the victim just before Caroline. The Slasher will kill you before he kills her. I had to break the chain, and I sensed I had to break it with you."

His eyes widened more with every word she spoke, and he searched her face. "You came up with this whole crazy scheme to protect your sister?"

"At first. But almost as soon as I met you, it became just as important to me to keep you alive, Ash. *You* made me feel that way. You let me think...and all the time... God, I made love to you, Ash! How could you let me do that when you knew, when you were only pretending?"

"Joey, no. I wasn't—"

"You let me fall in love with you! Damn you. Damn you, Ash!" She got to her feet and started for the door.

"Wait!"

She froze, but didn't turn to face him.

"You...you *love* me?"

Her spine stiffened. God, he'd played her well, acting as if he cared when in truth... Tears streamed over her face, but she wouldn't let him see. Tearing the fake ring from her finger, she dropped it onto the floor. Then she raced down the stairs and out the front door, never looking back. She dashed through the rain to the car, started the motor and took off, spinning the tires on the wet pavement, fishtailing before lurching forward.

CHAPTER 16

Ash picked up the simple gold band, stared at it. Dammit to hell, she was a freaking lunatic! Angry at him for lying to her when she'd told a whopper as big as his. Bigger. Blaming him for letting her fall in love.

In love.

My God, she loved him. He stood stock-still in the bedroom and let that information seep into his bones, into his heart. He felt something stir deep inside. That old longing. That little boy he'd tried to lock away, the one who had yearned for love more than for air or warmth or even light. The deep pit inside him wasn't so empty anymore. And it shook Ash to realize that it hadn't been for some time. Because even though she hadn't vocalized it, Joey had been steadily filling it up with her words, her touch, her presence. God, her kisses, her body, her very breaths, had all been filling that well inside him. It wasn't empty at all anymore. It was filled to bursting; *he* was filled to bursting. No wonder he'd had such confusing emotions about Joey. He loved her right back.

He heard the car pull away. He couldn't lose her. Not now. He had to make her understand why he'd done what he had.

He started for the stairway to go after her. Then he realized he couldn't do that. She'd left him without wheels. Think! Hell, he couldn't let her go on another minute believing what she'd just accused him of—that none of this had meant a thing to him, that he'd been playing a role all along. He hadn't been doing that any more than she had.

He paced some more, then stopped at the telephone still on the floor. He'd call her. He'd talk her into coming back, or just tell her what he had to tell her on the phone. He'd make her listen. God, he was only just beginning to realize why she meant so much to him. She'd done what he'd believed could never be done. She'd healed that child inside him. She'd given him the ability to love. He had to tell her that.

Her cell phone went straight to voice mail, so he tried the landline. It rang endlessly, but no one answered. Frustrated, he slammed the receiver down. Okay, she just hadn't had time to get home yet. He'd give her five minutes. Five minutes, no more. Then he'd call again. And if she still didn't pick up, he'd get to her if he had to crawl. And in the meantime, he'd ponder this some more, decide how best to explain this to her, what to say. It would have to be perfect. She was angry.

He paced the bedroom floor, rehearsing lines, tucking the ring into his pocket.

When he heard the car in the driveway, he stiffened. She was back! His heart skidded to a halt in his chest when he realized it would be now or never. He'd have to make her understand or....

His heart sank when someone else appeared in the doorway instead of Joey. "Damn. What are you doing here?"

Joey paced. Then she cried. Then she paced some more. It was nothing. Ash felt nothing for her. He was hard-nosed, stubborn, ready to do anything necessary to get this story. He'd used her all along. God, he'd used her own lie against her, even slept with her. While she'd been losing herself to him, heart and soul, he'd probably been laughing at how far she'd go to carry off her charade. But she hadn't made love to him to convince him the marriage was real. She'd done it because she loved him. She loved him...still.

She groaned deep in her throat and realized this was going to hurt for a long, long time. Then she stilled as grim laughter filled her mind. Not her own. Nothing this evil could come from her.

The Slasher.

The maniac prowled somewhere out there tonight, enveloped in darkness, sheltered by the storm itself.

Her vision! God, how could she have left Ash alone when she knew he could be next? What if it was too late?

What if that blade had already ripped across the tight skin of his throat? She ran to the phone, yanked up the receiver. She would call, just to make sure he was okay. Then she would get back to him. She'd...

No dial tone. The phone is dead.

Okay. It doesn't mean anything. Think! Think of the vision. Try and see the area around Ash, when he's lying on the floor. Could it be Caroline's house? Could that be where it happens?

She strained to conjure the vision in her mind, but instead of Ash's body on the floor, she saw Caroline's. She lay facedown, on a brown sculpted carpet. It could have been the carpet in Joey's own living room. Her long, multicolored waves were loose and spread over her back. The ends had soaked some of the blood from the back of the oversized gray T-shirt and—

Joey went perfectly still and her heart seemed to trip to a stop in her chest. The T-shirt in the vision... She glanced down at herself. It was the one she was wearing right now. Again she sought details in the image she'd foreseen. It could be her, not Caroline at all. Their hair was alike. She'd only assumed she saw her sister in the vision because of the signature clothing the woman on the floor wore. But the face hadn't been visible. And Joey was wearing those exact clothes right now.

And the phone was dead.

Her heart began functioning again, hammering so hard against her ribs that her body shook with the percussions. She had to get to Ash. The killer would hit him before her. She was certain of that. And she might already be too late.

She turned toward the door. Thunder rattled the windows and lightning flashed for an instant. A dark silhouette was framed beyond the curtains of the sliding-glass door. Not Ash, and not a woman. A man.

The Slasher was here already. Finished with Ash. It was Joey's turn now.

"God, please, no," she whispered, limping slowly on trembling legs toward the stairs. "Please don't let Ash be dead. Please." Maybe he was still alive. Maybe, if she could get help to him in time, he could survive. He'd been lying still in the vision, but that didn't have to mean he was dead. It didn't...it couldn't.

She found the stairs and climbed them. She walked softly, trying not to make even the tiniest sound, into her bedroom, to the nightstand. Carefully she opened the drawer, pulled out the gun.

She extracted the clip, made sure it held all the bullets it could hold, then slipped it inside again.

Glass shattered downstairs. She clapped a hand to her mouth to keep from screaming and tiptoed fast to the bedroom door, closing it and turning the lock. She retreated to the far side of the room and huddled in the corner, gun ready.

Footsteps sounded on the stairs. Heavy ones. Then they sounded in the hall. They stopped.

Joey trembled from head to toe as she waited for the knob to jiggle, or for the door to splinter beneath a heavy blow. But nothing came.

She waited longer, and still nothing. Not a sound, or a step, or anything at all. What was happening? Maybe the killer had given up, or left to search somewhere else. She had to find a way to get to Ash. She couldn't huddle in this corner all night while he might be bleeding to death at her sister's house. She had to help him.

Slowly, silently, she crept back to the bedroom door, the gun held in a two-fisted, white-knuckled grip. She moved closer and closer, straining to hear a sound or movement. She opened her mind and tried to home in on the evil presence that had invaded her home, her very being. But she found nothing there. She bent low, pressing her ear to the door.

It smashed open suddenly, cracking the side of her head and sending her sprawling. The gun skittered across the floor and under the bed. The door hit the wall behind it. Joey shook her head to clear it and scrambled to her feet.

The Slasher stood in the doorway, soaked in rain. There was a thin layer of dark, curling hair on muscled arms that ended in fine black gloves of kid leather, with those two tiny buttons she knew so well. And clutched in one of those gloved hands was the double-edged dagger, its jeweled handle glinting in the dim room. The face was one she recognized, but still it took a moment to sink in.

Radley Ketchum.

Ash fought his way to consciousness, a single, blood-chilling phrase ringing over and over again in his mind. "Where is the little woman?" Rad had asked.

Ash had turned to grab his still-wet jacket. "Her place. And I'm glad you're here, cause I could use a ride."

That was it. One large blow to the back of his head, and he'd gone down in a heap. He had no idea how long he'd been out. But he knew Rad had hit him.

Joey. Rad was after Joey, and he'd blurted out where she was. Home. Alone.

God, he couldn't believe it was Rad. Ash struggled to roll over, then pulled himself into a sitting position. His head was screaming. He was dizzy. He reached for the phone on the nightstand and brought it to his ear, dialing quickly. He asked the cop who answered at the station to put him through to Beverly, then waited until he heard her voice.

"Bev...it's Ash."

"You don't sound too good. Been drinking?"

His voice was slurred, but not from alcohol. "The Slasher...it's Radley."

Silence.

"You hear me? It's Radley."

"No. it's not."

"Then why did he just bash me over the head and take off?"

"He what?"

"He's on his way to Joey's house right now, and she's there alone. Get out there. Hurry."

He slammed the phone down as she began shouting questions. Then he picked it up again and punched Joey's number. It rang endlessly, but no one answered.

His heart was rapidly turning into a lump of stone in his chest. Either she'd changed her mind and was on her way back, or the storm had knocked the phones out...or he was too late.

He got to his feet, still unsteady, staggered down the stairs and out into the rain. The car was gone, but in front of the shop beside the house, Ted's pickup sat. Ash loped crookedly to it, yanking open the door.

No keys.

Panic was trying to set in, but Ash fought it. He had to get to Joey. He ran to the shop's door, peered through the glass. Yes. The little key rack had one set dangling from it. Ash smashed the door in with his shoulder, grabbed the pickup key, and took off.

"Why?" Her entire body quaked in fear as she saw the solemn determination in Rad Ketchum's eyes. "God, Radley, why?"

"I have to protect her." He spoke softly, almost kindly. "I'm sorry, Joey. I like you, I really do. And Ash...Dammit, I didn't want to hurt him."

"But you did, didn't you? Did you kill him? Is Ash dead?" The backs of her legs hit the bed, and she began edging sideways, toward its foot.

"Amelia is sick. She's so sick. It's not her fault."

She didn't want to hear it. All she wanted to hear right now was that Ash wasn't dead, or dying. But she had to buy time, keep him from killing her until she could get away from him. "Ash said it was cancer. I'm really sorry Radley."

"Not cancer," he said. "That's what I told people to explain it away when she would act so...." He shook his head as if shaking away a memory. "Freaking quack psychiatrist said she was a psychopath. Dangerous. Wanted to lock her away. I couldn't let that happen." He glanced at the dagger in his hand and seemed to remember his mission. He focused on Joey again. "I can take care of her. I was doing fine until she realized I was drugging her to keep her calm. Docile. Bedridden, really, but it was better than letting her keep hunting. She fooled me though. Stopped taking the pills, got out of the house."

"And committed more murders," she said softly.

"I just have to watch her better, that's all. I just have to watch her better."

She said, "Amelia's the Slasher."

He closed his eyes, shook his head. "She can't help it. She doesn't even know she does it, she just...hell, you just don't understand."

She shook her head rapidly. "I'm trying. Really I am."

She'd edged around the bed, and was almost to the bathroom door now. Distract him, she thought. Distract him and then run.

"She feels you inside her head," he said. "She told

me so. She wanted to kill you, but I wouldn't let her. I really didn't want it to come to this. I was gonna frame Bev Issacs for the murders. Put an end to all of this. But Amelia was right. You're too close. You're gonna figure it out and then they'll take her away from me. I can't live without her. I can't."

He was looking at her, violence coming to life in his eyes.

"W-Why do you think she does it, Radley?" Anything to buy some time, she thought. She'd come up with something. She'd find a way out of this.

"She was a ward of the state as a little girl. Terribly abused by a foster parent. I think he's the one she really wants to...hurt."

Joey nodded as if she understood. "But...there was a female victim. In Vegas...."

"That wasn't Amelia," he said. "But she saw Amelia. I couldn't let her tell the police."

Chills raced up Joey's spine and over her nape. So he'd killed too. All to protect his beloved wife. Joey's hand inched toward the door that led to the bathroom. Rad took another step toward her. His gaze caught the movement of her hand and he lashed out with the blade. She shoved the door open and ducked through it, slamming it behind her just in time. Then she sprinted across the bathroom, through its other door into the hall and down the stairs. She ran straight through the living room to the sliding-glass doors, shaking hard, her thigh screaming, her blood pounding in her temples, the echo of her pulse deafening in her ears. She bent low and tore the broom handle out of the track, then flicked the lock up, grasping the handle to pull the door open.

Radley grabbed her from behind and spun her around

so hard her head snapped back as if her neck were made of rubber. One hand caught her hair cruelly, tipping her head to expose her neck. The other lifted, clutching the dagger.

She brought her knee up for all she was worth, heard the forced expulsion of air from his lungs when it connected, and then the thud of the dagger falling to the carpet. He doubled over. She dropped to her knees, her eyes never leaving Radley as she patted the carpet in search of the knife. Then her hand closed on its cool handle.

Touching the weapon caused myriad faces to appear in her mind, and an instant later she realized they were the faces of the Amelia's victims. Innocent, frightened faces. She reached behind her for the door. Rad straightened and took a step toward her. She swung the blade in a wide arc, felt it drag across his chest.

Radley gasped and dropped to his knees in front of her, blood spreading over the front of his shirt. But he was still conscious, and she couldn't turn her back to try to make it through the door. She darted past him, running for the kitchen and those stairs, hoping to make it to the back door. But before she even reached the kitchen, she felt his arms come around her from behind in a brutal bear hug. He tackled her, knocking her to the carpet, squeezing the breath from her body, crushing her ribs, his weight adding to the burn in her thigh. She felt the half healed wound tear open, felt it bleed.

He came down on top of her back, and she could feel the warmth of his blood soaking into her shirt. She swung backward with the dagger, her arm twisted so awkwardly it was painful. The blade sank into his side, and when he jerked instinctively away from the pain, she wrenched herself out from beneath him, scrambling to her feet.

Horror like nothing she'd ever known surrounded her, pummeling her senses, and hysteria tried to take over. She fought it, taking a step back, waiting for a chance. Her stomach lurched as he made it up to his knees, reached down and jerked the blood-slick dagger from his side. He looked down at the blade, then his eyes rolled and he fell forward.

She screamed and jerked away still farther, but her back met the wall. Radley didn't move. He lay motionless, blood steadily seeping into the carpet beneath him.

Trembling so violently her muscles felt as if they'd tear free of her bones, Joey bent low, reached out. Slowly, slowly, her hand inched toward the still bloody one that held the dagger. She gripped the bloody blade and pulled it from its owner's grasp.

He didn't move. He was dead. She'd killed him. He wasn't moving. Why was she still so terrified?

She lifted one foot to step past him, to move toward the door. Then she lifted the other. One more step and she would be beyond his reach. She made her legs move. He was behind her now. The door was only a few feet away.

A warm, sticky hand closed around her ankle with crushing force. She fell forward at the sudden tug on her ankle, cracking her head on the corner of a table before she hit the floor, facedown. She felt the knife fly from her hand, saw it land on the carpet, leaving the outline of its shape, drawn in blood, on the pile.

He was getting up on all fours. He was dragging himself forward. She had to move! She lifted her head, though it screamed in agony when she moved it. The blade lay on the floor ahead of her, and she stretched her arm to reach for it. But her fingers fell short of their goal, and then her mind slowly sank into the depths of a black quagmire.

Through the sliding-glass door, Ash witnessed a nightmare. Joey was lying on the floor, facedown. Her back was covered in blood. She wasn't moving.

Rad stood, hunched over, a grotesque, bloody mess. He stared at Joey and took a step forward.

Ash leapt for the door, knowing it would be locked, intending to kick it in if necessary. But when he jerked on the handle, it slid open. He hurled himself at Radley, smashing him in the face twice, before the big man tottered backward and crashed to the floor like a felled redwood.

Ash dropped to his knees beside him, noticing for the first time the blood pulsing from Rad's side and wondering if it had been his punches or this wound that had brought the man down. The flow of blood slowed. Ash frowned and reached for Rad's neck. There was no pulse.

Agony twisting inside him, he whirled toward Joey, and it hit him that what he was seeing was precisely the image she'd described to him. Except that she'd thought the woman on the floor, her back coated in blood, was Caroline. The truth was too much to take. She had foreseen her own murder. Not her sister's.

"God, Joey, don't die. Not now."

He bent to lift the T-shirt away from her back, hoping he could stop the bleeding and keep her alive until help arrived. Already he heard the sirens in the distance. He bent low, squinting in the poor light to see how bad her injuries were, but he saw only a coating of blood. No cuts. No slashes. No punctures. Not even a scratch.

Frowning hard, he caught her shoulders and gently rolled her onto her back. "Joey? Joey, baby, can you hear me?" His eyes scanned her throat and found it smooth and untouched. Her forehead was gashed open and blood trickled over one side of her face, but it wasn't a mortal wound.

The sirens grew piercing, and then flashing lights came through the still-open glass door, bathing Joey in color. "Joey?"

Her eyes opened. She blinked. "Ash?"

"You're okay..."

"He didn't kill you," she muttered. "He didn't kill you." Tears coursed down her face as he gathered her to him. Her arms tightened around his neck and she clung to him, sobbing softly, words tumbling from her lips the way the tears fell from her eyes.

Bev came in and started barking questions, but Ash held up a hand to silence her.

"It's Radley's wife, Ash," Joey said. "She's the Slasher. She doesn't have cancer at all. She's a psychopath. He's been drugging her to keep her bedridden, and trying to cover for her, protect her. That woman in Vegas was a witness. He killed her to protect Amelia."

"My God. All this time...and Amelia broke her hand," Ash said slowly, rocking Joey in his arms.

"What?"

"Rad said Amelia took a fall, broke her hand. That's why the killer switched from right handed, to left." He closed his eyes, shaking his head.

Bev spoke to an officer behind her. "Get someone

out to the Ketchum residence. Bring Amelia Ketchum in for questioning. And give her a coffee or something so you can get a DNA sample from the cup. That's going to clinch it." She walked back outside, still giving orders.

"Thank God you're all right," Ash said softly, looking Joey over once more to ensure himself that she was.

"I am. I love you, Ash. I do. I don't care about the lies we've told each other or anything else. Just you. It tore me apart to lie to you. I hated it. But you're alive. You're alive and I love you. I love you."

Her tears made it tough to understand all of her words, but Ash knew exactly what she was saying. He still couldn't believe she was all right. He'd thought her dead when he'd first seen her lying there, so still. He stood, scooping her up into his arms as the room filled with cops and an ambulance pulled into the driveway. He ignored the shouted questions, the restraining hands on his arm, and carried her outside, toward the rescue vehicle and the paramedics spilling out of it.

He bent over her, kissing her again and again as he carried her to the ambulance. Then he lowered her to the stretcher the men had just pulled from the back of it and fell to his knees beside it.

"You'll have to get out of the way, sir," one of the medics told him.

"I'm not going anywhere except with my wife." He saw her eyes widen at his words, and he reached into his pocket, pulling out the ring she'd thrown away before. He caught her left hand in his and slipped it onto her finger. "I want you to keep wearing this, Joey."

She frowned at him, ignoring the hands that fastened safety straps across her waist and took her pulse and probed at her injured forehead. "Ash?"

"Just until I have a chance to buy you a real one." He pushed her hair off her face and kissed her lips softly. "I love you, you know. I'm not letting you go. You said you were my wife, and I'm holding you to it."

Another vehicle came bounding up the driveway and skidded to a stop. Matthew Bradshaw, looking frantic, leapt out and ran toward the ambulance. "What's happened? Where's Joey? What's—? My God!" He spotted her, and raced toward her, stopping across from Ash, on her opposite side. Ash had never seen anyone so pale or terrified.

"She's all right, Matt. Just a bump on the head," Ash assured him. "She's gonna be fine."

Matthew leaned over her. "Are you?"

She nodded, lifted a hand and closed it around her father's. "I am," she told him firmly. With her other hand she clasped Ash's, her eyes brimming with love as she stared into his. "I am, Dad. We all are. We're going to be from now on."

"Damn straight we are," Ash told her. "This frog prince is more than ready for his happily ever after."

She smiled as he bent to press his lips to hers, and she knew that happily ever after was exactly what they would have.

Sometimes, ESP was an awfully good thing to have.

EPILOGUE

Joey, Toni, and Caroline sat side by side in lawn chairs near the riverbank, sipping fruity, girlie drinks and watching as Britt and Beth gave the men fishing lessons from the dock, nearby. Toni's puppy, Ralph, took turns racing from one little girl to the other, and they were loving every minute of it.

Joey and Ash had tied the knot as soon as she'd been released from the hospital—on a wild weekend in Vegas. Caroline and Ted were falling in love all over again, it seemed. And Toni was engaged to former FBI agent, Nick Manelli and planning a huge wedding next spring. They were buying a big Victorian near Ithaca, only an hour away.

Joey didn't think she'd ever been happier. And then Toni reached into the tote bag that hung from the back of her lawn chair, pulled out an envelope, and handed it to her.

Joey frowned as she took it. "What's this?"

"Something that's going to piss Caroline off, I'm

afraid," Toni said. She sent Caro a sheepish look. "Another sister you're gonna share her with."

Caroline lifted her brows. "More Christmas and birthday gifts for my girls," she replied. "What's not to love about that?" Then she smiled and sat up in her chair. "Which one did you find, Toni?"

Joey opened the envelope and pulled out a sheaf of papers as Toni said, "Meet Caitlin Rossi, our sister."

A photo of a the most beautiful and sophisticated looking blonde Joey had ever seen, graced the top of the stack of papers. The woman in the photo was leaning against a red Porsche Carrera, holding a pair of designer sunglasses in one hand, and there was a mansion in the background. The shot could've been a cover shot for *Billionaire's Weekly*.

Joey stared at Caitlin, looking for a resemblance to herself or to Toni, and not finding any.

And then suddenly she was behind the wheel of that very car. Her wipers beat against pounding rain and her headlights fought to cut through the pitch black of the night. A hairpin curves appeared as if from nowhere, and she realized with a gasp that she was going too fast. She jerked the wheel and pressed hard on the brake pedal.

But nothing happened.

The car careened toward sharp corner, and she yanked the wheel harder, stomping repeatedly on the useless brakes. She was still stomping as she crashed through the guardrails and sailed into the darkness. And then she began to plummet.

Joey blinked. Her sisters were on either side of her, talking to her, touching her, shaking her. She didn't know when she'd got up onto her feet, but she was standing. The black night and slashing rain had faded away, and she was once again in the bright sunshine of her own backyard, surrounded by her family.

"What is it Joey? What happened?" Caroline asked.

From the dock, Ash was looking her way.

Joey blinked and said, "I think I just saw Caitlin."

"And?" Toni asked.

"I think someone's trying to kill her."

-THE END-

Don't miss the rest of the
SHATTERED SISTERS SERIES.

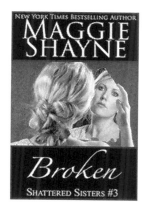

Continue reading for an excerpt from:

BROKEN

Some there be that shadows kiss; Such have but a shadow's bliss.
—William Shakespeare

The pain lanced her head like a dull blade, sawing its way through her skull. At first, that was all she felt. Then, slowly, as if the lights were coming up in a dark theater, other sensations came to life. The hard, irregular shape of her pillow. Her fists clenched around it. The words "steering wheel" surfaced in her brain. She wasn't even certain what that meant. Then it came to her.

Next, she noticed the warm, steady trickle along her neck. She lifted her hand to touch the spot, only to find it soaked and sticky. Her fingers moved upward to trace the source, and located the gash at her temple. She pressed against it and a sharp pain made her wince. Still, she held the pressure there. It would stop the bleeding. She didn't know how she knew that, but she did.

Sounds filtered through the dense fog surrounding her mind. Sizzling...like bacon in a frying pan. No. Rain. It was rain.

Lifting her head slowly brought on a rush of dizziness as she peered through the darkness. Rainwater cascaded in sheets over a shattered windshield. She could see nothing beyond the spiderweb pattern of the broken glass and the rain. Only darkness, filled with the howl of a vicious wind.

At first, she thought the wound to her head was what made her feel off center, out of balance. But when she tried to sit up straighter, she realized the car was at a strange angle, tilted up on its side with the driver's door down.

"I've been in an accident." She said it aloud, trying to take stock and finding it difficult. But the sound of her own voice made her gasp and jerk herself rigid. It wasn't her voice. It couldn't have been. It was the voice of a stranger, a voice she'd never heard before in her life. She blinked rapidly, looking around the car's interior, though she could see little detail in the darkness.

Then there was a flicker of light, a snapping sound, an sharp aroma.

Fire!

Clasping the door handle, she shoved desperately, again and again. It wouldn't budge. Of course it wouldn't, it was pressed to the ground. Panic wasn't doing her any good. She had to think. Gathering her strength, she released her seatbelt and immediately fell against the driver's door. As quickly as she could, she got herself turned around and started to climb up the sloping seat toward the opposite door. Her knee banged against something, a stick shift on the floor. Her skirt caught on it when she tried to move. She tore it free, and the sound of ripping fabric somehow added to the fear exploding inside her mind.

Her body shaking, she groped for the door. It barely moved when she shoved at it. It wouldn't open.

Yes it will, she told herself. *It's not locked and it's not jammed. It's just heavy.* Gravity made it far heavier than a car door ought to be, that was all. The car was tipped up on its side. Her escape hatch was nearly horizontal above her. She pushed with all her might, bracing her feet against the center console. The door lifted, and she summoned every ounce of strength she possessed and pushed harder. It wouldn't remain open on its own. She could only hold it up, her arms straining above her head, as she made her way up and out. She braced one foot on the dashboard, the other on the seat's headrest and shoved herself upward, still holding the door with one hand while trying to find a grip on the outside of the car with the other. Halfway out, her arm buckled, the door dropped onto her back, and she yelped in pain. And yet she kept going, wriggling her way inch by inch out from beneath the weight of the door, and finally out into the punishing rain and brutal wind. She didn't hesitate, but kept going, right off the upright side of the car to the ground below.

Her legs gave way as soon as she hit the slick, muddy earth. She fell, curling into a small ball in the mud. Pain screamed through her entire being. She could barely tell up from down, she was so dizzy. She was cold, and afraid, too. So very afraid.

She only struggled to her feet again when the flames began to spread. Brilliant tongues of fire licked a path from the front of the vehicle toward the rear. The smell of gasoline burned her nostrils. She pulled her mesmerized gaze from the hungry flames and bolted, only to skid to a halt in the mud. A sheer drop stretched endlessly into blackness and pouring rain. And behind her, a steep, slick embankment angled sharply upward. She and her car had landed on a small outcrop that had prevented her plummeting to certain death far below.

And yet, unless she could put some distance between her and the flames, she'd be dead anyway.

Cold rain beating against her face, pummeling her body, frigid wind buffeting her every step of the way, she started up the bank. She clawed with her fingers and dug with her toes. She wore no shoes. She had no idea what had happened to them.

Countless times she slipped, losing more distance than she'd gained as the cold, wet soil scoured her palms, her knees, her chin. Each time, she gritted her teeth and began once more. She'd be damned if she would die here in this mud and misery. She gripped every protruding twig or rock that she was fortunate enough to encounter. Slowly, agonizingly, with blood spilling over her neck and dampening her shoulder, she made her way to the top...to the twisting, narrow, deserted stretch of road.

An explosion rocked the ground beneath her, and she nearly fell from the force of its percussion. Bits of metal and glass flew so high that they rained around her and she shielded her face with her arms, frightened beyond rational thought. The car from which she'd escaped became a blinding ball of flame, and she had to turn her eyes away. The pounding in her head and the pressure against her temples grew stronger with every ragged breath she drew.

She heard the sirens then. In the road ahead of her, vehicles with flashing lights and flapping wipers skidded to a halt. Men emerged, and several hurried toward her, shouting.

268 | MAGGIE SHAYNE

Again she felt inexplicable fear. She whirled from them and ran headlong in the other direction, bare feet slapping cold wet pavement, raindrops ricocheting in front of her, lashing her face and legs. Headlights rounded a curve. A car swerved to miss her, skidding to a stop on the shoulder. She went rigid as the driver's door opened and a man emerged.

She could only see his outline. He stepped around the car, the headlights at his back, rain pounding his body, and came toward her, a powerful, menacing silhouette. A shadow.

Her heart hammered and she couldn't draw a breath. It was more than fear she felt. It was stark terror. He would hurt her, she was sure of it. He would kill her. He kept coming, closer, closer.

She screamed. It was a shriek of unbridled horror, and it froze the shadow-man in his tracks. Again, she turned to run blindly. The paramedics were in her path, hands held out as if to gentle a frightened pony, voices soft. "Easy now, just calm down. We're here to help you. Easy."

She shook her head, pressing her hands to the sides of it. One came away dripping crimson and her throat closed off. She backed away from them, turning again only to find the shadow-man there, so close she could smell the rain on his skin.

She screamed again when he lunged closer and his arms closed around her like a steel trap. She fought, thrashing in his grip, kicking, pounding him with her fists.

"Dammit, Caitlin, that's enough!"

His voice was deep, frightening. But it wasn't his voice that made her stop her struggling. She blinked the rain and blood from her eyes, looking up into a face that was no more than a grouping of angles and planes in various shades of gray. A square, wide jaw. Full lips. Heavy brows.

Her voice a croak, she whispered, "What did you call me?"

His grip on her eased. She felt, rather than saw, the shock that rippled through him. "Caitlin." His arms freed her, but his large, hard hands gripped her shoulders. "Caitlin," he said again.

She was aware of the others closing in behind her. She shook her head, and dizziness swamped her like a small boat in a hurricane. "That's not my name." Her legs seemed to dissolve and her upper body sagged. She fought the sensation and managed to remain standing.

"Then what is?" It was nearly whispered, but there was a coarseness to the words that rubbed at all her nerve endings.

She closed her eyes, searched her mind. It was a simple enough question. What was her name? She squeezed her eyes tighter, trying to extract the information from her mind like juice from an orange. Nothing came. Her answer was an empty hole. A dark, empty hole in her mind where her identity should have been.

"I don't know."

"You don't know?" He seemed to be searching her face but she could barely see his. All crags and harsh lines and beaded droplets of rain. Deep-set eyes. Wet hair that looked like a windstorm. No colors. Only shadows.

Fear closed her throat. She didn't know who she was. She didn't know where she was. But she did know that she was afraid, terribly, paralyzingly afraid. Of what, or whom, she had no clue. Right now, it was of everyone, everything. Most of all, this hard-faced man. She tried to pull free of him, but he wouldn't release her.

"Let me go!" She twisted her shoulders back and forth, heedless now of the icy rain pelting her, the streams of it running between her shoulder blades and soaking her clothes. "Let me go!" Again and again she screamed the words until the dizziness returned. The varying grays around her lost their form and blended into one cold, dark color. And then, even the pain in her head drowned in the gray sea.

Look for **BROKEN**
Now Available

ABOUT THE AUTHOR

New York Times bestselling author Maggie Shayne has published more than 60 novels and 23 novellas. She has written for 7 publishers and 2 soap operas, has racked up 15 Rita Award nominations and actually, finally, won the damn thing in 2005.

Maggie lives in a beautiful, century old, happily haunted farmhouse named "Serenity" in the wildest wilds of Cortland County, NY, with her husband and soul mate, Lance. They share a pair of English Mastiffs, Dozer & Daisy, and a little English Bulldog, Niblet, and the wise guardian and guru of them all, the feline Glory, who keeps the dogs firmly in their places. Maggie's a Wiccan high priestess (legal clergy even) and an avid follower of the Law of Attraction

Connect with Maggie

Maggie's Website: www.MaggieShayne.com
Wings In The Night: www.WingsInTheNight.com
Maggie's Bliss Blog: www.MaggiesBlissBlog.com
Coffee House Blog: MaggieShayne.com/CoffeeHouse
Twitter: www.Twitter.com/MaggieShayne
Facebook: www.Facebook.com/MaggieShayneAutho

28069755R00162

Printed in Poland
by Amazon Fulfillment
Poland Sp. z o.o., Wrocław